SHE SAID, THREE SAID

DAVID B. LYONS

Created with Vellum

PRAISE FOR DAVID B. LYONS

"An outstanding craftsman in the thriller genre" – No. 1 Bestselling author Andrew Barrett

"Lyons is a great new voice in fiction" – Critically-acclaimed author John A. Marley

"This year's must-read author" – No.1 Bestselling author Rob Enright.

"Lyons certainly knows how to get readers on the edge of their seats" – No. 1 Bestselling author Sharon Thompson

"Best book of the year" – BooksFromDuskTillDawn

"Incredibly clever" – The Writing Garnet

"A devastating twist" – Irish Independent

"Keeps you guessing right until the end" – Mail On Sunday

WANT TO STAY UP TO DATE WITH DAVID B. LYONS'S NOVELS?

Visit David's official website

www.TheOpenAuthor.com

Or

Sign up here to become a David B. Lyons insider and receive exclusive information on his latest novels.

www.subscribepage.com/dblinsider

For Kerry

… as always.

1

They line up to enter the room like school children.

Brian stops in the doorway to wave everyone through as if he's the conductor of this orchestra. In general, this would be viewed as a polite gesture. But at this stage — five weeks in and with patience stretched — his eleven peers just think he's acting like a twat.

None of them offer him a thank you. The politest reaction he receives is a twitching of the lips from Number Three as she wheels past him.

Number Ten sits down, then stands immediately back up and walks to the far side of the oval table, settling on a seat next to Number Four.

'Jee, undecided already?' Brian says as he enters the room. He chuckles. Nobody else laughs. They're not in this room to laugh. But spitting out a joke only to be met by silence is nothing new to Brian Hoare.

A lack of humour isn't the only blemish he has. Hell no! Brian's unfortunate in a multitude of ways. He's awful looking for starters. He was bald by the time he was twenty-one. Some guys can carry off a shaved head, not this guy. The top of his crown is too bulbous and the bottom of his head… well, it just doesn't seem to exist. He has no chin. His jaws just sink into his neck. The overbite doesn't help either. Nor does his lisp. He produces a squelching sound as if he's bursting saliva bubbles with his back molars when pronouncing a lot of 's' sounds. It doesn't happen all the time, but it is quite a harsh squelch when his lisp does take over. He also has really bad breath. He doesn't know he has; only people who happen to be within a two-foot radius of his mouth know he has. And right now, Number One and Number Eleven are the unfortunate ones within that vicinity.

'Ah – six-all again,' Brian says, leaning over to tick his box on the lunch order. He regrets it as soon as he's said it; is aware he has already overstated his fascination with voting numbers over the course of the past five weeks. This wasn't the first time he'd counted up the lunch orders and barked the 'result' across the table as if it held any sort of significance.

'Jusht my idea of a bit of humour,' he whispers to Number Eleven when he sits down. Number Eleven smiles at him sympathetically; not hiding the fact that it's a sympathy smile either. She kinda just throws the smile at him, hoping it will shut him the fuck up. This lack of respect would sting Brian had he not grown thick skin years ago. You'd have to grow thick skin to be a politician. And you'd certainly have to grow thick skin if you looked like Brian Hoare.

He could've compensated for his unfortunate appearance had he developed some sort of personality over his thirty-two years. Aside from his miss-timed jokes, Brian takes himself way too seriously. When Number Four gave birth to the idea that the jurors should be known by their juror number rather than their real names over the course of the trial, Brian just had to be the awkward twat he always seems to be by going against the grain.

Most of the jurors were well aware that this trial would be splashed over the front pages of every national newspaper for weeks on end. Some of them were paranoid about the effect it could have on their lives. When this was all over they just wanted to return to normality; out of reach of the press, out of reach of the public, out of reach of each other.

They took a vote at the time. Nine voted *for* the use of juror numbers — three against. So they went with it. All except Brian. He opted to scribble his real name on his sticker badge. It sparked a succession of tuts around the table when he first stuck it to his chest, but his flaunting of the first rule the jurors made inside this room was never mentioned again. Nobody wanted to give Brian the satisfaction of having to explain himself.

He would have liked to have shared his reasoning though. His take on it was he didn't have anonymity anyway. He assumed everyone in the room already knew who he was.

They didn't.

Far from it.

Before this trial started, only Number Eight recognised Brian Hoare. Brian is a long way away from being as important as he thinks he is. By the time he was twenty-four, Brian made waves within the Labour Party; running for the party's leadership having shown drive and ambition when helping his hometown of Ongar pull through the financial crisis unscathed. Seventeen separate businesses opened in his small constituency through the crash over a three-year period. Most in Ongar knew he was just a jammy bastard, though. He happened to be in the right place at the right time. The plans for the majority of those businesses were in place well before Brian was elected as local TD.

But Brian wasn't backward in claiming credit for the

successes, gloating about his achievements in the national press at any given opportunity.

The positive PR didn't go unnoticed by the big wigs in the Dail and suddenly Brian was climbing the ranks of the Labour Party. Though that didn't mean he wasn't deluded when he ran the leadership race in 2011. He never stood a chance. After six weeks of bluffing to the press, he eventually fell out of contention. He's been back in Ongar ever since; half hated, half adored by his constituency and becoming more and more frustrated in his attempts to be re-elected as the local representative. He easily could have been excused from jury duty as of right — being a former politician — but he relishes the prospect of judging too much to pass on such an opportunity.

Brian's self-delusion was highlighted to his fellow jurors within the first twenty minutes of meeting them. He challenged Number One for the position of Head Juror as soon as they entered this room. In a secret ballot for the position, Number One thrashed Brian eleven-to-one. Everyone shifted awkwardly in their fake leather chairs when it became apparent that Brian was the only person around the table to vote for himself.

As soon as all jurors have taken their seats around the table, Brian is the first to pipe up.

'I propose we conduct an early verdict vote just to shee—'

'Scuse me,' says Number Five, cutting Brian's sentence in half. 'You're not the Head Juror. Let Number One do the talking.'

Brian rubs at where his chin should be, then motions towards Number One to get the ball rolling.

The trial ended just over ten minutes ago, the judge's closing statement ringing fresh in their ears, yet they still hadn't begun deliberations. Ticking a box on the lunch order and finding a seat in the jury room took a hell of a lot longer than was necessary.

'Okay everybody — this has been a long, drawn out five weeks,' says Number One after clearing his throat. 'And it all boils down to our discussion in this room. The fate of those three men lie in our hands.'

'And hers,' snaps Number Five.

'Yes. And Sabrina's too,' says Number One, swinging his jaw. 'I was just about to say that, thank you. I've been thinking of the best way for us to approach these deliberations from the get-go and it is my opinion that we should go through the whole night in chronological order. We should start our discussions about what we think happened just gone seven o'clock, when they all first met each other. Then we can continue through to the end of the night... until the incident is believed to have taken place, somewhere between midnight and half-past midnight.'

'We need to do an early vote,' Brian calls out, disrupting Number One's flow.

'What do we need a vote for?' Number One asks, his brow furrowing.

The rest of the jury begin to mumble; Number Ten doing nothing to disguise her annoyance by holding her two palms over her face and sighing heavily into them. Number Four holds one finger to the middle of his forehead and stares down into his lap. This kind of body language is standard practice in a jury room. But very rarely before deliberations had even begun.

The jury rooms in Dublin's Criminal Courts are specifically designed to spark discussion and debate – and they work. Debates arise in here all the time; like ping pong back and forth across the table. But it just so happens that a large percentage of those debates have fuck all to do with the trial they've been tasked with examining.

When twelve random strangers are forced together, the chances of no ego making itself known in the room is extremely rare. It turns out that way more people than you would actually imagine love the sound of their own thought process. In fairness to most of them, they *are* in these rooms to share their thoughts. It's just that the majority of people placed in this situation don't know how to filter between a significant thought and an insignificant thought.

'We need a vote because it'sh important we take note of how we are feeling at every point of the deliberations,' Brian says, trying to justify himself. 'It would be beneficial if we all gave our gut instinct after five weeks of listening to the evidensh. The evidensh is fresh in our minds now. Fresher than it will ever be. I propose that it'd be advantageous to us as a jury if we all knew where everybody stood before we even begin deliberating. It's the besht place to start.'

A mumble of discussion fills the room; a nodding of heads almost running around the table like a Mexican wave. Most of the jurors agree with Brian's sentiment, but they also loathe to give him the satisfaction of gaining a minor victory. Number One sighs before raising his voice again.

'Listen... hands up if you think we should start with a verdict vote?' he asks.

'Hold on... we're having a vote about whether or not we're having a vote?' says Number Twelve, shaking his head. The delivery of his line produces a snort of laughter from a few around the table. Others just sigh.

Four jurors raise their hands in the hope that it will quicken the process. And then four more swiftly follow.

'Okay... so that's eight of twelve. Majority rules. We *will* have a verdict vote to start proceedings,' Number One says.

Brian smiles into his chest. His obsession with voting has bordered on fanatical at times. But this isn't an ordinary vote; it isn't a lunch order, it isn't a vote about the jurors' name tags, it isn't about electing a Head Juror. This is the real deal — a verdict vote. Brian can't wait to see what way his fellow jurors have been swayed over the course of this trial. He is dying to know how many agree with him: *not guilty*. He'd made his mind up half-way through the trial and isn't for changing. Brian is adamant the prosecution didn't do enough to prove the case.

'No need for formalities,' continues Number One. 'This will be an open vote. So we'll just raise our hands. There will be three options for now: guilty, not guilty or undecided.'

Number One takes a deep breath, then bounces the butt of the paperwork he's holding off the table.

'Okay… so raise your hand if – at this stage, immediately following the trial — you feel strongly that these three men are guilty.'

Each juror's head pivots around the room. Three hands fly up; Number Five's, Number Three's and Number Six's. Silence fills the air for a moment, in anticipation of any other hands being raised. None are.

'Okay, and those who at this early stage feel that the three men are innocent, please raise your hands.' Brian's hand shoots up, followed almost reluctantly by Number Twelve's.

'And those undecided at present?' asks Number One, pointlessly. He even proceeds to count the hands in the air aloud, including his own. 'Okay,' he says, scribbling down the result on the sheet of paper in front of him. 'That's three guilty… two not guilty… seven undecided.'

He coughs, scribbles nonsensical notes on the paper just to bide time and then falls silent again. He doesn't know where to take things from here.

'Let's do what you were gonna do,' Number Twelve speaks up. 'Let's go through the night in chronological order. Starting with when Sabrina first bumped into the three lads... or when the three lads first bumped into her – depending on who you believe.'

'Yeah – there's disagreement from the outset,' says Number Ten. 'Sabrina says the three guys approached her first. They claim she approached them. Who do we all believe made the first move?'

19:00
Sabrina

I tug at the V in my jumpsuit again, adjusting it for what must be the fiftieth time since I left my apartment half-an-hour ago. I don't know why. My breasts aren't going to fall out. But because it's cut so low, almost down to my belly button, my eyes are constantly catching the end of the V and I instinctively keep running my thumb under the fabric to pull the two sides tighter together.

It's a beautiful jumpsuit, but I really don't feel comfortable in it. It's making me feel too self-conscious. I'm normally self-conscious, but particularly so this evening. Perhaps I overdid it, especially for this place. I've never been to the Hairy Lemon before; assumed it was a bit classier than it actually is. It's just a basic old-school after-work inner-city pub; after work for everyone else in here, the beginning of work for me.

'You do a non-alcoholic wine?' I shout over the other voices to the barman.

He bends down, pops his head back up in a matter of seconds, holding a small bottle of Ebony either side of his face.

'The red, please.'

'You alone?' a boy-cum-man asks, squeezing behind a girl at the bar so he can talk to me.

'I am,' I reply, 'but not for long. Sorry.'

He trundles away, his head bowed. It's tough for men. What are they supposed to say when they see girls in a bar they find attractive? Where would you even begin? I've heard it all over the years; from cheesy one-liners to outright advances. None of it works. Certainly not with me. There's just an unnatural chemistry that ignites as soon as somebody attempts a chat up line. It makes the process unattractive. Chat up lines are cheesy. Cheesy is uncool. Uncool is unattractive. Or maybe I'm just a fussy bitch. Probably why I've only ever had one-and-a-half boyfriends my whole life.

I hand over the five-euro the barman asks for, pick up my glass of red and make my way towards the stairs, slaloming through a host of bodies as I take my first sip. This place is pretty much packed. It's not going to be easy to locate my target tonight.

When I reach the top of the stairs I check my phone. Still no text message. But it'll come through soon enough. It always does.

I soak in the atmosphere. Most people in here likely arrived just gone five o'clock, as soon as their working week ended. They're all out for fun. But I don't envy them. Not at all. The idea of being cooped up in an office all week doesn't sit right with me. Never has. I can't understand why that's the route most people in this city take to earn money. It seems like slave work to me; working forty hours a week to make somebody else rich. How does that even make sense? I guess it's just routine, tradition, conditioning. Everybody feels they have to have a career and rather than thinking outside the box, they all just do as their parents did: work for somebody else.

It's a real shame. Though I do sometimes feel that if I wasn't genetically blessed I'd probably have to join everybody else in that rat race too. I don't earn an awful lot of money — a modest amount, enough to keep fresh food in the kitchen and a roof over my head. But I guess I'm as happy as I've ever been. I'm managing to stave away my depression most days — and that's probably as good as I can ever do. There are times when I feel down, but I don't feel as lost in life as I have done in the past. There's a tiny glimmer of light at the end of my tunnel. I just have to fixate on it, keep walking towards it.

I pull at the V again as I reach the top of the stairs; noticing a man stare me up and down, licking his lips in appreciation. I've never fully known for certain whether men lack subtly in these situations or whether they genuinely just don't give a shit about getting caught staring. I don't even laugh when I clock the wedding ring on his finger and watch him stroll over to a table on the far side of the room, kissing a girl I hope is his wife. She's pretty — certainly better looking than him. He should count himself lucky. He doesn't need to be perving at me.

I check my phone again and let out a sigh. Still no text. I probably should have waited outside, until the message came through. It's not a great idea for me to be in here before him. Especially in a packed bar. I'm courting way too much attention. I polish off my glass of wine, plonk it on a shelf next to the toilet and make my way through the swinging door; not because I need to use the loo, but because I'm getting a little too self-conscious standing out there on my own. I'll hide out in here for a while, until my phone buzzes.

'Nice jumpsuit,' a young girl says staring at me through the reflection in the mirror.

'Oh thank you.'

'Yeah, ye look deadly. Jaysus, I wish I looked as good as you do when I'm … eh… sorry, what are ye twenty-nine, thirty?'

I look into the mirror, just to see if her estimation is justified. She overshot my age by five years. Bitch. That stung. Maybe she meant it as a put down. I'm used to girls being jealous of me; but to portray jealousy within five of seconds of seeing me is probably a new record.

'Just gone twenty-five,' I say. She holds a hand up to her mouth in apology.

'Well… if I look as good as you in seven years I'll be over the moon,' she says, twisting the nub of her lipstick back down. She wings the door open, leaves me in peace – just me and my reflection. Maybe I do look older than I am. My depression has added those years, I'm sure.

The lack of sleep when you suffer with bouts can be torturous. But I still look good. I know I do. I just don't feel good. And I'd take feeling good over looking good any day of the week. Looks are overrated. I know that for a fact. I'm living proof of it.

I touch up the winged tip at the sides of my eyes and purse my lips at my reflection. Eyeliner is the only make-up I ever wear. I'm lucky; I don't have any blemishes on my face to hide. In fact, I don't have any blemishes on my body at all. I'm not quite sure where myself and my sister got our sallow skin from – neither of our parents have it. I guess we just won some sort of gene lottery. We got looky, but not lucky.

I hover inside the middle cubicle, trying to kill time. But time doesn't want to be killed – certainly not quickly enough. I check my phone: 7:16. Lorna said I should receive the text anytime between seven and seven-thirty. Another sigh. I can't stay locked up in this little cubicle for much longer. I'll just head back outside, try to blend in. I sigh as I push through the swinging door, my eyes focusing on a group huddled into the far corner of the pub. None of them were there before I went to the toilet. I place my phone back into my purse and pace over to see what the fuss is all about. A group of lads seem to be lining up to take photos of a tall red-haired guy. I feel a wave of excitement wash through me. I bet he's famous. I squint to focus on his face, but can't place him. I always wanted to be famous… in fact I always felt destined I would be. But it never happened. Not yet anyway. Though sometimes I wonder why I hold on to that dream; parts of the celebrity lifestyle must be horrendous. I can't imagine I'd have the patience to pose for a hundred photos and sign a hundred pieces of paper every time I walked into a pub. Though this fella seems to be enjoying it. Either that or he has mastered the art of maintaining a fake smile. He's been handed two pints of beer in the one minute I've been standing here. That's kinda ironic. If this guy is super famous then surely he has money. Why do the people feel the need to help fund his night out?

'Sorry love, who is that guy?' a girl asks over my shoulder, her eyes squinting as much as mine.

'No idea.'

'He's cute.'

I take in his face again. Yeah... he is kinda cute. I mean... I don't think I've ever fancied a red-head before, but he wears it well; the beard offsets the ginger somewhat — it actually suits him.

'Yeah he is kinda good looking... kinda has a—' I stop, realising I'm talking to myself. The girl who approached me has gone. I take a step forward and focus on his face again. How do I not know who he is? I stay on top of celebrity news. I could even name all of the past contestants on *Big Brother* if they were lined up in front of me.

'I'll get you a selfie,' a guy says startling me, his Dublin accent not fitting his Asian appearance.

'Sorry?'

'C'mon... I'll introduce you to Jason,' he says.

19:05
Li

We laugh out loud walking up South William Street. It's been so long since the three of us have been out together and it always paints a grin on my face when I realise just how seamlessly we fall back into the old routine of slagging each other's mothers.

We've been stinging each other with 'yer ma' jokes since we were fourteen. After I just said I never get sick of the Hairy Lemon, Zach replied 'yer ma never gets sick of my Hairy Lemon' and the three of us literally burst out laughing; the laughter rasping from our mouths like fart sounds.

We know that line isn't funny to anybody else in the world but it happened to be the humour our friendship evolved on. I couldn't care less if anyone labelled us immature. That kind of humour isn't immature to me. It's golden. It's rare. Not every group of best friends from primary school are still best friends thirty years on. I'm proud of our banter. I actually find it quite magical that when the three of us are together we can turn easily back into those innocent little kids we were when we first met.

For some reason the three of us decided to be mates on our first day at Mourne Road primary school. There must have been about three hundred kids in the school at the time, but on day one the three of us somehow happened to cower into the same corner of the large playground. I often think we found solace in each other because we were the three strangest looking kids in the playground that day. Jason's hair was orange. Not ginger. *Orange*. Bright orange. I don't know why Mrs Kenny didn't have it cut short. She just let him walk around with a giant orange bush on the top of his head. He kept it that way until he was fourteen.

19:05

Zach looked like a midget. Still kinda does. He's small, though he always seemed to be the one who got the girls. Before Jason became famous, that is.

There was no doubt I was different. 'Chink' they called me all the way through primary school. 'Chink', I'd later find out, derived from the word 'Chinese'. I don't think the lads understood there was a difference between Korea and China. I'm just certain anyone with Asian eyes in Dublin those days was called 'Chink'. It used to bother me, but all in all I think I survived being of a different race pretty well. I wasn't really bullied at school… just made fun of. Things could have been a lot worse.

'Ah, Jason Kenny,' the bouncer calls out, throwing his hand out for a shake. Zach and I get offered a grabbed handshake too. That's not one of the perks of having a famous friend. I'm a bit of a germaphobe. I wipe my hand against the inside of my blazer as we step inside. It's busier in here than I thought it'd be.

'Whatcha want?' Zach shouts over the chatter, muscling his way towards the bar.

'Here, I'll buy,' Jason pipes up.

'T'fuck you will, big shot.'

'Go on then, get us a pint of Heineken.'

'Same,' I say, even though I hate beer. I only drink it because I feel that's what I'm supposed to drink. I'd love a cocktail. Some bright-red, iced concoction that tastes like a Slush Puppie. I could drink that kinda stuff all night. But there's no way I'd order one. I'd look like a right mug.

I sip on the beer Zach hands back to me wondering how the hell my gut is going to feel in the morning after I've poured about seven pints of this piss into it.

'Will we go upstairs?' Jason asks, pinching his shoulders in so he doesn't bump into anyone.

'C'mon,' Zach says, leading the way.

Heads cock as Jason walks through the crowd. He's often said his height helped make him a success, but that it's a bastard to be tall and famous. He gets noticed everywhere he goes.

A bout of 'Boom, boom, boom, lemme hear ya say Jayo' sounds out. This is nothing new. The Irish fans started chanting that when Jason was in his prime, about eight years ago. It follows him everywhere he goes. Only me and Zach know that Jason genuinely hates that chant. It makes him cringe. He hates being called 'Jay' or 'Jayo'. He only answers to Jason.

We shuffle up the stairs without anyone asking him for an autograph or a selfie and manage to squeeze ourselves into a corner of the pub opposite the toilets. The chatter's not so loud up here. Gives us the chance to do what we came out to do: catch up. Jason hasn't been home in almost a year.

'How's Jinny?' he asks me.

'Great. Doing her Leaving next year, can ye believe that?'

'You're fuckin' joking me!' he says, holding his fist to his face in surprise.

'Yeah… she's seventeen in a couple of months.'

'Jaysus Christ. I still imagine her being four.'

Jason's always had a soft spot for my little sister. Well, he kinda has a soft spot for my whole family. We're an odd little bunch, us Xiangs. My mam and dad met pretty much the night I was conceived. They're still together… sort of. He mainly lives in Korea, and has still barely bothered to ever learn how to speak English. I've tried to learn Korean; can just about get by to share a polite chat with him whenever he decides to come to Dublin. But I'm not great at it. It's a tough language to nail. Jinny hasn't bothered. She doesn't seem as interested as I am to get to know Dad better. She just can't forgive him for being away from us for most of the year. Mam gets by. She's used to it. Everybody loves my mam.

She's just one of those loveable oul' dears. The type that would do anything for anybody. She runs the community centre on Mourne Road; helps out at the charity shop on Galtymore. All for nothing. Just for the reward of being part of a community.

'And your ma?' Jason asks.

'Still the same. Hasn't changed.'

'Good to hear it. Tell them I was asking for them.'

'Sure, pop in to them before you go back.'

'Yeah, I'll—' he stops, distracted by somebody holding a pint of Heineken in front of his face.

'Here ya go Jason. For that goal against Holland, ye legend ye!'

'Thank you, mate,' Jason says smiling back at the stranger.

'I knew as soon as you shaped up to hit that that the ball was gonna fly—'

'Sorry, my friend,' Zach interrupts. 'It's just Jason here is trying to have a quiet night out with his buddies. We haven't seen him in ages and—'

'Course, sure thing, sure thing,' the fella says, reaching out for Jason to shake his hand. 'I'll leave ye to it, Jason. Have a good night, me oul' mucker. Ye fuckin' legend ye!'

We're used to it. But the unfortunate thing about the first person approaching Jason when we're out is that it opens the floodgates for everybody else. I'm pretty sure that within the next five minutes, Jason will have at least three more pints of Heineken handed to him and will have signed a dozen autographs and appeared in a dozen selfies. He handles himself so well. I know he hates all this shit, but it's par for the course.

I raise my eyebrows at Zach as a crowd begins to form around us.

'We'll just have the one here,' I whisper into his ear as Jason does his thing. 'I didn't think this place would be so busy this early. Forgot about all the work crowd on a Friday evening.'

'No problem,' he replies. 'We'll just play it by ear.'

'Here mate, will ye take a pic of me with Jason Kenny?' a young fella who must be just about bordering on the legal age limit to drink asks Zach.

Zach doesn't hide his impatience with these fans. He sighs while taking the phone off the young fella. I take in the crowd gathering. It's small – only about eight or nine people. It'll all be over in five minutes. Then we can get back to catching up.

I sip on my pint as I'm forced out of the pack. This always happens. Me just standing aside.

I turn around, take in the artwork on the walls. It's not much to look at, just framed posters of old movies. Most of them are of John Wayne. I'm not quite sure why the pub's decorated this way. I don't see the connection.

I squint, then blink at the reflection in one of the glass frames, barely believing what I can see.

Now that *is* a work of art.

I spin to look at her. She's gorgeous. The white suit she's wearing is really hot. Cut all the way down to her bellybutton. She has a sheen right down her cleavage. It's like she's bloody photoshopped. But that's not what's most attractive about her. It's those big brown eyes. I'm not one for approaching girls, have never had the courage, but I find myself walking towards her and I can't stop.

'I'll get you a selfie,' I say to her.

'Sorry?'

'C'mon... I'll introduce you to Jason.'

'Who... who is he?' she asks me.

A lot of girls do this. Play dumb; pretend they don't know who he is — thinking that's how he would like it to be. It's all very transparent, though. I don't expect everyone to know who Jason is, but if you've been queuing up looking for an autograph or a selfie, then it's not particularly logical to play the I-don't-know-who-you-are card. But she's super cute. So she can kinda get away with it.

'Hey Jason, this is… this is…?' I ask turning to her.

'Sabrina,' she says, smiling. 'Sabrina Doyle.'

2

'Listen,' Number Twelve says. 'We won't know for certain, but if you sorta boil it down to logic, it's more logical that she approached them. People were approaching Jason. We know that. There's evidence to support that.'

'They cudda approached her,' Number Five says rather dismissively, turning to look Number Twelve square in the eyes.

'Yeah but…' Number Twelve pauses. 'Where's your logic?'

'Where's *your* logic,' Number Five snaps back.

'But that's what I said… I said it's more logical that she approached Jason because Jason is famous – people must approach him all the time.'

'Well you need to look up what logic stands for in the dictionary,' Number Five says.

It's rather ironic she said that. She may have said it as a reflex of what she was thinking, because she isn't entirely sure what the word logic means herself. She always thought she did, but Number Twelve's use of it just now kinda threw her. Number Five isn't normally this stupid but she's been overwhelmed by jury duty. Her anxiety has played up over the course of this trial. She's not entirely sure what her role is supposed to be. She feels a bit out of her depth amongst the eleven others serving alongside her. Feels she has to compensate for her lowly-paid shopping centre shelf-stacking job by ensuring she has one of the loudest voices in the room.

Number Seven speaks up, more so to ease Number Five's discomfort than anything, though she did have a valid point to make.

'I don't want this to sound wrong, sexist... I suppose,' she says. 'I guess it's best I say this rather than a man. But... I kinda think there could be some logic in the boys approaching her. I mean... we've seen photos of the night in question right; how stunning was Sabrina? She doesn't look that striking in the courtroom — still a lovely looking young woman... but on the night—'

'What the hell has this got to do with how hot the girl is?' Number Five snaps back, her voice all high-pitched. She hadn't realised Number Seven was actually supporting the point she was initially trying to make. Number Seven sucks air in through her teeth; an attempt to stop her blood from beginning to boil.

'That's not what I'm saying,' she says as calmly as she can, a polite smile on her face.

'It's exactly what you just said. You were comparing how hot she was on the night to how she dressed in court. We're not here to judge that kind—'

'Number Five, please!' Number Seven finally snaps, placing both of her palms face down on the table, almost standing up. 'It *does* have a lot to do with what she looked like on the night, okay? It does.'

All of the jurors except Number Five stare at Number Seven. She hadn't been exactly shy over the past five weeks, but nobody would have predicted she'd be the first one to lose patience. And the jury are only twenty minutes into their deliberations.

Number Seven is a secondary school teacher from inner-city Dublin. Her real name is Roisin Gorman; a twenty-two-year-old who shares a small two-bedroom apartment in the centre of town with a work colleague. Number Seven is nearest in age to Number Five in this room; they're the only two still in their twenties. Their maturity levels are decades apart, though. Number Seven raised her hand as undecided in the initial verdict vote about twenty-minutes ago, but is veering towards the Not Guilty camp; though she loathes the idea of Jason, Zach and Li getting away scot free, if they did in fact rape Sabrina.

'Ish it even conceivable that both parties just happened to bump into each other and therefore nobody necessarily approached anyone first... they jusht struck up conversation in passing?' Brian asks slowly, trying to cool the temperature of the discussion.

'None of the witnesses allude to this,' replies Number Twelve.

That was accurate. Six witnesses from the Hairy Lemon were called to the stand over the course of the trial. The defence found three witnesses who were willing to testify that Sabrina deliberately made a bee-line towards Jason as soon as he arrived at the bar. But the prosecution were also able to call on three witnesses who testified in complete contrast to that. Two of them said Sabrina was led towards Jason by his friend Li. One other said that he was pretty sure Jason signalled to Li that he should bring Sabrina towards him.

It's justifiable that the jurors are genuinely torn on which side to believe in this instance. There was no CCTV footage, just three witnesses on each side cancelling out each other's perception of what really happened.

'The problem here is,' Number Twelve continues, 'one party or the other is lying all through this case. Straight from the bat somebody is lying and that could, conceivably, lead us to believe that they are lying about everything else.'

The jurors begin to talk over each other, most debating against Number Twelve's argument. But he raises the palm of his hand to silence them. He hadn't finished what he was saying. 'Sorry, if you don't mind me just finishing my point with this... the truth is, if we look at all the evidence, little that there is in this case, we don't and never will know who approached who first. All we have is our gut feeling. Our opinion. And that's not enough in this room.'

The jurors soak in Number Twelve's last sentence. They know this, were told this by the judge. Yet it's so easy to lose track of such instruction; so easy to be swayed by instinct, by opinion.

The judge had eyeballed each and every juror before setting them off on their deliberations after the trial ended this morning. He tried to get through to them that they could only convict Jason, Zach and Li if they felt the prosecution proved beyond all reasonable doubt that non-consensual sex occurred on the night in question. But some of the jurors still aren't entirely sure what 'reasonable doubt' means exactly. Number Twelve and Brian made attempts at defining the phrase for them, but at least five people sitting around this table are still genuinely confused by the phrase. This is not a new phenomenon in these jury rooms. This lack of understanding of the legal processes occurs on a daily basis in here; jurors unclear on the exact protocol they should follow when examining a trial. The judge had told jurors that they shouldn't use their gut instinct, shouldn't use opinion, should only go by the evidence they heard at the trial. Number Five has been totally thrown by this. She can't comprehend that her opinion holds no value.

'It can't be proven,' Brian raises his voice again, his Dublin accent thickening, 'beyond reashonable doubt that Sabrina approached the boys or that the boys approached Sabrina first. So we'll have to chalk this down as an even reshult.'

'What the hell do you mean even result?' Number Three asks. 'It's not a bloody football match here. We're each entitled to our own individual feelings on this and I genuinely believe that the lads were on a mission — as they probably are every time they go out — to find the hottest girl in the pub to bring to Jason. There is a witness who confirms this.'

'There are witnesses who say the opposite,' Number Twelve bites back. But his point is barely heard over the murmurings of everybody else around the table. They all have their own views. And they all want to be heard.

'Can we calm down please?' Brian says, standing to attention. 'Number One, please...' he says to his nemeses, almost embarrassing the Head Juror into curtailing the behaviour around the table.

'Okay... okay,' Number One says, shuffling the butt of his paperwork off the table again. 'We have heard from six witnesses and this matter of who approached who first practically evens itself out, just like Number Twelve said. We will not know who approached who first. Perhaps we should move—'

'If we believe — as Sabrina testified on the stand as well as in her original police statement — that she didn't know who Jason Kenny was, then surely we can believe that she didn't approach him,' Number Three says, opening up another branch of the same argument just as Number One seemed to be bringing it to conclusion. Number Seven sighs as the debate ripples around her. Then she rises from her seat.

'I'm pouring myself a tea, anyone want one?' she calls out,

hoping a quick break will offer everyone a chance to digest the argument and calm down.

'Go on,' Number Four says. He's the only one who paid any attention to her question.

The rest of them are still mumbling their views on who approached who first in the Hairy Lemon.

Number Four rises from his seat and follows Number Seven towards the tiny table that stands just inside the door. The only facilities the jurors have inside the jury room rest on this table; a silver dispenser that produces both cold and boiled water, different flavoured tea bags, a jar of instant coffee, a jug of milk and a choice of either plain or chocolate digestive biscuits. The only other object taking up floor space is the mahogany conference table. It's oval, a bit like a rugby ball; six chairs either side of it. A black carton, about shoe-box in size, rests atop it. The carpet's bright red, just as it was in the courtroom – the exact shade of red you'd normally find a movie star gliding across at a premier. Everything else is white; the walls, the ceiling, even the modern rectangular lampshade hovering over the table is a bright white. The bulb is always switched on, shining an unflattering light down on to the top of the juror's heads. They will be given a break in the corridors soon, just to stretch their legs. At lunch time they'll be brought to a different room, left alone to further discuss the trial over their beef or chicken dish if they so wish. But that won't be for another three hours.

'Whaddya think of this handjob?' Number Four whispers to Number Seven as he pushes down on the tap, releasing cold water into his glass.

'Not a chance. Four minutes?' she replies, raising an eyebrow.

'Ah... I don't know,' Number Four says, shaking his hand side to side. Number Seven snort-laughs, then holds up an apologetic hand over Number Four's shoulder towards the rest of the jurors. Their faces had swivelled towards her at the sound of her snort. She waits until they all resume talking, then whispers back into Number Four's ear.

'That how long it takes you, yeah?'

'It does actually.'

They both stifle their laughs. Number Four and Number Seven had already decided to be friends via body language within the first week of the trial. Their friendship had now developed to a level where they would make eye contact with each other whenever one of the other jurors produced a tic; like when Brian would talk over somebody, or when Number One would bounce his paperwork off the table, or when Number Five would say something close to outlandish, or when Number Twelve would use the word 'logic'. When any of these tics occurred, Number Four and Number Seven would stare at each other, then twitch a muscle in their cheek to signal a stifled smile.

'So what do you two think then?' Number One directs at the pair of them from the far side of the conference table.

The whole table stares at them.

'Sorry?' Number Four says, turning to look back over his shoulder.

'Will we leave that discussion there? I mean we could get back to it at some point… but shall we move on?'

'Sure,' says Number Four. Number Seven nods her head, mouths a silent 'yeah', then sits back down. She offers a purse of her lips to Number Six who is sitting directly across from her; has felt sorry for the woman since the first day of the trial. Number Seven has an inkling that Number Six really doesn't want to be here. But she couldn't be more wrong. Number Six is revelling in this. Nobody has been able to put an accurate age on her. Physically, she looks older than her sixty-eight years; her face is worn, wrinkles wedge deep into her forehead and cheeks – most likely because she has smoked at least twenty cigarettes every day for the past half a century – but although she is mostly quiet, she's not bored, just observant.

'Unless... Number Six, do you have anything to add?' Number Seven suggests, directing her hands across the table.

Number Six peels her back, vertebrae by vertebrae, from the fake leather chair in almost slow motion, pokes her chin out so that it's parallel to the table, looks at the faces of all six jurors sitting on the opposite side to her, then forgets to speak. Everybody sits wide-eyed, staring at her... waiting. She picks up the cold glass of water in front of her, sips from it, swirls the water around her mouth – making much more noise than most would deem appropriate – then places the glass back down with a thud. She lets out a gasp of satisfaction.

'I'd like to move on to the handjob,' she says.

19:15
Zach

I'll never understand why grown men and women don't have enough cop on to leave Jason alone when he's out with his mates. I've already brushed one of them aside, but there are too many gathering now. Too many to hush away without making Jason look like a prick.

'Here mate, will ye take a pic of me with Jason Kenny?' some youngfella asks me. I sigh, let him know this isn't why I fucking came out tonight, but take the phone he's offering anyway, guide him towards Jason and call Jason's name so they're both facing the lens while I take the pic.

'Here ye go,' I say, handing the phone back. The youngfella pinches at his screen.

'Ah, will ye take another one, mate, my eyes are half closed in—'

'No,' I snap back at him, turning towards Li.

Li normally laughs at how short I can be with Jason's fans. But he's not there. He's scooted away from the small crowd, pretending to stare at shitty movie posters on the wall instead.

I don't know how Jason has the patience to keep that fake smile on his face while he does this shit. I wouldn't be able for it. It's a good job he's the one who made it as a professional, and not me. I'd probably be locked up by now for punching fucking idiots who felt it was appropriate to ask me for an autograph while I'm out having fun with me mates.

Getting an autograph just seems so tedious to me. It used to be bad enough when people wanted just that – Jason's name scribbled on a piece of paper — but camera phones have changed the game. All people want now is a photo –

proof that they've actually bumped into Jason as if it's some kind of achievement for them. Sad fuckers.

The frustrating thing about the camera phone is that the cunts never have the bleedin' setting ready. They're always fumbling around with their buttons, trying to find the camera app while Jason stands there waiting with a fake smile plastered across his face.

Maybe I got lucky missing out on all this shit. I was always a better player than Jason. He'd even admit that himself. But he got the breaks. I didn't. I think it's to do with the fact that he grew into himself. I'm still the same height I was when I was fourteen. His natural physique is more in tune with being a professional footballer. Plus – and I only realised this later — Jason had more support from his family. His da practically coached us from when we were about nine years old. His family would be on the sidelines of every home match in Benmadigan Park, cheerin' us on. He had a stable upbringing. Mine was shite in comparison. My ma and da couldn't even tell you what position I played in. My brothers used to play a bit themselves, but by the time I was fourteen, fifteen — that kinda age — they'd already fucked off to live in different corners of the world.

They couldn't stand living in our fractured home, couldn't stand living under the same roof as our folks. Callum moved to Sydney when he was just eighteen. He was supposed to go travelling for a year — is still there twenty years later. Brad was twenty-one when he fucked off to Toronto. I've often felt like following one of them overseas. To getaway from Drimnagh, get away from Dublin. But I don't think running away from problems is what will make me happy. I genuinely think my older brothers are cowards. I face up to my problems. I've even told me ma and da that they are the reason I didn't make it as a professional footballer. But they couldn't give a shit. They've no interest in what I'm doing, let alone what I'm not doing.

I sip on my beer, wait for the small crowd to go away and try to dream up an epic night out for the three of us. It's been ages since we've been out together. Jason barely drinks anymore. Just on the odd occasion that me and Li persuade him to. We always have a session in Dublin when the footie season ends. It's the only time each year that we get to spend some quality time doing what we used to do. A few times over the season myself and Li fly over to games, sit in the VIP area of some of the best stadiums in England to take in the games. But the novelty of that died off years ago. It's actually a bit of a slog to go over now. Almost boring. Jason has to be super professional. So when we do call over to see him, it's normally beans on toast suppers while watching Netflix in his gaff. Pretty much the same as I do at home with me bird.

I sigh as another youngfella offers me his phone.

'Sorry mate, it's not my job,' I say before he leans in towards Jason, holds his phone out, fumbles with the button and tries to take a selfie.

'Ah, here – gimme the fuckin' thing,' I say before taking a picture of him with a footballer he probably doesn't even rate that much.

After handing the phone back, I decide to walk away from the crowd, do as Li normally does; step aside and pretend it's not happening.

I look towards Li, notice him walking the most amazing lookin' bird towards us. Fuckin' hell. She's deadly. I love brunettes. There's something more naturally sexy about a brunette than any other hair colour.

I shuffle towards Li, try to eyeball him, try to say well done, mate. But his eyes haven't left the girl's face. That's unusual for him.

19:15

I watch her shake hands with Jason and as I approach I hear him offer to buy her a drink. Bastard. He got in there before me.

19:20
Jason

I'm sure there are worse things to be experiencing than having a queue of people lining up to take a picture with you. I try to remind myself of that on a consistent basis. But the awkwardness of this never fades. Especially when someone mumbles the word 'legend' in my direction. I hate being called that, as stupid as that sounds. I'm far from a legend. Nobody in the football world would class me as a legend. But people just want to say that word to me when they meet me, as if they feel a need to sensationalise my ability. It's just verbal diarrhoea. Utter bullshit. And it makes me feel instantly awkward.

It happens a lot more here than it does in the UK. Probably because the Irish are a lot friendlier by nature. But it's probably more to do with the goal I scored for the national team against Holland. A saucy half-volley that guaranteed we qualified for the 2012 European Championships. It was a freak. I'm not a goal scorer, never was. It's rare Irish supporters have much to celebrate, much to remember. But that goal is up there. If I tried that half-volley another hundred times, it wouldn't end up in the net once. But that's football. It's much more a game of luck than anyone cares to admit. And I'm one of the luckiest fuckers around.

I watch Zach take another phone from another fan and almost laugh out loud as he takes the pic. I'm well aware he'll be boiling inside. I've often joked with him that it's a good job I became famous and he didn't. He doesn't have the patience to be a modern-day professional footballer. Truth be known, he didn't have the ability for it either. Not that I've ever said that to him.

'Hey Jason, this is… this is..?' Li says to me, pointing out one of the most stunning-looking girls I've ever seen.

'Sabrina,' she says, flashing a smile. 'Sabrina Doyle.'

Wow. She's hot.

'Lemme get you a drink, Sabrina Doyle,' I say. It's probably as unoriginal as opening lines go – offering to buy a drink – but it was the first thing that popped into my head.

'Eh… sure. A… red wine,' she says.

'C'mon,' I say, ushering her towards the bar with me. She seems as nice as she looks; shy almost. Actually reminds me of the first girl I ever fancied. Valarie Byrne. She went to Mourne Road primary school with us. All the boys fancied her. But I didn't stand a chance. A pretty little brunette with a dimple on each cheek was never gonna look at the pasty-skinned, freckly ginger kid.

I actually never had a girlfriend until I found fame. I'll never know what it's like for somebody to actually like the real me, not the celebrity. My therapist tries to drill into me that I *am* a celebrity, it's part of who I am and that if fame is attractive to some people, then that's great; because I have fame. He says I shouldn't be too paranoid about it. I don't know… celebrity is just so complex that I'm of the thinking it's pointless even trying to understand it. And fuck knows I've tried for long enough.

I'm ninety-nine per cent certain I wouldn't have wound up depressed if it wasn't for my celebrity, though. All I remember from before I made my first-team debut for Everton is happiness. Even when my brother Eric was born — and diagnosed with his heart condition — our family were still happy. It was a big blow, but us Kennys just bandied together. We didn't let the fact that one of us had a ticking bomb for a heart get in the way of us all enjoying our lives — however many years they were going to last.

Mam and Dad's outlook was always positive. I'd give up

all of the money I have now, all of my fame, in return for an ounce of their positivity. I don't know where mine went. It's almost like I had to sacrifice my happiness to become a successful footballer.

FifPro released a survey they carried out a couple of years ago about depression in footballers. Their research found that thirty-eight per cent of professionals end up clinically depressed within a decade of retiring from the game. That shocked the world. Didn't shock me. I pal around with pro footballers. Most of them are unhappy. Not that they'd admit it though.

'So, what do you do?' I ask Sabrina as I hand her the glass of red.

'Me? What do you do more like? Why is everyone keen to get a picture taken with you?'

'I'm a green grocer,' I tell her. It's my usual line. Especially to girls who play dumb.

'Well your apples and pears must be the best in the business if people feel they need to get a photo with you,' she says laughing. Fuck. That's a helluva laugh. I could fall in love with this one.

'I'm a footballer,' I tell her, giving in.

'Ah... who do you play for?'

'Well... actually, y'know what,' I say, puffing a small laugh out of my nostrils. 'I don't play for any team anymore. But don't tell anybody that. Nobody knows. That can be our little secret.'

I wink at her. Not sure why I feel the need to be so honest with a girl I met literally two minutes ago. Perhaps a pretty face is more powerful than I ever thought it could be.

'It's eh... difficult to talk in here,' I say, leaning towards her. 'Fancy going outside for a minute?'

19:25
Sabrina

'Eh... sure. A eh... red wine,' I answer before checking the time on my phone. 7:25. My text should be coming through any minute now, but fuck it — it's not every day a celebrity ever offers to buy me a drink.

I'm supposed to stay sober when I'm working, supposed to only drink non-alcoholic wine. But it's impossible sometimes. The target almost always wants to buy me a drink.

I stare at the back of his head after following him to the bar. One or two people call out his name, wanting to be heard to acknowledge him. It must be great being a role model. I've probably dreamt of fame more than I've dreamt of anything in my entire life, though I know that doesn't make me unique. I'm sure most people have fantasised about being a celebrity. I play the name over and over in my head. *Jason Kenny*. It doesn't ring any bells.

'So, what do you do?' he shouts at me as he leans on the bar. It's difficult to hear in here. The bar area is a lot louder than where we'd been standing.

'Me? What do you do more like? Why is everyone keen to get a picture taken with you?' I shout back, cupping my hand towards his ear.

'I'm a green grocer,' he lies, a big grin stretching across his face. He's getting better looking the more I stare at him. I like his freckles, they look like they belong on his face; as if his face wouldn't work without them.

'Well your apples and pears must be the best in the business if people feel they need to get a photo taken with you,' I shout back, aware it's getting quite obvious that I'm flirting. I'm so uncool. I've never had the nerve to be flirtatious. Unless I'm on the job, of course.

'I'm a footballer,' he relents.

'Ah… who do you play for?'

'Well… actually, y'know what. I don't play for any team anymore. But don't tell anyone that. Nobody knows. That can be our little secret.'

I don't really know what he means by that. Assume it's some football transfer thingy. He's probably waiting on another club to buy him or something. But I feel quite chuffed that we have our own little secret. It's such a shame I'm working tonight — it'd be really cool to hang out with Jason; see how the other half live.

'It's eh… difficult to talk in here,' he shouts at me. 'Fancy going outside for a minute?'

I agree by nodding my head and standing aside, letting him lead the way. I notice the crucifix on his chain as he brushes past me. Jaysus, my dad would be delighted if I brought this fella home; not only a footballer, but a bible believer too. They're the only two boxes a man would need to tick to make Dad happy. Dad still goes to church every Sunday. Myself and Amanda would join him on the rare occasion, especially around Christmas and almost certainly around the time of Mam's anniversary. But that's it. They both tried their best to raise two Catholic daughters, but they raised two atheists instead; probably by trying to force us to be Catholics. In truth, it wasn't anything they did or didn't do – it's just a generational thing. The difference between our generation and their generation is that a world of common sense opened up to us. Media, TV, the Internet — our generation don't have to believe fairy tales to explain some of life's mysteries. We have all the answers at our fingertips. Dad is hugely disappointed that we don't believe the fairy tale he happens to believe in. And he *really* believes it — is deluded enough to think he's going to spend eternity with Mam, even though we burnt her body to a crisp eight years ago. But neither Amanda nor I would ever debate the subject with him. We're happy that he's happy to believe. Perhaps believing is the key to happiness. Because there's definitely a key to happiness somewhere that I've not been able to find.

I can't hold his faith against him though. Not when he has an ass like that. I stare at both of his cheeks snuggled into his jeans as he leads me towards the door. The crucifix is a bit cringe… would most likely put me off most other fellas, but when am I ever going to be flirted with by a professional footballer again?

Jason motions for us to walk around the corner when we get outside, to the side of the pub, and I already know I'm going to kiss him. Jesus, if I still kept a diary this would be one hell of a Dear Diary moment. Before either of us offers up another word, his lips are locked onto mine; his tongue circling my mouth. This all happened so fast. I shouldn't be enjoying it so much; shouldn't be giving myself over so easily, but I am enjoying it. Lots. So much so, I can hear the little devil on my shoulder giggling. It's unusual he gets his way.

My stomach flips a wave of excitement through me. This guy is so cute; he's a footballer; he's famous; he's rich; he's mine — for this moment anyway. He'll probably be snogging someone else in ten minutes' time. But right now, all of his attention is on me.

'You're so hot,' he whispers into my ear after gnawing his mouth away from mine. But then he's back in, his tongue now circling in the opposite direction. It's a cute technique; new for me. His left arm squeezes me closer, his right hand working its way up my back, then around to my chest. I allow him to cup me, because the thrill is working. I haven't felt this wanted in a long, long time. Certainly not by anyone I want to want me.

'Touch me,' he whispers. I just continue kissing him, unsure of what he's asking exactly. Until I feel him unzipping his jeans.

I don't move my hands. Not at first. I just continue to kiss him, until I notice my right hand slipping inside his zip; rubbing at his dick through his boxer shorts. Average size. I think. This is only the third dick I've ever touched. It's certainly the average one by my experience.

'I can't,' I say, pulling my hand away. I'm not sure how long I had it in there. Seconds, I'm sure.

I sigh, place my hands either side of his face and bring him in for more of that tongue circling. He wrestles his zip back up, then stops kissing me so he can fasten his top button. I hear the phone vibrate in my bag; a quick buzz that lasts less than a second. But I know it's going to take me away from this moment forever.

'Sorry,' I say, leaning off Jason. I unzip my bag, take out the phone and open Lorna's text message.

'I eh… need to go back inside,' I say, tilting my head and pursing my lips. 'This has been… well… it's been lovely.'

19:30
Li

Zach strolls back to me, a beer in each of his hands.

'Here y'are, fella,' he says holding one towards me. Now I've got one and a half pints. Zach's already downed his first. That's nothing new. It's almost as if he sees drinking alcohol as a sport. A competition. I try to swig back the rest of my first pint, but I almost regurgitate it back into the glass.

'I didn't see Jason at the bar, where'd he go?' Zach asks.

'Signing autographs,' I say. 'We came to the wrong bar. I didn't think it'd be this busy this early. Fancy heading somewhere else?'

'Relax Li, we've only just got here.'

He seems worlds away, his head cocking around the room. He hasn't even looked at me since he got back from the bar. Zach and I have always had a strange relationship. We're definitely best mates. But I think we'd both admit – even though we never have out loud – that we're best mates by default. If Jason wasn't living in England, he'd be both mine and Zach's best mate. But as it is, me and Zach are the ones who regularly get to see each other these days. Yet, bizarrely, we've never been really close. Like *really* close.

I know everything about Jason, and he knows everything about me. Not only about our families, but about everything: our feelings, opinions, insecurities. I don't really know Zach that intimately. But only because Zach isn't interested in talking about himself. Well, aside from how good a footballer he used to be. He would never share anything about his feelings. Would never ask after my family, ask how I'm genuinely getting on. I think it's because he had a bit of a shitty upbringing. He's just used to keeping everything bottled up.

I've had a shitty upbringing too though, in fairness. Hasn't stopped me from opening up.

My mam raised Jinny and me on one hundred and ninety pound a week. That's how much she got off the social welfare when we were younger. I'll always remember that figure. It just sticks in my mind. Mainly because I remember transitioning from thinking that's a lot of money to realising 'that is nothing!' as I slowly began to fathom how much things cost.

I watch as Zach pivots his head around the room again.

'Where's yer one gone… that Sabrina bird?' he asks.

'Oh… haven't seen her in a while.'

'She's not with Jason, is she? I'm into that. Don't want him getting his hands on her first.'

'Don't think so,' I say, finishing off my first pint, staring at my second as if it's going to be responsible for me feeling like shit tomorrow. 'I think he's signing autographs somewhere.'

That's just an assumption. Jason often goes missing when we're in pubs together, only for us to find him in the middle of a tiny scrum, scribbling his name down on peeled beer mats.

'Where do you wanna go anyway?' Zach asks.

'Somewhere a little quieter. Didn't think this place would be so jammed. I wanted to have a word with the two of you.'

'About what?'

'Ah… I'll tell you later.'

'It's not… it's not about…' Zach says, his eyes narrowing. 'It's not about the secret is it?'

'Jesus no!' I say, noting further evidence that the secret never really leaves Zach's mind. It has affected all three of us, massively. But Zach, I'm sure, is the one who has suffered the most.

Jason and I can keep the secret to the back of our minds. But I just know Zach carries it around with him on a daily basis. He's still as paranoid about it now as he was back then. He still thinks we're all going to get found out. Put behind bars.

'Fuck sake, mate. You've gotta let it go. That was years ago. It's over. No... I just have something to say to my two best mates. We haven't been out in – ah here he is now,' I say, nodding as Jason strolls towards us.

'Where've you been?' Zach asks him. 'Y'haven't seen that Sabrina bird have ye? I'm dying to chat her up. She's amazing lookin'.'

'Eh...' Jason hesitates. I know he's about to lie. I know Jason inside out. 'Nah, haven't seen her since I bought her that drink, mate,' he says.

19:30
Jason

I usher her around the corner of the pub, along the pathway. And as soon as she stops walking, I kiss her. Couldn't help myself. I actually brought her outside to have a chat, to get to know her a little better, but she just looked too pretty to not kiss.

I squeeze her tighter, feeling her breasts against my chest, then bring my hand back around, just to feel one. It would be a lie to say I haven't moved this fast before — I have — but certainly not with anybody I genuinely like. This just feels right.

'Touch me,' I say, almost regretting it as soon as the two words come out of my mouth. My dick has shot up since I started kissing her. It's almost calling out for her to touch it. But what a stupid fucking way to ask a girl to give you some intimacy. *Touch me.* Jee... I'm such a twat. I cringe inside. Yet for some reason I've popped the button of my jeans open, and pulled my zip down. I leave my jeans hanging on to my hips, wondering how stupid I've made myself look. I contemplate zipping back up and apologising when Sabrina's hand slips inside my jeans, her fingers twiddling at my balls, working her hand up to my shaft. Jesus, this is a hell of a turn on. How the fuck can one woman be this good looking and this dirty?

'I can't,' she says, taking her hand back out, killing my bone instantly. She goes rooting in her bag, picks out her phone.

'Sorry,' she says, offering me a little smile. 'I eh... need to go inside. This has been... well... lovely.'

Bollocks! I'm a fuckin' idiot. I've treated this girl like one of the little sluts who hang around nightclubs in the north east of England; the ones who don't hide their ambition to spend the night with a footballer. Shagging a footballer is almost like a badge of honour to these girls. I would consider that really sad if I wasn't the beneficiary of a thousand orgasms because of that reality. Though I'm pretty sure that kinda thing has led to my depression. I sometimes hate myself for how easy it is for me to have sex. Literally any time I want it.

'I need to check through this,' she says pointing the screen of her phone towards me just after we arrive back inside the pub. I cringe again. Maybe she has a boyfriend. Maybe she feels guilty and is pretending she got a text message to cool things with me before they got out of hand.

'Okay, I'm eh... gonna go back up to the lads upstairs,' I say. 'Come see me before you leave.'

I curl my fingers back into my palms and stab with my nails into them as I watch her walk towards the toilets on the far side of the pub, my gaze only disturbed when somebody behind shouts out my name.

'Ye fuckin' legend ye!' a stranger says, pointing his two thumbs up at me after I turn around. 'Me cousin used to play for the Bosco as well y'know? Was coached by your old man.'

I'm famous throughout the breadth of this country. But me dad's more famous in Drimnagh than I am. Anyone who has any relationship to Drimnagh always talks to me about my old man. He must have coached three hundred kids, I reckon, at St John Bosco. He gave up his Saturday mornings playing golf with my uncle to coach my team when I signed up for the under tens. He coached me and Zach for years. I'd say I think of my dad about five times a day, every day. I miss him like crazy. Feel like I have nothing to prove if I don't have him to prove it to.

'Ah here he is now,' I hear Li say in the middle of his conversation with Zach when I stroll up the stairs.

'Where've you been?' Zach asks. 'Y'haven't seen that Sabrina bird have ye? I'm dying to chat her up. She's amazin'.'

Shit. I fucking knew this would happen. It's not the first time hot birds have come on to me, that Zach assumes he could just have for himself. I can't have this argument with him now. Not again.

'Eh... nah, haven't seen her since I bought her that drink, mate,' I tell him. 'Well, he wants to head off somewhere else,' Zach says, nodding towards Li. 'But I ain't going till we see that bird. I'm not leaving without her number. She's was a fuckin' ten!'

'Where d'ya wanna go anyway?' I ask Li, trying to change the subject.

'Somewhere quieter. We were supposed to come out for an early drink so we could catch up... have a chat. It's too noisy here.'

'Yeah – let's head off then,' I say.

But Zach's having none of it, his head swivelling in search of Sabrina. He's not gonna find her up here. She's down in the loo. Probably with tears pouring down her face because she cheated on her fella.

3

Brian raises his voice the loudest.

'Can we all jusht calm down one moment, please?' he shouts.

It's slightly ironic. It was he who started the jurors off on the tangent they were currently on. He then raises his eyebrows towards Number One, gesturing outwards with his hands.

'Yes... yes,' Number One says, taking the hint and rising from his seat. 'Let's keep perspective.'

He undoes one more button on his shirt, showing a bit more chest hair than most would deem appropriate. He is one of a few jurors who is finding the temperature in the jury room too hot. But while Number One is loosening buttons on his shirt, Number Six is pulling her cardigan tighter around her shoulders. She's freezing. Isn't the only one.

'Number Six, you mentioned you were keen to get to this stage of deliberations, do you mind giving us your take on it?' Number One says, sitting back down.

Number Six grabs her glass of water again, sips from it,

lets out another gasp and then sucks her lips, making a bizarrely loud pop sound.

'It's just… it's just,' she stutters. 'As Number Twelve said earlier. Somebody is lying through the whole night. And I feel that the handjob is the key aspect of the trial because whoever is lying about this, is lying about what happened at midnight… lying about the rape.'

'Yes,' Brian pipes up, resuming control from Number One. 'But what is your take on the handjob specifically – what do you believe happened just outside the pub?'

'Well, I'd rather hear from others on this,' Number Six says, her voice almost shaking.

'Number Six, at some point you have to realise that you are part of this jury too. Your thoughts count as much as anybody else's in this room.'

Number Seven says this sympathetically across the table. It isn't so much that she values Number Six's opinion, it's just that Number Seven wants everybody to be involved as much as they possibly can. She's a typical teacher and is tired of listening to the same two voices all the time. Both Brian and Number One had gone beyond irritating her weeks ago.

'Well, I think that maybe he wanted her to give him a handjob but she refused,' says Number Six, giving her first genuine opinion of the trial.

'Why didn't she say that in her teshtimony, or to the police when she first made the allegations?' Brian retorts. 'If it was a case that Jason tried to get a handjob from Sabrina, why didn't she mention this? Trying to get a handjob ishn't what we have to deliberate here. Nobody argued about trying to get a handjob. Jason is saying she *definitely* gave him a handjob, while Sabrina is saying she kissed him and that was it; that she didn't go near his… eh… his penis.'

'Well in that case, I don't believe it happened,' Number Six says, reaching for her glass again, her fingers shaking.

'So you've changed your mind in the space of—'

'Calm down, Brian,' snaps Number Five. 'You asked for her thoughts, let the woman speak.'

The room falls silent as Number Six finishes her sip, then lets out another gasp that almost turns into a burp. Number Four has to stifle his laugh at the sound.

'I just think four minutes is just not... I don't think much happened in that time,' she says.

The jurors have just finished watching three re-runs of the CCTV footage from the entrance of the Hairy Lemon pub that showed Jason leading Sabrina outside the main door at 19:32 p.m. and then back inside at 19:36 p.m. Unlike the earlier argument of who approached who first, there was at least some hard evidence of this encounter. But it didn't really help either side of the argument.

Sabrina admitted, even as early as her first interview with police almost eighteen months ago, that she did share an early kiss with Jason Kenny on the pathway to the side of the pub. She insists he was trying to kiss her more passionately than she felt appropriate, given that they had only just met. She confirmed that at one point she gave in and kissed him, testifying on the stand that it was 'a very small kiss, didn't last long.' Jason's testimony was quite different. He said he was surprised they were only outside for four minutes, because he remembers them kissing for quite some time, said Sabrina even went so far as unzipping his jeans, fondling his penis outside of his boxer shorts before reaching inside and performing manual stimulation on him.

'If I may raise my concerns here,' says Number Eight, looking at the plasma screen hung on the wall, still showing a paused image of Sabrina and Jason arriving back inside the pub. 'Sabrina doesn't look embarrassed or at any kind of unease coming back in. Don't you just think that if she had given a stranger a handjob, then she might be a bit self-conscious? A bit embarrassed, perhaps?'

'But sure it's black and white footage. She could be red-faced for all we know,' says Number One.

'True. But she's not even trying to hide her face. She shows no sign of unease at all. I genuinely think from this evidence,' Number Eight continues, pointing at the screen, 'this handjob never happened. I think he's making it up. It suits his defence. I wouldn't be surprised if his whole expensive defence team just made this part up.'

Number Twelve lets out an audible sigh before getting to his feet.

'I know we're all frustrated at this particular juncture. But what do we have – apart from the CCTV footage which only proves they went outside for a few minutes... which neither side actually deny? We have her word against his. It's not much to go on.'

'Well I think I may have a good point to raise,' Number Ten says, before clearing her throat. 'Don't forget that the defence are brilliant, right? They are an expensive, operation – we all know this. Think about this for a second... if Sabrina opened Jason's zip, why didn't they try to prove this? Why didn't they have the jeans examined to gather confirmed evidence of her finger prints on his zipper?'

The jury room falls silent, only the noise of a couple of jurors shifting their seating positions creating any sound at all.

'That's a very good point, Number Ten,' claims Brian. 'You're right. If these guys are the besht of the besht in terms of defence lawyers, surely they would have looked into that. And I'm sure they did look into it. But why wasn't it brought to court?' he says, shrugging one of his shoulders.

'Because they didn't find her finger prints on his zip,' says Number Ten. Number Eight stares at Number Ten, meets her eye and then raises his eyebrow in appreciation of her nous. Number Ten is proving that first impressions shouldn't count; certainly not in jury rooms.

Number Ten's real name is Janice Dean, she's a thirty-two-year-old self-labelled geek from Mulhuddart in west Dublin. She's a massive superhero fan. Like her dad, Number Ten read both Marvel and DC comic books as a kid. She has worn an overly big T-shirt for every day of this trial, normally emblazoned with the name of a rock group she's into. Today's T-shirt is blank, but throughout the course of the trial she had worn T-Shirts with the logos of Black Sabbath, Led Zeppelin, AC/DC and Deep Purple — bands her dad had forced her to listen to as a child, bands she still listens to today. She has her face pierced in seven different places; two piercings on each ear, two on her nose; one on the side of her right nostril, the other a ring that forms a bridge between both nostrils like a cute dairy cow. And she also has a rounded stud just below the centre of her bottom lip. It would be difficult to tell from looks alone that Number Ten is one of the highest earners in the room. She works as an engineer on construction sites — again, influenced by her dad. She remains undecided on a verdict in this trial, but is tipping towards not guilty because she thinks the expensive defence team would have done a better job of proving the rape had it in fact really happened. That's how her brain operates. No other juror has looked at it from that point of view.

She sits back on her chair and wallows in the praise that is coming her way from fellow jurors.

'Yeah… why didn't they do that?' Number One asks. 'Really good point, Number Ten. Very smart.'

'Well why didn't the prosecution prove that the jeans didn't have Sabrina's fingerprints? You could argue both sides,' rasps Number Twelve.

'I applaud the point being made', Brian says. 'But given that that is circumstantial, does anybody feel particularly strongly about this handjob claim? Is there anyone here who feels this definitely happened or definitely didn't happen? Let's do it this way... quick and easy. Hands up if you feel strongly that Sabrina did *not* give Jason a handjob just past seven-thirty on the night in question.'

Number Three, Number Five and Number Six raise their hands. This is no surprise. The three of them had already let it be known that they were in the guilty camp from the outset.

'And hands up if you think Sabrina *did* give a Jason a handjob at this juncture?' says Brian as he reaches his own hand into the air. Number Twelve also holds his hand aloft. So too does Number Eight. At least there's been some movement on their earlier verdict vote. But not necessarily a move in the right direction. If anything, the jury room is more split down the middle now than it had been at the start.

'Three for, three against,' says Number One. 'Six undecided.'

'It's not undecided,' says Number Ten. 'It's just that we have no way of knowing for certain. I'm not undecided. I genuinely don't know — and neither does anyone — whether or not Sabrina gave Jason a handjob outside the pub. So I find it quite interesting that anyone would raise their hand for any of those verdicts with any degree of certainty at all.'

'Hold on... I am entitled to my—' Number Five begins to argue. An argument she doesn't even need to have.

'Calm down, Number Five,' Number One shouts, interrupting her. It was the first time the Head Juror properly raised his voice.

Number Five sits back in her chair, folds her arms across her chest. She was just about saved by Number One from uttering the word 'opinion' once again. She lets out a sigh that only she can hear. When talk resumes around the table she lifts her head, takes everybody in and begins to wonder why she feels as if she is the dumbest in the room when she certainly doesn't look the dumbest. She stares at six female faces, five male. Then pictures her own face, and tries to imagine what the other jurors are thinking when they look at her. Her sentiment is skewed though. They weren't making judgements on her looks, they were judging her based on what she was saying. She's beginning to wish she hadn't been picked for this trial at all.

The prosecution had tried hard to lean the jury selection gender-wise. They were determined to have as many females on the jury as possible; assuming that women would be more sympathetic to Sabrina's story. The defence did a fine job in limiting the number of female jurors to just seven; almost celebrating the seven:five gender ratio the judge settled on when jury selection was completed. Both the defence and prosecution were actually flawed in their ambitions though. Contrary to the long-held assumption that female jurors find in favour of a female victim of rape, research of over one-hundred rape cases in Dublin's criminal courts show that female-dominated juries are less likely to convict in this type of circumstance. It's almost difficult to believe. But the understanding is that women are more fascinated by this subject. They watch this type of trial through their television screens on a regular basis. Between *Law and Order, The Good Wife, LA Law, Crime and Punishment* and plenty of other Americanised TV courtroom dramas, women – who are the main target audience of such shows – are exposed to trials more readily than men. But the trials they watch on TV are dramatised versions of the real deal. And when set up in a real jury dock, suffering the endless silences of a trial and putting up with legal arguments that can go over most people's heads, they find themselves presented with a scenario that does not match their perception. They are not granted the same indicators and clues that pop up on TV dramas, and — as a result — they are less likely to convict. Though in truth, the toying between both sides pre-trial when it comes to selecting a jury can be a largely pointless exercise. Jurors are mostly swayed, not by their gender or even their past experiences, but by the most dominant voices in the jury room.

In this instance, the Number One versus Brian Hoare arguments — that continue to enrage most jurors, most of the time — hold a lot more significance to the outcome of this case than anything else.

19:40
Li

Zach can get a bit like this. Manic. Obsessive.

He won't shut up about that Sabrina girl all night now. I'm sure Jason lied to him, told him he didn't know where she was. Zach would have had a little strop if he knew Jason had got in there before him. That's how nuts he can be.

'Where d'ya wanna go anyway?' Jason asks, trying to pull the three of us together; to stop Zach's head spinning around the room.

'Somewhere quieter,' I say. 'We were supposed to come out for an early drink so we could catch up… have a chat. It's too busy here.'

'Yeah – let's do it then,' Jason says.

He clinks my glass, then holds his towards Zach, waiting a brief moment until Zach tunes back in to clinks glasses.

'C'mon man, we're gonna head somewhere else,' Jason tells him.

'Ah wait… lemme see if I can find that hot brunette. Not leaving here till I try it on with her.'

I want to tell him he's wasting his time, that she's way out of his league. But Zach's sensitive about things like that. I mean, he's a nice guy, the funniest guy I've ever met — doesn't take himself too seriously most of the time. But there are two things in life he can't seem to get over. One, Jason becoming a pro footballer while he didn't even get picked up by a League of Ireland club and two, the fact that Jason is now the one who gets all the girls.

'Go and have a quick look for her then,' Jason says, sighing. He looks at me; knows that I know. Is aware the night could turn into a bit of a fuck up if Zach figures out Jason has already put a marker down on Sabrina.

Zach swigs the rest of his second pint down, gasps out loud then claps Jason on the back and sets on his way.

'Have you already been with yer one?' I ask Jason after Zach has disappeared into the crowd. He clenches his teeth and nods his head.

'Ye shudda just told him, for fuck sake.'

'Ah… thought it best if he didn't know. He didn't even tell me he fancied her. The usual shit. Thinks he has first dibs on everything.'

'Poor Tina,' I say.

'And Scott. And Charlie.'

Zach's been married around ten years now. Him and Tina have two sons; one they had before they wed, the other straight after. He's often told me and Jason that he wouldn't have married Tina if she hadn't fell pregnant. As if it was all her fault. But I actually think they're a good couple. Zach needs Tina. He'd go off the rails without her. He'd be fucked.

Still, it doesn't stop him cheating on her almost every time he goes out. He can't help it. Feels a night out isn't a night out unless he's pulled. He's always felt that way. He's the only one of us who cheats. Jason's only had one serious girlfriend, which lasted about two years, but all through that period he stayed faithful to Jessica. I still can't quite figure out why they broke up. 'We just grew apart,' has never really been fully explained to me. That's because Jason can't fully explain it to himself, I bet. My genuine feeling is Jessica got sick of him moping around the house. Jason used to be always in good spirits, certainly was when they first met, but his happiness seemed to erode a few years ago. He's become a lot more introverted. I think it's because his career is coming to an end. Think he might even be suffering from a touch of depression these days.

His current state of mind reminds me of the Jason immediately following The Secret. He shut down back then, kept all of his thoughts to himself. His depression didn't last too long though. Hopefully it doesn't now.

Getting away from Ireland helped after The Secret. So did the excitement of a promising Premier League career. He was sixteen when Everton snapped him up. Three years later he was making his first team debut against Manchester United; with me and Zach chanting his name from the stands of Goodison Park.

'Can't find her. She must be gone,' Zach says arriving back to us. That's a relief. I had visions of him coming back here after her telling him she'd already snogged his mate. It would mean Zach would be breathing heavily through his nose for the rest of the night, barely talking to either of us. It's happened before. Lots of times.

'She must be gone. Sorry mate,' I say. 'Plenty more fish in the sea.'

He spins his head around one more time, then shrugs his shoulders.

'You done with that pint, Li?' he asks.

I stare at the drink in my hand. It's still full. The two lads' glasses are empty.

'Ah... fuck it, I'll leave it,' I say, stretching to place it onto the shelf next to us.

'Fuck that,' says Zach, swiping the pint from me. He takes a deep breath before swigging from the glass, swallowing it all in one go. Then he looks at both of us, his eyes watering.

'Let's get the fuck outta here, boys,' he says.

19:40
Sabrina

I click the latch of the door, slap down the lid of the toilet and sit on it. Then I open the text message, squinting my eyes at the photograph. The face doesn't ring a bell. I definitely haven't copped this bloke since I've been here. Maybe he's just arrived. The text message isn't clear on that.

Target in place. Downstairs bar in Hairy Lemon. Be careful. Best of luck. Lorna. x

The guy looks pretty handsome in the pic. Not normally my type, but it helps my job if they're good looking because it makes everything more believable and less awkward. I click into my emails, recall the notes even though I've read them about eight times today.

Niall Stevens. Age 27. Car mechanic. Lives with his fiancée. Hobbies include watching Formula One, TV shows like Top Gear & Robot Wars. Loves Will Ferrell movies.

I stare at his picture again. Then place my phone back into my bag and stand up, open the lock and pace towards the mirrors. This toilet is pretty packed now. I have to stare over some girl's shoulder to get a good look at my face. I still wish I had worn something a little more comfortable, though this little number certainly worked on Jason Kenny. That was quite intense; never had somebody grab me up against a wall before, throwing their tongue in my mouth after literally meeting them two minutes prior. I enjoyed it. Probably shouldn't have put my hands down his pants though. It's most likely put him off me. He's probably moved on to his next girl already, thinking I was too easy — not enough of a challenge for a professional footballer. It's a pity work called for me when it did. If he's still around when I'm finished with Niall, I might go and speak to him. He did invite me to, after all.

I take one last look in the mirror, pull the V in my jumpsuit closer and decide to just get on with it. I almost see Amanda staring back at me. I think the older I get, the more I look like her. Amanda was a known model in Dublin. Signed up by Assets Agency when she was just seventeen. She used to appear on morning television all the time; me and my folks crunching on our Corn Flakes as she posed on our screens wearing the latest trends for some five-minute fashion item.

I used to think she had the most glamorous existence anyone could ever have. I was crazy jealous when I was a young teenager, though everyone kept assuring me my time would come. Apparently I was even better looking than my older sister. That's what they used to tell me. My time never really did come, though. I did a couple of those morning TV shows after I was signed up to a much smaller agency than Assets about eight years ago. It wasn't the glamorous gig I had assumed it would be when I was younger. Far from it. While Amanda spent ten years modelling, I only lasted two. Not even two. About twenty months. Casting agents used to tell me on a regular basis that I was 'too pretty' and 'too commercial' to land the jobs they were specifically looking to fill. I took myself way too seriously. Barely cracked a smile all through my teens. I'm sure this had an impact on casting agents. It's not just about looks — personality comes into it too, no matter how hard that is for anyone who's not a model to believe. It's a shitty business, modelling. And that's exactly what it is – a business. It's not glamorous from the inside at all. Modelling isn't about being pretty, it's about being a saleswoman. It's too corporate. Takes itself way too seriously. And I became a mirror of it. I'm pretty certain my aspirations of becoming a model, which I held from the age of twelve — when Amanda first started out — is the reason I'm introverted; the reason I haven't quite figured myself out; the reason I don't have much of a personality; the reason the prude angel on my shoulder always wins out over the devil. It's also the reason I don't have many friends.

School was torturous for me, though the torture happened long before I became a mirror image of the modelling industry. One day – my memory tells me it was in the first year of secondary school, but that may be fuzzy – I accused Thomas D'Arcy of punching me on the arm, just so the teacher would move him away from me. I hated sitting beside him; he smelt. I punched myself in the arm repeatedly, until it bruised, then walked into the classroom, sat beside Thomas and raised my hand. 'Miss, Thomas just punched me,' I said, forcing some tears out of my eyes. My plan worked. I was moved. But because Thomas was more likable than me, the students took his side. I was left alone in the playground for pretty much the next six years until I got secondary school out of the way.

I pull open the door of the ladies, the noise of the music causing me to tut. I'm sure somebody's turned the volume up since I've been to the loo. I suck my lips, take in every face before me, searching for the guy who's in to Formula One, who's into Will Ferrell movies.

'Wow,' says some guy, standing back a bit so he can take all of me in. I just purse my lips at him in an almost sorrowful way, then walk on by. Turning lads' heads isn't a thrill for me; it never has been. I thought being good looking was a blessing when I was younger, only because it would help in my ambitions to become a model. But it genuinely isn't any advantage whatsoever. Anyone who thinks being good looking is advantageous is one of two things; either they are an idiot or they've never been good looking themselves.

Amanda and I are perfect examples of looks not counting towards happiness. We're both genetically blessed; both miserable at finding love. Sure take the hottest women on the planet: Halle Berry, Jennifer Aniston, Angelina Jolie, Charlize Theron… All hot as fuck. All miserable in love.

I'm pretty sure being good looking is a disadvantage because if you are good looking then that almost seems enough for most guys. They don't need to look past that initially, they don't need to go deeper. Once the novelty of the good looks wears off, which it inevitably does in every relationship, then the guy who hasn't bothered to get to truly know you doesn't know why he's dating you anymore. If it can happen to Halle Berry – constantly – then it can happen to anyone. I'd love to trade my looks for a better personality. I'd love to lighten up, be more outgoing. My new job is helping me come out of my shell, though. I'm getting better at it. I feel more confident now than I've ever felt in my life.

I rub at my palms. They always get a bit sweaty moments before I have to approach a target. They'll stop sweating once I'm talking to him. That's always the way; like an actress waiting backstage before she goes on. She shits herself behind the curtain, is cool as a cucumber as soon as that curtain rises. It's just adrenaline clamming my hands up. I'll be fine. I always am.

'Lookin' for someone, love? It's not me, is it?' some fat guy asks me. I just smile at him. Walk on to the end of the bar. And that's when I see him. Niall Stevens. Taking a sip from his pint, before continuing a conversation with his mate.

I take a deep breath and think through my plan. I've got this.

I mutter the words 'excuse me' as I brush between a

couple talking and make my way to the bar leaning into it beside Niall.

'Non-alcoholic red wine,' I say to the barman. I notice Niall has already clocked me. He took a peek over his shoulder after his mate pointed me out. I pretend not to notice. Then, after another deep breath, I knock into him – jarring my elbow into the small of his back just as he's taking a sip of his pint.

'Shit… I'm so sorry. So sorry,' I say, holding my hand up to my mouth. Then I reach out and brush my fingers through his shirt as if I'm trying to wipe away the beer he's just spilt.

'Please, lemme buy you another drink,' I say.

19:50
Jason

Li leads us down the stairs. He seems overly keen to get out of here; thinks it's too busy. He says he wants to have a talk with us, somewhere quieter. That's nothing new. Li likes to open up, values the opinion of his two best mates. Especially me. We're almost like brothers, Li and I. We share everything. Zach's a bit more insular. A bit reluctant to open up.

When we're half-way down the steps I notice her. On the far side of the bar. I turn to Zach, just to try to block him from seeing her. I pull him in for a headlock, keeping his eyes down.

'C'mon Zach, cheer up, mate, this is gonna be a great night.'

'I'm alright, I'm alright,' he says into my armpit. 'Lemme go, for fuck sake.'

I only let him go after we've both reached the bottom of the stairs, Sabrina out of sight. Another bout of 'Boom, boom, boom... lemme hear ya say Jayo,' sounds out. I acknowledge it by holding my hand in the air, but head straight towards the exit without stopping to shake anyone's hand or signing another autograph. I turn to my two best mates as soon as we get outside.

'Hang there one more sec, will ye lads?' I say. 'I told a bloke in there I'd sign a quick autograph for his son before I left. He's just at the far side of the bar. Won't be long.'

I jump back inside. The chant starts up again, but I keep my head down and pace towards Sabrina. I can't let a girl like her go. But it dawns on me quickly that I have to. She's talking to some other guy. Probably her boyfriend. I watch as she laughs at one of his jokes. Damn it. I shudda known.

I turn on my heels, head for the exit again.

19:50

'Jason, can I have a quick pic—'

'Sorry man,' I say, rushing by.

It's unusual I'd snub a fan. But he just caught me at a wrong time — in a moment of self-pity. Those moments seem to come to me more often these days.

'Right!' I say, rubbing my palms together as soon as I get back outside, trying to gee myself up for a rare night out with my two besties. 'Where we off to?'

'Your call, Li,' Zach says as he lights up a cigarette.

'I just fancy a nice quiet Irish pub, somewhere we can sit down, have a chat. I thought it'd be quiet in there,' he says nodding back at the Hairy Lemon.

'Jaysus... a quiet chat? Are you sure this is not about... y'know, The Secr—'

'It's not about The fuckin' Secret,' Li snaps back at Zach.

My stomach turns itself over. It's been ages since any of us have talked about that. At least a couple of years since the subject's even been broached by any of us. Not that it's out of our minds. Jesus no. All three of us still live with it most days, I'm sure. I pray about it every night; offer my apology to God and thank him for his forgiveness.

The three of us agreed years ago that we'd stop letting it consume us; that we'd stop talking about it with each other. It was over half our lifetime ago now. Twenty years ago this summer in fact. It happened just a couple of months after I'd signed for Cherry Orchard. I'd been putting in great performances for the Bosco for five seasons. Either me or Zach would end up with the Player of the Season award every year. In fact, I won it three times, him twice in the five years we played together. A few scouts from bigger teams around Dublin started to turn up at our matches. It was obvious they were looking at us two. Cherry Orchard offered both of us a trial, the chance to play in the highest divisions of schoolboy football. A chance to be spotted by proper scouts — scouts from England's biggest clubs.

They ended up asking me to sign for them. But not Zach. I had to lie to Zach. Tell him that the only reason the Cherry Orchard coaches didn't want him was because they already had too many strikers and didn't need another one. He couldn't understand it. Couldn't quite get his head around the fact that I'd leapfrogged him; that I was playing at a standard much higher than he was.

We were fifteen at the time. There's only two weeks between me and Li. Zach's four months younger. Me and him had to stay disciplined at weekends if we wanted to make it in football. But Zach started to slide. He felt we needed more fun; that we needed to let our hair down at the weekends. He started drinking and smoking. Li gave in to the pressure, started drinking himself. But I didn't. I had no intention of throwing away the opportunity I'd been given at Cherry Orchard.

Zach used to wait till his dad went down to the Marble Arch for his usual Saturday night drinks before stealing his car keys and taking the three of us out for a joy ride. We'd head to the coast, out towards Howth, just for something to do. The two lads would be swigging back warm cans of cider. Zach would drive out, I'd normally drive back. But it didn't happen that way this night. Li took the wheel. He just said he fancied it. And I let him. Even though he'd downed about four cans.

Though in fairness to Li, she appeared from out of nowhere. We genuinely didn't see her. Not until the car skidded to a stop.

4

Brian holds his palms flat to the wall and pushes his left calf back to stretch it as if it's half-time in a football match. The judge did tell the jurors they would receive five-minute breaks 'to stretch their legs', but it's not supposed to be taken so literally. It certainly can't be literal in Number Three's case because she doesn't have the use of her legs. She's wheeling her wheelchair up and down the corridor, humming to herself while most of the other jurors have huddled themselves into different corners of the corridor, talking. Not about the trial – they're all staying loyal to the rule that they can only discuss the trial when all together – but about their lives. Weirdly, although they don't know each others' names – for the most part – they know an awful lot about each other.

'Okay jurors,' says a young man dressed all in black, opening the door to the jury room with an overly-big bunch of keys. They file back in one-by-one, Brian deliberately standing at the door and motioning with his hand that everybody should enter ahead of him again. He read about this approach in a self-help book about how to treat the general public and felt it would help him become a more popular politician.

'So...' Number One pauses, gazing down at his notes. 'We... eh... move on to ... yes, Copper Face Jacks. Did Sabrina or did she not—'

'Hold on for one second... if you don't mind me interrupting you, Number One, sorry everybody,' says Number Twelve. 'I just found a small flaw in the way we are deliberating. If we are going through the night in chronological order, then we are missing some of the picture. We're missing out some of the background of these four people. Some of the eh... the...'

'The character witnesses,' says Number Ten.

'Exactly,' Number Twelve says, sitting more upright. 'Like the photographer and the journalist. The fella who testified against Sabrina, and the other fella who testified against Jason and Zach. This kind of evidence – if you can call it evidence – gets ignored if we are just talking about the night in question.'

'Good point,' Brian says. 'We should discuss the character witnesshes at some point. What do we even think of the first photographer teshtimony – about Sabrina?'

'Yes... a Mr Patrick Clavin. Does anyone even find his testimony that pertinent?' Number One asks nobody in particular. It's been one of his biggest flaws as Head Juror — he doesn't direct his questions at anyone specifically. He just thrusts them out there, to the middle of the conference table.

Patrick Clavin has had a photography studio on Thomas Street in Dublin since the late eighties. He started off photographing weddings, communions, confirmations, that kinda thing; made quite a few quid for his troubles. But as he evolved his business, he evolved his clientele and has been working with top talent agencies for the past decade. He is a genuinely nice guy, never once even considered cheating on his wife and their four kids, though he still gets a kick out of photographing pretty actresses and models for a living. He testified on behalf of the defence that Sabrina Doyle had been a client of his back in 2012, seeking nude shots. He proved to be a very honest witness, certainly amongst the jurors. But some wondered if his testimony was even worthy of being heard during the trial. The defence, doing their due diligence in search of some dirt on Sabrina, contacted a number of people she had worked with over the years, many not able to help their cause. Nobody had anything bad to say about Sabrina Doyle, aside from the fact that she could be a bit moody every now and then. But Clavin let slip that she had done some nude modelling for him six years prior and suddenly they pounced on him, believing his testimony would paint an image in the minds of the jurors that Sabrina was in some way fascinated with both sex and celebrity.

Clavin believed he was just following protocol by agreeing to confirm this information at the trial, but as he sat in the stand giving his evidence, he began to feel really guilty. He looked at Sabrina, knew he had been spun by the defence into painting a negative picture of the claimant. And he actually liked Sabrina. He just answered the questions coming at him as honestly as he could and then kept his head down as he exited the courtroom. Sabrina insisted his testimony was 'mostly made up' when she was called to the stand. 'I did indeed attend Patrick Clavin's studio in August twenty-twelve, but I never posed nude,' she said. The jurors were perplexed by this, couldn't understand why Clavin would lie. Unless, perhaps, he was coerced by the defence. It was an argument worth raising.

'I don't know,' says Number Eleven. 'He was definitely nervous on the stand, but I just got the impression he was telling the truth. Let me hold my hands up now and say I am genuinely leaning towards guilty — I think those lads took advantage of Sabrina that night, raped her. But I actually feel she might be lying in this particular instance. I don't know what it is... I believe her every time she speaks, but not here... not about the nude photos.'

'Clavin's testimony was believable,' agrees Number One. This also went against what Number One believed overall — that Jason, Zach and Li were all guilty of raping Sabrina Doyle. But he too found it difficult to dispute the photographer's testimony; didn't believe the defence were evil enough to ask somebody to just make a story up in order to discredit a claimant. Number One's real name is Albert Dwyer, a fifty-five-year-old car mechanic from Rathcoole in Co Dublin. He looks wise – sports glasses, wears his thick head of silver hair neatly split from left to right. It was on appearances alone that led to his fellow jurors electing him over Brian as Head Juror. But Number One hasn't been great in this role at all. He's too indecisive, and lacks the balls to keep everybody in line. Another example of appearances being deceiving.

Number One found himself feeling the defendants were guilty pretty early on in the trial. He couldn't bring himself to believe a beautiful young woman like Sabrina Doyle would consensually have sex with three men in one night. Number One is married with two daughters. It had been advised by the judge that personal experiences shouldn't enter the consciousness of the jurors when considering a verdict, but that's impossible advice to curtail. Number One's daughters aren't far off Sabrina's age. He sees them in her. Her in them. For that reason, more than any other, it would be extremely difficult to persuade him into the not guilty camp. He's adamant that Jason, Zach and Li deserve to do time behind bars.

One of the big question jurors find themselves stewing over their mind when it comes to rape cases is the difficult-to-comprehend notion that a woman would cry rape when in fact she hadn't been raped at all. Jurors find this more difficult to morally accept than they do actual rape. For some reason, crying rape when you haven't been raped constitutes as a harsher crime than actual rape in the mindsets of the general public. It's bizarre. Sabrina's case is a fascinating one to consider under these terms: what does she have to gain from claiming these three men raped her? Is she after Jason's money? Or – as is the question most jurors morally ask themselves when examining trials like this – did Sabrina have consensual sex with all three men and then only afterwards feel she was raped? Number Nine raises this point to the room.

'It's possible,' Number Eight answers first, staring straight ahead.

'Yeah, I think that kind of thing is a big possibility,' Number Twelve follows up with. 'A girl feeling guilty the next morning for the... y'know... whatever happened the night before.'

'You can't rule it out,' says Brian. 'Ugh... I don't know. I just... I genuinely think we have to find them not guilty. There jusht isn't enough evidensh—'

'Hold off, Brian,' scoffs Number One. 'We aren't having a bloody verdict vote at the minute... we're not saying what we think overall.'

He sits more upright, elbows on the table, staring down at Brian. He's almost sporting a grin as if he has something in his armoury that will bring Brian down a peg or two.

'So you think not guilty overall, yeah?' he says, swinging one of his hands as if he has adopted a teenage attitude. 'So do you believe Sabrina Doyle is lying about not approaching the three men initially in the Hairy Lemon?'

Brian nods his head slowly, sits back in his chair, almost welcoming the test.

'And you believe she is lying about the nude photos...

about the handjob… about going to that nightclub Copper Face Jacks?'

Brian nods again, shrugs his shoulders too.

'You believe she's lying about the rape too, yeah? Lying about everything?'

'Yesh, yesh I do,' says Brian, leaning forward again, placing both of his elbows on the table to mirror his nemesis in body language.

'Why?' asks Number One, his face glowing pink.

'Why what?' asks Brian.

'Why would she lie about everything? What does she gain from making all of this stuff up?'

'Well that ish one question I can't answer,' Brian says.

Number One scoffs, but Brian continues.

'And I know I can't answer it because I have had that question running through my mind all through this trial. For weeksh I've had that spinning around in my head. And for weeksh I've failed to justify an answer.'

It is believed, though it can't be proven, that in ninety-two per cent of rape cases the claimants are not lying. A massive majority of women who claim they were raped, claim it because they were indeed raped; or certainly believe they were raped. Only a tiny fraction of rape claimants have ulterior motives. Sadly, even though it's believed that ninety-two per cent of rape claims are genuine, only a pitiful eighteen per cent of rape trials end with a guilty verdict, though those numbers are growing — both the number of rape claims and the percentage of guilty verdicts. Unfortunately the former is growing rapidly, the latter very slowly. This particular trial is the two-hundredth and sixty-sixth rape trial that has taken place in Ireland this year, and yet it is occurring in the first week of July: the half-way point of the calendar year. Last year Ireland saw a significant spike in rape reports. In 2016, five hundred and twelve claims of rape were reported, there were six hundred and fifty-five in 2017. This year there is projected to be over seven hundred and twenty. The graph line is practically pointing north on rape claims throughout the country. But sadly that is not the most alarming statistic when it comes to rape. The most jaw-dropping fact is that these growing numbers only take into consideration rapes that are reported. A vast majority go unreported. It is believed, although impossible to prove, that up to eighty per cent of rapes are never reported to police.

'She may have just wanted his attention, his money, his fame,' says Number Eight.

'Well, she's not getting any of that is she?' Number Ten says. 'She's been hiding – and rightfully so – behind the name Ms X in the newspapers, she's not getting any attention, not getting any money, any fame.'

'I don't know... I'm just trying to answer the question,' Number Eight shrugs. 'Maybe she's planning on selling her story down the line. I mean, she must try to court attention in some ways, right? She's a model after all. And if she did do these nude shots, then what sort of attention are you trying to court?'

'Yeah, but that's only if you believe she did the nude shots,' says Number Ten.

20:05
Zach

Every time I mention the two words *The* and *Secret* I get hushed. It's been twenty years since we first labelled it 'The Secret', and vowed never to talk about it again; decided to leave what happened in the past exactly there — in the past. But sometimes I wish we could all sit down and talk about it... get it all off our chests.

The three of us stroll towards Aungier Street almost in silence; the fact that I mentioned those two words playing on all three of our minds. I wonder how often Jason and Li think about it; wonder if they think about it more than I do.

I recommended The Swan Bar, felt it would be one of the quietest pubs around. Li can tell us whatever the hell he wants to tell us in there, then we can get on with our night. Have some fun. We'll probably end up in Copper Face Jacks now that we're heading in this direction. I know it has a piss-poor reputation, but I love Coppers. It's rare I'd leave there without scoring some bird. Everyone who goes there is practically out for their hole. I certainly am tonight. I'm sick of the same pussy every night. Ye can't beat a bit of strange. I genuinely don't believe in monogamy; think asking a male mammal to stick with one female is asking a bit too much. We're just not cut out for it.

I didn't cheat on Tina for the first four months after meeting her. I was kinda proud of that, but four months was my limit. I love sex, certainly sex with strange birds, but it's more the chattin' them up that is the drug for me. I just love the back-and-forth of the chase; the flirting, the bullshit. I'm a great bullshitter. I'm pretty sure I could bullshit any bird into bed. If I saw Margot Robbie out in a club, I'd have no hesitation in chatting her up. And I'd probably score her too. When it comes to scoring birds, it's not about looks – that's not what they look for in a man. They just want to be charmed, made to laugh. No better man to make a woman laugh than me. I wish that Sabrina bird hadn't left the Hairy Lemon so quickly. She was definitely a few levels above me when it comes to looks, but I'm pretty sure I could have scored her.

'Where is this place?' asks Jason. He doesn't really know Dublin as well as me and Li. Never really took advantage of the nightlife this city has to offer. Even when he lived here, he stayed in at the weekends. Football always came first for him. Fun comes first for me. Always has. I'm sure some think that's why he made it over me, but I don't buy that bollocks for one second. Some of my favourite ever players could handle a few drinks as well as a football career. If Ireland's greatest ever player – Paul McGrath – could balance a social life and a professional football career, then so could I. I just didn't get the breaks. No point in wallowing in it now anyway. At least that's what I tell myself regularly.

'Just on the next corner,' I reply, pointing up Aungier Street.

'Don't think I've been in this place before, is it rough?' Li asks.

'Yer ma's rough!' I fold my fingers into my palm, hold it out, and take a fist bump from both Li and Jason for the gag.

'Ah, it's just a quiet bar. We'll have one in there, then head up to Harcourt Street, will we?' I say.

'Coppers?' Li asks.

'Fuck it, why not!'

'Yeah – fuck it,' says Jason, laughing.

I swing the door of The Swan open and spot a free table at the front window.

'Right, big shot,' I say to Jason, 'your round, mate. Three Heinekens.'

Li and I take a seat at the table. I stare at him, wonderin' what the hell he has to tell us. I love this fella to bits, I'd do anything for him. But he can kinda do my head in sometimes. He takes everything too seriously. I don't know why he feels the need to be formal all the time; don't know why we all have to be sitting around a quiet table when he has somethin' to tell us as if we're havin' a bloody office meeting. If I had something to say to my two best mates, I'd just bloody say it to them.

It's too far back for me to remember fully, but when we were kids I'm pretty sure Li was as outgoing as I was. But ever since The Secret, he lost his edge. But maybe he carries more guilt than me and Jason. He was the one driving after all. I can still hear the thump of her hitting the car. I opened the passenger door, stared at her lying on the ground in front of us. It all seemed to happen in slow motion after that. I don't even recall hearing sounds as Jason got out of the car and ran towards her. Li followed him. I just stayed in my seat, a wave of sobriety splashing me in the face.

'Get the fuck back in the car,' I screamed at them when I clicked back to reality. They did. Both of them.

'She's breathing,' Jason said to me, almost hyperventilating as he jumped in the back seat. Li was more composed. In fact, he set The Secret in motion. That's my memory of it anyway. We probably all have different versions of that night. But seeing as we've vowed to never talk about it again, I can't be entirely sure what their memories of that night are. But I definitely remember Li suggesting we drive off; leave her.

So we did. Li turned the car around, headed back towards Drimnagh. Each of us silent for the whole half-hour drive. We even turned the car radio off. It was the most silent silence I've ever heard.

20:05

'Here y'are,' Jason says, plonking the three pints in front of us.

'Cheers,' I say, holding my pint glass up.

We clink. Again.

'Now,' Jason says, looking at Li as he sits himself into the chair between us. 'What've ye got to tell us, buddy?'

20:05
Sabrina

I like this guy. He's polite enough to include me in the conversation, but also loyal enough to his girlfriend to indicate he has no interest in me. We've shared a couple of anecdotes, a few laughs. But he's mentioned his fiancée to me twice already. If he was interested in pursuing me, he'd have kept his relationship schtum. He's a good guy; cute, honest, funny. His fiancée is a lucky girl.

'Can I get you one back before we leave?' he asks.

'Oh no, thank you. I owed you that for spilling your pint,' I reply.

He waves his hand.

'Ah... let me get you one back.'

He motions to the barman.

'Glass of red for the girl please.'

'And a couple of pints?' the barman asks.

'Nah, sorry — we have to head off now,' Niall says back to him.

Shit.

'Are you eh... are you leaving now?' I say.

'Yeah – we've to meet another mate.'

'Well, I'm only going to have that one you ordered me if you're having one,' I say, finishing off my wine. He looks at his friend, then back at me.

'G'wan... two pints of Miller as well,' he shouts over to the bar man.

Great — he's staying. I've got to work harder on him. Everything seems very positive so far, but I don't have enough information. Not yet anyway.

'So, what is it you do?' his friend asks me. 'Lemme guess, you're a model?'

I sniff a laugh out through my nose. Quite a few people take that guess with me. Perhaps they're right in some way, but only if they use the past tense.

My modelling career basically involved multiple meetings, eight five-minute TV appearances, and sixteen catwalks — some of them in front of about eight people. That was it. I spent most of my twenty months as a model being peered at by casting agents and hearing the word 'no' over and over again. No wonder I became an introvert. People with positive mindsets certainly don't work in an industry plagued by rejection. You think I'd have been well prepared for it. I had an older sister who had been through the ringer before me, who could pass on appropriate advice. But Amanda almost seemed embarrassed by the fact that her job wasn't as glamorous as her younger sister assumed it was. She didn't want to ruin the fantasy for me. Not once did she ever say anything negative about her work — not to me anyway.

My agent – Anne Ray – was a good confidante . I got lucky there. I'd heard horror stories about other agents. She did her job perfectly and was completely transparent and trustworthy. She always got me in front of the right people. But I couldn't close the deal. I'd say I was recruited for about two per cent of the jobs I'd present myself for. It was Anne's idea for me to visit Patrick Clavin. She even paid half of the fee. She felt my commercial face would benefit from his work; that he could put a portfolio together for me that would define what path I should take in the industry. He was a lovely man, Patrick. I felt at ease with him straight away.

Even though he'd shot a thousand models before me, he wasn't boring company at all. He was personable, asked me about me, not about work. He'd heard of my sister, had never shot her though. He was very sympathetic when I told him of her plight.

'You are very beautiful, very commercial,' he told me. 'But so too are ninety five of the last one hundred girls I've shot.'

I'd heard this loads of times and had already begun to realise my looks didn't really help me at all in this industry. Casting agents aren't looking for pretty faces, they're looking for unusual faces.

'Have you thought about glamour?'

I sighed, almost rudely.

'It's been mentioned,' I said. 'Anne has said it to me a few times, but I just... it's just not why I wanted to be a model.'

'I totally understand,' said Patrick. 'Look, the money is good. And it's all about hotness. In the glamour industry, all that's required is good looks. You certainly tick that box.'

I chewed on my lip, trying to let on to Patrick that I was thinking about his proposal. But the truth was, I'd already thought about it; already decided glamour modelling wasn't for me. I couldn't imagine my dad opening up a magazine to see me smiling back at him, my arms folded under my bare breasts.

Patrick rang Anne, had her on speakerphone for about twenty minutes as the three of us discussed the prospect. Patrick cut a deal with Anne; said he would destroy his negatives, that he'd send digital versions of the photos to her and insisted she would be the only one who held copies. So I agreed. I took off my clothes, changed into some sexy lingerie he had in storage, then let him take some risqué shots – some of them nude. Nothing too graphic. Everything was nicely lit; sexy, classy and I certainly didn't feel as uncomfortable as I feared I would. But I knew these photos would never see the light of day; that I'd have a conversation with Anne the next time I was speaking to her and tell her I didn't want them to be sent out to anyone. And she kept her word; took it with her to her grave two years ago. Anne Ray was always honest with me. It's actually a must-have trait in the fashion industry. Everyone's honest with everyone. Too honest, I would say. I worked with Patrick again, trying to perfect a commercial portfolio for myself, but it didn't get me anywhere. There are just too many commercial girls in this world.

I tell Niall and his friend a brief synopsis of the truth. I *had* been a model — tried it out for a couple of years. Got nowhere. Neither him nor his mate could believe it.

'But I see models all the time in ads and stuff that aren't half as good lookin' as you,' Niall says.

I thank him for the compliment, touch his arm as I am doing so and pause to see if he will reciprocate my approach.

'Yeah sure, if it was just about looks, my fiancée cudda been a model too,' he says. That's so cute. Too cute in fact. I'm almost feeling a bit neglected here. I would be hurt if rejection wasn't my actual aim.

I watch Niall drain down the last of his pint of Miller, trying to work out whether or not I had enough information on him. I think I do.

'Claire, it has been a pleasure meeting you,' he says, holding out his hand for me to shake. And I do shake it, as if we're professionals who have just ended a work meeting. Niall has no idea I'm the only one working right now.

'Yeah – I enjoyed our little chat,' I say. 'And you too, Martin.'

I hold my hand out for his mate to shake and suddenly they are on their way, heading for the exit. Before they've reached the door, I have the phone to my ear.

'Hey Sabrina,' says Lorna answering. 'Have you completed the job?'

20:10
Jason

'Three Heinekens,' I say to the barman as Zach and Li take a seat. I get the sense this could be one of those shitty nights where we let Zach's mood dictate everything. Though that could all change depending on what Li has to tell us. It can't be anything to do with The Secret. Li's been the best at brushing that under the carpet. In fact, I'm pretty sure it plays less on his mind than it does mine and Zach's. Li's the nicest bloke I know. But he can be cold and calculated when he needs to be.

'First round is on us, Jason,' the barman says after placing the three pints on the bar and winking at me. 'For that goal against Holland.'

I thank him, almost apologetically, then plonk my arse onto the seat between my two best mates.

'Slainté,' Zach says as we clink glasses for about the eighth time tonight. And we've only had a couple of drinks. It's just so rare that the three of us get out these days that we can't help toasting each other. We're not toasting much. Just the fact that we're in a pub. It's such a rarity these days.

I know it's my fault, I'm the one who moved away, who got a career that meant I had to be disciplined — but I don't think anyone's complaining. I sometimes wonder how our friendships would have gone if I hadn't moved to England. Perhaps we'd have all pissed each other off by now. We probably wouldn't be such good friends if we'd spent every single weekend of the last twenty years doing what we're doing now: drinking beer and talking shit.

'Now, what've ye got to tell us, buddy?' I say, turning to Li.

He picks up his mobile phone, scrolls through it then turns the screen towards me and Zach.

'Fuckin' hell – yes! Congratulations mate,' I say after my eyes focus to take in the photo.

'I've ordered it online. It's gonna arrive next Wednesday.'

'She'll be fuckin' delighted,' says Zach. 'How ye gonna do it?'

'Well, we're going to Lanzarote next month aren't we – I'm gonna do it there.'

'Hold on, you're gonna get engaged in Lanza-fuckin-rote?' Zach asks.

'Y'know, on the beach when the sun goes down or is coming up, or something romantic like that.'

'Don't mind him, Li,' I say pulling my best mate in for a hug. 'Why would you take tips on romance from this fuckin' eejit, huh?'

The three of us hold each other in a bit of a huddle. We're good like that, good at noting milestone moments in each of our lives. When we want to be, we can be right in the moment, all of our stresses and strains miles away; The Secret all but forgotten. But these moments happen way too infrequently these days.

'And I want you as best man,' Li says after releasing us from the huddle. 'And you as groomsman, Zach.'

We don't answer, not verbally anyway. We just reform the huddle and soak in the moment again.

'Bottle of champagne,' I shout out to the barman. 'Most expensive one you have.'

I walk up to the bar, a smile wide on my face. I'm so happy for Li. And for Niamh. They're an ideal couple. Perfect for each other. They're both so headstrong – it makes me a little jealous actually. I don't think anybody would have thought when we were younger that by the time we all got into our thirties, Li would be the only one who had his shit sorted out.

'A thousand and ninety-nine euro,' the barman says, holding up a black bottle. I can make out the word Krug-something or other on it.

'T'fuck,' I say. 'Over a grand?'

'You said the dearest one.'

I stare over at Li, watch him smile as wide as he can while Zach ribs him again for planning on getting engaged in Lanzarote.

'Fuck it, go on.' I say, handing over my debit card.

Li deserves it. I had two reservations when I left for England; one was that I would be leaving my little brother Eric behind. I knew he looked up to me, would miss me terribly, and two; I would be leaving Li behind. For the exact same reasons.

Playing for Cherry Orchard put me in front of the world's most influential scouts. I'd heard rumours that head scouts from Manchester United, Arsenal and Celtic were looking at me, but that's all they were – *rumours*. Besides, I wasn't the only good player on the pitch. At the level I was playing at with the Orchard, every one of the twenty-two players on the pitch at any one time had something special about them. I'd often walk out of the dressing room after a match, hoping a scout would call after me and offer me a trial. But that's not how it happened. I was hanging around a street corner with Li and Zach one Tuesday evening when my dad shouted my name out from the hall door of our house. I thought I was in trouble, until I got closer to my old man and could sense he was trying to stifle a smile.

'This fella wants to talk to you,' he said, motioning to the living room.

'Jason Kenny, how are you?' the stranger boomed out as if he was an actor on a stage. 'I'm Billy Kirby — Everton football club.' I stared at my old man. He wasn't stifling his smile anymore.

'Here we are, boys,' I shout out, getting back to the table with the black bottle of whatever-it-is and three flutes. 'Let's get this into us.'

I pour each of us a glass, hold mine up for our ninth clink of the night, but one of significance; so much so that I think it deserves a little speech.

'I'm so proud of you, Li, and proud of Niamh too. Here's to many, many years of happiness and eh... loyalty,' I say, meeting Zach's eye. He laughs. He knows he shows absolutely no loyalty to Tina. Doesn't hide that fact from anyone, except for her, of course. 'Congratulations man.'

We each clink glasses and take a sip.

'Uugh,' says Li as Zach makes a face, almost gurning with disdain at what he's just poured into his mouth. I'm certain my face is mirroring his.

Wow — a fucking grand for this piss.

20:20
Li

I scroll through my phone, pull up the picture of the engagement ring I've ordered for Niamh, then twist the screen around so it faces both Jason and Zach. I dart my eyes between both of their faces, waiting on the penny to drop.

'Fuckin' hell – yes! Congratulations mate,' Jason says, his mouth wide open.

'I've ordered it online. It's gonna arrive next Wednesday.'

'She'll be fuckin' delighted,' says Zach. 'How are ye gonna do it?'

'Well, we're going to Lanzarote next month aren't we, gonna do it there.'

'Hold on, you're gonna get engaged in Lanza-fuckin-rote?'

Typical Zach. He can't let me have my moment without taking the piss somehow. But I know he's delighted for me. I tell them I'll ask Niamh on the beach at sunset, or sunrise, then Jason drags me in for a hug. I hook my arm around Zach and bring him into the huddle too. I'm such a lucky bastard. Two great mates and a girlfriend who's going to be mine forever. If she says 'yes' of course. Though I'm pretty certain she will. She loves me as much as I love her.

'Don't mind him, Li,' Jason says. 'Why would you take tips on romance from this fuckin' eejit?'

I stare up at them both.

'And I want you as best man,' I say to Jason, 'and you as groomsman,' to Zach.

They both grab me in to repeat the hug, the three of us soaking in the news.

'Bottle of champagne,' Jason calls out over my shoulder to the barman.

'So where we gonna have the stag?' Zach asks after Jason runs to the bar. 'Should probably go to Kiev, I heard the birds there are fuckin' amazing.'

'Was thinking of something a little quieter,' I tell him. 'Out to the west coast; Galway, Kerry maybe.'

'T'fuck!' he says, before sipping on his beer. 'What are we supposed to do, fuck some traveller birds on a stag?'

Zach has never noted mine and Jason's loyalties to our girlfriends. He always includes us in his plans for cheating, as if it relieves some of the guilt from within him. A bit like The Secret.

The story circulated in the news for two full days; in both the newspapers and on the tele. Caitlin Tyrell was only nine years old at the time. Her dad had trusted her to go to the chipper as a late night treat. It was only a five-minute walk from her house, the only hurdle being the road she had to cross. And then we came along. Fuckin' eejits.

Bizarrely, the newspapers reported the police were on the lookout for a red saloon car. A car matching that description had been noted as speeding nearby around the time we hit Caitlin. That piece of information, given to the Gardaí by a witness walking their dog, was all the cops had to go on. And it was all they did go on. We got away with it. In the eyes of the law anyway — we certainly didn't escape the guilt. Well, I didn't anyway.

'I'm so proud of you, Li, and proud of Niamh too,' Jason says, after passing around a flute of champagne to each of us. 'Here's to many, many years of happiness and eh... loyalty — congratulations, my man.'

We each clink flutes.

'Uugh,' I say, almost spitting the drink back out. 'That's disgusting!'

Zach just rests his flute back on the table, squelches up his face to show how much he hated what he's just tasted. Jason follows suit.

'I just paid over a grand for that,' he says.

Zach and I burst out laughing.

'Fuck it, let's get outta here,' Zach says. 'Let's go celebrate in style. Pick up some chicks.'

'Where we off to?' Jason asks, standing up.

'Coppers?'

The three of us look at each other, nod our approval, then head out the door.

'I'm bringing this piss with me,' Jason says, picking up the bottle of champagne.

He strolls out of the pub behind us, slurping from the neck of the bottle, then passes it to me. It tastes just as revolting from the bottle as it did from the flute – like fizzy dishwater.

The three of us saunter up Aungier Street, passing the bottle between each other. I'm certain each time it comes back to me, none of the champagne is missing. The other two must be doing the same as I am, pretending to drink from it.

I'm delighted the night has turned around. Zach had threatened to turn it into a bit of a messy evening with trying to cop off with that Sabrina girl, but he's in much better form now – singing football songs with his two arms held wide over his head.

I was looking forward to tonight, couldn't wait to tell them both that I had just ordered an engagement ring for Niamh. She has no idea. Only five people know now; me, Jason, Zach and my mam and Jinny. They both helped me look online for the perfect ring that would suit Niamh's finger. Mam insisted Niamh would like a Number Nine cut stone, similar to the one Dad bought her. So we settled on a white gold version of a Number Nine cut. It cost me nine hundred and ninety quid — the most expensive thing I've ever bought.

I'm going to ring Niamh's dad in a few weeks' time, bring him for a pint down his local, do the decent thing and ask for his permission to marry his daughter. It's all planned out, except what I'm actually going to say to Niamh when I ask her. I want to say something meaningful, from the heart. Ensure it's the best moment of her life.

We turn onto Harcourt Street, Zach still chanting some sort of nonsense. He's probably improvising. He used to do that as a kid; make up chants about himself and ask me to sing them on the sidelines of the Bosco's matches. I think he was deadly serious, though you never quite know with Zach.

'Scuse me,' the bouncer says holding his hand to Zach's chest. 'Think you might have had a few too many.'

'He's with me,' Jason says, stepping forward.

'Ah, Jason Kenny! How are ye, my man? Listen, you'll have to get rid of the bottle, or finish it outside, then come in.'

'Here y'go, love,' Zach says, passing the bottle to a group of girls walking by. They take it from him, laughing their heads off.

'Copper Face Jacks mutha fuckers!' he screams out, smiling at the bouncer as he passes him by. Jason looks back at me and rolls his eyes.

Then we follow Zach inside the club.

5

Number Five lets out a yawn; doesn't even think to try to hide it. She's not tired, just bored. She isn't the only one. Number One hasn't been doing a good enough job as Head Juror. Not because he fails to rein in the arguments, but because he lacks authority.

He has been going through the night in chronological order, yet despite the jury being almost two hours in to their deliberations, they are only ninety minutes through the night in question. The numbers don't add up.

'It's insignificant,' Number Five whispers to Number Six as Brian repeats his argument for the third time. She didn't mean for anybody else to hear her, but she wasn't as discreet as she'd hoped to be.

'Sorry Number Five,' interjects Number One. 'What was that?'

Number Five lets out a deep breath, stares at Number Six for support and when none is forthcoming decides to speak her truth.

'Isn't it kinda insignificant? I mean we've been arguing this for almost half-an-hour alone. So what if she did have nude photos taken six years ago, so what if she didn't. What does it have to do with her possibly being raped years later?'

'Patrick Clavin is a character witness,' Number Twelve spits out. 'He is suggesting that not only is Sabrina Doyle interested in sexy images but she is also a liar.'

'Whoa, hold on there,' croaks Number Eleven. 'Clavin is not suggesting anything of the sort. He just gave a contrasting account about his work with Sabrina than she gave — that's all. Having said that, his testimony is significant in some ways. I believe Clavin, I think Sabrina did do nude shots and is too embarrassed to admit to them.'

'Well, we've had a deep enough discussion about it,' says Number One, bouncing his paperwork off the table again. 'I think it's fair to say most jurors agree with the testimony of the character witness. But that's all it is — a slight on Sabrina's character, not a certain indication that she was or wasn't raped.'

'It isn't insignificant, of course not,' says Number Twelve, 'but I guess we can all calculate just how significant it is in our own judgement.'

Number Twelve is doing his best to remain patient. He's normally smug, arrogant. Is already certain that the rest of the jury will eventually swing around to his way of thinking: *not guilty*. Twelve's real name is Dave Barry, a thirty-seven-year-old insurance broker from Inchicore in Dublin. He's happy enough with his nine-to-fiver, content with the bang-on average €38,000-per-year salary he accumulates. Has figured out a way to make it work for him, his fiancée of ten years and their now eleven-year-old daughter Molly. He could do better — certainly has the intelligence to carve out an enviable career for himself — but chooses not to. He's fine as he is. He complains about life, but is happy to complain. Number Twelve was initially intrigued about being called up for jury duty; his excitement growing when he realised he would be involved in the Jason Kenny case. He lied during the jury selection process: said he didn't know who Jason Kenny was. He wasn't the only one.

'Should we have another verdict vote now?' Brian offers to the table.

'You and bloody voting!' Number Three calls out, slapping at the arm rests of her wheelchair.

'Let's just hold off,' says Number Twelve. 'Maybe we can have one in another hour... see how our talks go before lunch.'

There is no protocol when it comes to juries having verdict votes during their deliberations. Some juries, like this one, start with a verdict vote. Some like to dive straight into their arguments, starting with the main points of the trial. This jury decided to discuss the night in chronological order, which is not an unusual tact when it comes to rape trials. Because these type of rapes tend to follow a similar pattern of victim-meeting-accused, victim-not-liking-accused-as-much-as-accused-likes-victim, victim-and-accused-ending-up-in-same-place, victim-taking-advantage-of-accused, it makes sense for jurors to examine the night in order. Though it's no surprise that the most significant debate lays heavily in the back end of the deliberations. The whole trial boils down to whether or not the jurors feel consent was or was not given during the sexual encounters both parties admit occurred sometime between midnight and half-past midnight during the night in question. Quite often a juror will have a very set verdict in their mind that they arrive at during a rape trial... until it comes to the final argument. Then, they can easily be persuaded they had it wrong all along. The truth is, during final arguments, gut instinct can easily be eroded.

'Well, let's move on to something that *can't* be considered insignificant then,' Number One says, without prompt this time. 'The defence's key argument, I guess, is that Sabrina knew who Jason Kenny was and sought him out for sex. I guess their strongest argument is that they believe she followed the men all the way to Copper Face Jacks. Now, we have solid evidence at this point that backs up their claims.'

Number One presses at a button on the conference table just in front of his Head Juror's chair.

'Can we see the CCTV footage of Harcourt Street, please?' he says into the speaker beside the button. The TV screen on the wall blinks on again.

'Okay… yes, this is the footage of Jason, Zach and Li all entering Copper Face Jacks at exactly eight-forty p.m.,' he says pointing towards the tiny white digits in the corner of the screen.

'Can we have the footage of Sabrina at eight forty-one on Harcourt Street?' Number One says, pressing down on the button on the table again. The screen blinks off. When it blinks back on, there is no mistaking the woman strolling past Iveagh Gardens, a mere five-minute walk from the nightclub the men had just entered. Even though the footage is grainy, Sabrina's white jumpsuit sticks out like a sore thumb in the centre of the screen.

'So as you can see, around about the same time the men are entering the club, Sabrina is close by having left the Hairy Lemon pub a good half-an-hour earlier,' Number One says.

'The one thing that bothers me about this,' says Number Twelve getting up off his chair, is that Iveagh Gardens, where she is walking right here,' he points at the screen, 'is past Copper Face Jacks. So she actually walked *past* the club. Not only that, this isn't the only time she walks in this direction. CCTV footage has her here about fifteen minutes later, right?'

'Yep, at eight fifty-six, she made the same trip,' Brian says, checking his notes. 'She practically walked around the block. She must have been waiting for them, then followed them into the club. She was after Jason in this inshtance, I've no doubt about that.'

'Can we totally rule out coincidence?' Number Three poses.

'A coincidence that they ended up in the same nightclub after being in the same pub some ten minutes walk away?' Number Nine responds, raising an eyebrow.

'Copper Face Jacks is a well-known club in Dublin, probably the most well-known. If you are on that side of town, and you fancy going to a club, then Coppers is the most likely destination.'

'Not when there's a nightclub directly across from the Hairy Lemon where they'd all been. Break For The Border. If she just fancied a dance, which is the reason she gave for going to Coppers in her testimony, why not go for a dance in Break For The Border... why walk all the way up Harcourt Street – *alone,* let's not forget — just to end up in the same place as the three men she'd already been talking to, one she already admits to kissing?'

Number Nine hates bringing up this argument, because she feels so sorry for Sabrina. But this is the one part of the night in question that irks her the most. It stopped her from voting guilty in the earlier verdict vote even though she really wanted to. But she's certain Sabrina followed the three men into Coppers; is starting to get swayed towards not guilty after putting her hand up as undecided earlier on.

'I agree with you,' Number One says. 'I find her testimony here very brittle. It can't be just a coincidence. Plus, we kinda have proof here, right? She was walking around in circles... she was killing time. Surely she was just waiting on the men to settle in the club.'

Sabrina had testified that she often attended Copper Face

Jacks — sometimes with her former boyfriend, the odd time alone. One bouncer even testified at the trial that he knew Sabrina's face to see in the club, if not her name. He said she used to go there with her boyfriend, that she always stood out to him because she was so much better looking than her other half. He did admit though that he hadn't seen her in there for 'quite some time' before the night in question. His testimony was the only crack of light Sabrina's legal team could cling to in this argument. They tried to suggest that visiting Copper Face Jacks wasn't unusual for Sabrina Doyle. Her own testimony on the stand, which did add up to what she had told police when she first reported the rape claim, was that she wanted to take in some fresh air after downing 'a few red wines' in the Hairy Lemon and just as she was walking around Iveagh Gardens, she thought "to hell with it, I'll go into Coppers for a dance, before going home". No matter how innocent she looked on the stand, passing off her bumping back into the three men in Copper Face Jacks as "mere coincidence" was difficult for each juror to buy.

There was one moment within the trial that helped bridge the coincidence theory somewhat though. Li never took the stand during the trial; a position most defendants take when faced with a rape charge. It's just too risky for them to put themselves in the position of being pelted with questions from the prosecution who are obviously intent on trying to trip them up. In Ireland – unlike most other European countries – juries are instructed that they must not draw any inference whatsoever about a defendant's decision not to take the stand. Despite this, Jason and Zach argued against the wishes of their defence team, both opting to give evidence. They wanted to put their side of the story across to the jury. During their time on the stand, the prosecution asked them both if they had told Sabrina they were going to Copper Face Jacks. Both admitted they hadn't. It meant the 'coincidence' argument could not be ruled out entirely. After all, if Sabrina didn't know where the three men were going when they left the Hairy Lemon, and she couldn't possibly have seen them entering — given her location at the time — then how could she have followed them in there?

'It's true that Sabrina couldn't have seen them entering Copper Face Jacks, right?' Number One says pointing to the screen again. It was a rhetorical question. He knew the answer. Everybody did. 'Because we know she was on the other side of Iveagh Gardens when they went in. So either she knew they were going in there, or – as she puts it – it was merely a coincidence that they all ended up in the same club.'

'Do you reckon Li told her where they were going?' asks Number Seven.

'You'd think if he did tell her, then he would have taken the stand to confirm this,' answers Number Twelve, sitting back in his chair and combing his fingers through his thinning hair in frustration. 'Listen, I know I'm in the not guilty camp and have made my feelings on this known. But just everybody for one second… look at the evidence here. We have to admit that it looks very likely she somehow caught wind that the men were in Coppers and she followed them in there. We can't know for certain, but the CCTV footage at the very least paints a picture of a woman who seems a bit on edge. She walks around in circles for twenty minutes before going inside the club. This doesn't look good for her. I'm as certain as I can be, without full knowledge, that she followed them in there. I know it doesn't suit my overall verdict, but I believe Sabrina Doyle is lying in this instance.'

20:40
Zach

I turn around, notice a gaggle of birds walking past the entrance of Copper Face Jacks and hand them the bottle of champers.

'Copper Face Jacks mutha fuckers!' I scream out as I pass the bouncer and head in to the club. Fuck you, dude. I'm with Jason Kenny.

You have to readjust your eyes when you walk into Coppers, even this early in the night. The place is only open a few minutes but it's always dark; the low ceilings and lack of windows giving it a bit of a claustrophobic feel.

It's not packed - not yet anyway - but there must be a fifty or sixty people in here already. I kinda love Coppers. It's cheesy as fuck, but everyone always has a good time in this place.

It has the reputation of being the place to go if you wanna cop off with someone. Ye normally get birds from down the sticks coming up to Dublin just for a night in Coppers — in the hope that they can snare some bloke from the capital. And I've been that Dublin bloke for a load of those birds. I'm happy to do my bit. Give them what they want. I'll certainly be happy to do that tonight. I'm dyin' for me hole. I mean, I can get it off Tina whenever I want, but it's just not the same, is it? Having sex with someone who's supposed to have sex with you just isn't sexy at all. Having to talk someone into sex, filling them with the bullshit that will help dampen their panties... now that's a proper fuckin' turn on.

I take every face in as I head towards the bar. I haven't seen the perfect girl — not yet. But it's early. The night is young. I turn around, find the other two are yards behind me. I don't know what takes them so long. They're always chatting, always in each other's ears. I've often wondered if they discuss The Secret behind my back. They probably assume I'm the strongest out of the three of us, that I've handled it all fine. But I do think about it — every now and then. Especially when I'm lying in bed, unable to sleep. The pictures of Caitlin Tyrell that I saw in the newspapers all those years ago can sometimes talk to me. She sometimes calls out in pain.

I thought Li got over it all pretty quickly to be honest. Especially as he was the one who was driving. I often think it's just his secret and that me and Jason are helping him keep it from everyone else. But I'd do anything for Jason and for Li. I'm never envious of them. People think I got pissed off with Jason because he became a pro and I didn't, but that's bullshit.

He knocked on my door one Wednesday morning slightly earlier than normal before we headed off to school. Told me he had something important to tell me. I was surprised he had agreed to go to Everton. I tried to talk him into waiting until Man United or Liverpool came knocking, but I couldn't blame him. Course I couldn't. I probably would have jumped on that deal myself if it came my way.

Me and Li had just finished our Leaving Cert a few months before Jason made his first-team debut. Li had already made up his mind, years ago. He wanted to study marketing at Rathmines College. I really didn't have any plans… well aside from turning pro. But, as I was approaching eighteen, I knew that wasn't going to happen for me. I even trialled for a couple of League of Ireland clubs. Both St Patrick's Athletic and Shelbourne agreed to let me train with them, but neither offered me a contract. By the time I trialled for them my heart had already decided it wasn't in the game anymore, though. My passion for the sport had gone, even if my ability hadn't.

I didn't know what to do with my life after school. I thought about following my brothers to different corners of the world, but I didn't wanna miss out on Jason's journey. I wanted to be with him as he made a name for himself.

He didn't want me living in England with him, though — felt it would be a distraction for him to have me or Li with him all the time. That pissed me off a little, especially after all I'd done for Jason over the years. But I could kinda understand it. When it comes to football, Jason has total dedication, total discipline. He even had that when he was ten years old playing for the Bosco.

I tried a couple of different jobs. I worked in a paint factory in Walkinstown for a few months before getting bored. Then I tried my hand at a bit of security, but that was a load of me bollocks. I left that one after ten days. I'd spend most of my time in the local pubs, spending whatever money I could cobble together on pints of Heineken. It didn't take long for me to give in to everything I had been warned to steer clear of from the time we were in school. The Drimnagh gangs are notorious around Ireland – everyone knows about them because they're plastered on the front pages of the Sunday tabloids every other week. I was determined not to get involved. I wanted to prove to everyone who thought I'd easily get tangled up in the gangs that I was stronger than they thought I was. But I couldn't help it.

It wasn't just the money that attracted me to working for Alan Keating. It was the fact that I actually had somethin' to do — a reason to get out of bed in the mornings.

'Shots, shots, shots,' I chant as Li and Zach finally catch up with me at the bar.

'Not fuckin' tequila,' Jason moans as he reaches for his wallet.

'What then?'

'Get those Baby Guinness things,' he says, 'they're not so harsh.'

'Three Baby Guinness,' I shout to the barman. It sounds like such a shite name for a shot. Shots are supposed to be a proper drink, a drink for grown ups. They shouldn't have the name 'baby' in them at all. It sounds like a pussy's drink. But I have to agree with Jason – they do travel down the throat well.

'Okay boys,' Jason calls out as the barman places the three shots in front of us. 'Let's get the night truly started. Are we ready?'

Jason hovers his debit card over the reader until it beeps, places it back in his wallet, then hands each of us a tiny shot glass.

'One, two three… go.'

We throw the shot into our mouths, crease our face up at the taste of Sambuca hitting the back of our throats. Then we begin to nod our heads to the beat of the music and shuffle towards the dance floor.

20:45
Sabrina

I lean against a lamppost, scrolling through my phone and glancing up at the entrance to the kebab shop every twenty-seconds or so. It's starting to get cold. I should have brought a light jacket to go over the jumpsuit.

I tug at the V again, not because I'm wary of one of my breasts falling out, but because goosebumps are popping up right through my cleavage. I take a look at the digits on the top of my screen. 20:45. The night is young. People are buzzing around town; some arguing over what bar they should go to next. I spot a couple outside Break For The Border snuggling into each other. It makes me think of Jason Kenny, not that he's been far from my mind over the past hour anyway. I click into the internet browser on my phone and type his name into *Google*. Jaysus, he looked a lot more handsome tonight than he does when he's on the pitch. He actually looks alright in half of the photos on Google, not so cute in the other half. It seems to me as if he's grown into himself, has grown into his looks as he's aged. Ginger guys do tend to get more handsome the older they get. His hair is less orange in the more recent pics, more a dark shade of auburn. Plus, the beard he has now is brown — it offsets the ginger. I like him. A lot. Such a shame I rushed back inside when I got the text message from Lorna. I don't normally have much to get excited about; hooking up with a celeb is certainly a good night out for me. Getting his phone number and meeting up with him for a date would have been even better.

I click into his *Wikipedia* page, try to work out how big a deal he is. He's played for both Everton and Sunderland. Whatever that means. I've heard of both teams at least, so it can't be that bad. He's made four hundred and ten appearances for Everton, two hundred and eighty-eight for Sunderland. Has sixty-two Ireland caps. But only scored three goals. Maybe he's not that good. He grew up in Drimnagh, was born in 1983. He's exactly ten years older than me. It even mentions here that he is a devout Christian. It's the only blemish I can find. That and the fact that if we had kids together, they could end up with orange hair.

As I'm scrolling through his page, I look up again, to the entrance of the Kebab shop. They're coming out, both holding a plastic bowl filled with chips. They turn left, on to Aungier Street. I place my phone back into my bag and follow. Slowly. I don't want them to notice me. I'll have to stay a distance behind them because I stick out like a sore thumb in this bloody white suit. I guess it wasn't a good choice for loads of different reasons.

As I turn on to Aungier Street I notice a picture of Nadia Forde smiling back at me. She's lovely, Nadia. Has done so well for herself. But I often wonder what made her stand out over me. She seemed to be the model who landed most of the jobs I auditioned for.

I never really gave up modelling. I guess it gave me up. Anne always held out hope that things would pick up for me, but she used to send me for cheap marketing jobs just so I could earn some money. The jobs were petty tacky. I'd stand at food festivals or car festivals and hand out fliers for about eight hours a day. Or worse, I'd have to wear some poxy fancy-dress costume to interact with kids. I don't mind kids, hope to have three myself one day. But the job of having to pretend to be happy and upbeat for eight hours consecutively was a serious stretch for me.

By the time I turned twenty-one, marketing was pretty much my full-time job. Anne called me into her office one day, said she had to let me go from her books; that I was wasting my money handing her over fifteen per cent for shit marketing jobs I could easily get for myself without her help. I thanked her profusely for all she had done for me over the few years I was with her. Made her promise once again that the nude photos I did with Patrick Clavin would never see the light of day. I knew they wouldn't. I regretted doing that shoot as soon as it was over. Even though Patrick was lovely and even though I trusted Anne implicitly, I was hugely uncomfortable that those images existed somewhere.

I stay about a hundred yards behind the two of them, stopping anytime they slow down. I've no idea where they're off to. Hopefully they're heading home. But I know for a fact that they landed in the Hairy Lemon about an hour ago and had two pints with me. They can't be calling it a night. They must be off somewhere else. Lorna told me I didn't have enough information on Niall Stevens yet; that I must get some concrete evidence one way or the other for the job to conclude. It's not the first time she's made me do this. It's the main aim of the job. I know I haven't nailed it; not yet anyway. Just because Niall mentioned his fiancée to me a couple of times doesn't mean much. I haven't justified the money Lorna is paying me. But I will. I'll give her the information she needs as soon as Niall and his mate decide where they're going next.

They turn on to Harcourt Street, my old territory. It's where Eddie used to bring me all the time. He was obsessed with this area of town. In fact, we met there; in the beer garden of Diceys. I do some calculations in my head. That would have been four years ago last month. Jaysus. Time does fly, even when you're not having fun.

Niall and his mate walk past Diceys and I immediately know where they're heading for. I cross over to the other side of the street and watch as the bouncer stops them for a quick chat before allowing them in.

20:45

Fucking Copper Face Jacks. Typical. It must be a couple of years since I've last been in there. I bet it hasn't changed. But I can't follow them straight in. That would look too suspicious. So I take a walk, decide I'll do a few laps of Iveagh Gardens and give it about fifteen, maybe twenty minutes before I pop in. Then I'll get the job done. At this rate I could be in bed before ten o'clock tonight. Perfect!

20:55
Li

Zach's the only one with natural rhythm out of the three of us. But it never really stops any of us. We take to the dance floor every time we're out — throwing shapes, most likely off beat. Well, I certainly do. I've never been able to dance. Never know what to do, other than flail my arms and stomp my feet. Jason has some moves, but most of the time he looks pretty awkward. We don't give a shit though. Once Jason's on a dance floor, the sharks circle. Suddenly there are dozens of people around us. Celebs are a DJ's dream. They get the party started.

I like Coppers. Always have fun when I'm here; not that I'm here that often anymore. Not since I met Niamh. Not because she doesn't like me to go out, but because I'd genuinely rather stay in. Throwing back shots and downing pints of beer just doesn't seem like an ideal way to spend a night anymore. That's what you're supposed to do in your twenties, not your thirties. I should be curled up on a sofa watching Netflix with Niamh, having an early night so we can go to Homebase with fresh heads in the morning. That's the stage of life I'm at right now. And I'm happy with it. *Very* happy with it.

I stare over at Zach, watch him body pop and assume the life I live would be hell on earth for him. He's the same age as Jason and me, but he doesn't agree that you have to slow the social life down as you get older. He's just as hungry for it now as he was when we were twenty-one. I doubt he's ever been to Homebase. Certainly not with Tina. He doesn't go anywhere with his wife. I very rarely see them together. They met when they were eighteen, both still immature. I'm sure that immaturity still lives in their relationship. They can't shake off the mentality they had with each other when they first met. I know Tina can't be that easy to live with, but she deserves better than Zach. He treats her like shit. I was thirty-two when I first met Niamh, she had just turned thirty. We were both mature, both knew what we wanted in life by the time we hooked up. That's why our relationship works.

I was scrolling through Tinder one evening, as was becoming the norm back then, swiped right when I saw her profile, then kept scrolling, swiping right on other profiles too. But she got back to me within the hour and suddenly we were arranging a date. I probably swiped right on about a hundred profiles on Tinder over the course of six months. Only two ever arranged a date with me. The first girl I met was called Felicity. She didn't look anything like her profile picture – still, we had a good night out and she promised she'd ring me during the week to arrange a second date. That call never came.

I was genuinely beginning to think I'd never have a girlfriend; felt Irish girls just didn't fancy the Korean look. But it was never about looks between me and Niamh. I was slightly put off by her weight when we met for that first date, but after about ten minutes I just didn't give a shit. We were wrapped up in each other's company, immediately opening up to each other as if we'd been best pals for decades.

A week later, on our third date, we were both muttering those three special words to each other. It just felt right. I did love her. Now I'm totally besotted — not just with her, but with us. We are a great couple. And I love the fact that we're both each other's first real partner. We both suffered the same awkwardness through our twenties when it came to trying to find somebody to settle down with. We share so much in common.

At first we were amazed that we liked the same type of

music, that we gorged on the same TV box sets. But over the years, we've learned that that's not what 'having things in common' is truly about. Our politics align. We're both huge liberals. Feel the world has to pull together, not drift apart. We were dumbfounded that Donald Trump got into the White House on the promise of building a wall between Mexico and America. And we were even more flabbergasted that the majority of people in the UK felt it was necessary for them to draw a border between their shitty little island and the rest of Europe. I can never understand anyone who thinks the world should separate. Neither does Niamh. And it was through these types of beliefs that helped us fall head over heels with each other. I genuinely don't know what I would do without her. If I lost her, I think I'd just end it; jump off a bridge or tie a noose around my neck. My life wouldn't be worth living without her. Which is why I'm going to tie her to me permanently. I can't wait to open the box, crouch down on one knee and ask her to be my wife. I just need to figure out what I'm going to say. I want it to be super romantic. Maybe Zach's right. Perhaps getting engaged in Lanzarote is a bit cheesy. Niamh deserves better. I'll have to think it through; come up with something that will blow her mind.

'Shot, shot, shot,' Zach yells into my ear. 'Your round, homeboy.'

I smile at him, walk myself off the dance floor towards the bar. I don't mind doing shots. They're certainly a lot easier on the gut than beer. Though I know I'm going to regret the shots in the morning. Especially when I've got to get up at eight to trek out to Homebase.

Niamh wants a new dining table for the apartment. I'm not sure how she's going to reconfigure the whole room to fit a dining table in, but she insists us having breakfast, lunch and dinner in front of the TV isn't doing her waistline any favours. She's a heavy girl — there's no disputing that — but I love her just the way she is. Though if Niamh wants a dining table, a dining table she will get.

'Baby Guinness,' I say to the barman, holding three fingers aloft.

Before the shot glasses are put in front of me, the two boys by my side.

'Shots, shots, shots.'

'I gave eh… yer ma a shot,' I say back. It's met with the usual straight faces; no laughter, dead eyes. I can never quite nail a 'yer ma' joke.

21:00
Jason

The three of us bounce up and down on the dance floor, not giving a shit. It looks like we've started a tsunami – loads more join us, bopping away to Rihanna's vocals destroying another great Calvin Harris track.

I only really do this once a year these days. Normally in the first week of June – just after the season has finished and I fly home to Dublin to hang out with these two idiots. I'm chuffed Li decided to share his news with us. It's totally changed the dynamic of the night. All three of us are buzzing.

I watch Zach whisper into Li's ear and then Li leaves the dance floor. I didn't quite hear what he said, but I'm pretty sure he repeated the word 'shots' three times over, informing Li it was his round.

He takes his wallet from the back pocket of his jeans as he makes his way to the bar. I wonder how he's doing financially, especially with a wedding to plan soon. I could help him out, offer to pay for part of the day – but only if he wants me to.

It's quite odd being flush with cash. You never quite know where to draw the line of generosity. I walked into the Marble Arch – our local boozer in Drimnagh – after I'd signed my first big contract with Everton and offered to buy everyone in the place a round. A few people thanked me, but some barked over to me that I was being a show-off. You can't win. So I don't do anything like that anymore.

I've helped Li and Zach out a few times, but I don't really offer money for fear of looking like I'm being condescending. If they want me, if they want money, they know where I am. Not that I'm going to have money for long. The days of earning thousands of pounds a week have come to an end. I've a good few quid in the bank, a few property investments dotted around Britain. But there's no way I'm as rich as most people assume I am. People think all Premier League footballers are on hundreds of thousands a week. That's bollocks. Only a very small handful earn those amounts – the top guys; three or four players at the biggest clubs.

The biggest contract I ever signed was for twenty-eight grand a week. I was on that for four years at Everton. The tax man ate a lot of it for me, but I still had more money than I could spend. It seems like heaven from the outset, playing football and getting paid for it, but I preferred the days when all I was interested in doing was playing football. Playing for the Bosco, or for Cherry Orchard or even for Everton's youth teams gave me a lot more satisfaction than playing in the first team.

I leave the two lads at the bar, tell them I'm dying for a piss. I really wish pubs and clubs had VIP loos. The most awkward thing about being a celeb is getting approached while you're taking a leak. It probably happens nine times out of ten when I'm in public places. I think lads assume the toilet is a sanctuary where we can all be as one. I never can quite wrap my head around it. I've had hands held out to me for shaking while I'm holding my dick, have had people take photos of me at the urinal too. One bloke even asked me to sign his own dick once, holding out a marker pen. I told him I could sign 'Jay' but that was about all I could fit.

'Jason Kenny, ye legend ye!' somebody says, grabbing at my shoulders as I try to ensure my dick is spraying in to the urinal. 'How are things goin', mate? Still at Sunderland, yeah?'

I just nod my head. I don't even look at him. I don't want to be staring at blokes when I'm holding my dick.

'They're gone a bit shit, aren't they?'

Cheeky fuck!

'Who do you play for?' I ask, again without looking up.

'Me? I just play for me local team – St Eithne's out in Cabra.'

'Eithne's… never heard of them!' I say zipping up and grinning.

I walk out without washing my hands. Couldn't be arsed entertaining that ass hole.

And that's when I see her. On the stairs.

21:05
Sabrina

I spot him leaning against the wall, talking to his mate. So I inch closer to them, but don't approach. I'll let him spot me; that'll look less suspicious.

Lorna's instructions are still ringing in my ear: 'get a definite yes or no'. I already know it's going to be a 'no'– I've had that impression from the off. Yet it's still not definite, not certain. And I don't get paid for uncertainty. It needs to be a red light or a green light; amber won't do.

I hate having to do this in clubs. They're way too noisy. Especially in here. I don't know why Coppers is noisier than all other clubs, probably because the ceilings are so low; the whole space seems to be condensed. I circle the ring atop my glass of non-alcoholic red as I wait on Niall to notice the coincidence; that somehow I've ended up in the same nightclub as him and his friend Martin.

'Heya love,' some spotty fella says to me.

'I'm waiting on my boyfriend,' I tell him before he's even asked me a question. He just walks on by. I wish I could carry the confidence I have when I'm working into the real world. This job is certainly edging me in the right direction though. It's made me realise I should have more fun; have more courage. I check the time on my phone. 21:06. If he doesn't notice me soon, the goal of ending up in bed by ten o'clock is going to be impossible. Fuck it. I don't have the time to wait. Well... that's not strictly true, I *do* have the time — I've nothing else to do — but I don't have the patience to wait. I pace towards the two of them.

'Niall! Martin!' I say, all high-pitched.

'Ah, how-a-ya, Claire,' Niall says, embracing me with a

quick hug. I get the same from Martin before a silence settles between the three of us. They both stare at me, awkwardly. They're not taking this as a coincidence. They know I followed them here.

'Listen,' I say sighing and holding my eyes closed. 'I never do this, so I'm sorry for being so blunt but eh… is there any chance I could eh… is there any chance you and I…'

'Jee,' Niall says, getting the message without me actually saying much. 'I'm flattered. Three years ago, hell yeah. But now?' he shakes his head. 'I'm loved up, Claire.'

'It's okay, it's okay. I just thought… ye know… you only have one life – I liked you, thought I'd just go all balls out and ask.'

I laugh awkwardly as Niall drags me in for another quick hug.

'Your fiancée's a lucky woman,' I whisper into his ear, before turning on my heels.

They don't call me back. Fine by me. My job is done. I have a red light for Lorna. A definite 'no'. I remove my phone from my bag as I walk up the stairs that lead to the exit and then I pause, just to text Lorna the update. That's when I hear my name being yelled over the music.

'Jaysus, what are you doing here?' I ask after turning around. My heart rate rises, in that excited way it does when the boy you fancied in secondary school decides to talk to you in the corridor.

'Eh… dancing,' he says. 'That's what you'd normally come to a club to do. What are you doing here if you're not dancing?'

'Ah… I just popped my head in for old time's sake as I was walking by. I used to come here… for years. I've decimated that dance floor plenty of times,' I say. 'But I'm on my way home. I fancy an early night.'

'C'mon,' he says, holding his hand out for me to take. 'Come have one with us before you go. We're celebrating.'

I don't get an opportunity to ask what they're celebrating. By the time he has taken me back down the few steps I'd walked up, the music is so dominating that he'd barely be able to hear me anyway. We stroll across the dance floor, my heart thumping. I genuinely haven't felt this way since I was a kid. I certainly didn't feel this way when I first met Eddie. In fact, there were no butterflies at all, no excitement. I just decided to go out with him because I thought it'd be convenient.

Eddie's a friend of my cousin's. I assumed he was a genuine guy, and at that stage that was all I wanted — somebody I could trust. Somebody I met generically, not some twat who approached me in a club. I didn't really fancy Eddie, he certainly wasn't my type, and I still can't quite work out why we went out with each other for three years. I think I was just getting desperate. I felt embarrassed about being a twenty-one-year-old who had never had a boyfriend. I used to tell people I was single by choice; that I didn't want to be in a relationship. It was easy for people to buy that line from me. I was good looking and guys approached me all the time. Only I knew I was lying. Only I knew that I actually struggled to find a boyfriend and that I had wanted one for years.

'HEY!' the Asian guy shouts in my ear. The other one – the bald one – hugs me; not a half-arsed hug like Niall and Martin offered me, but a proper squeeze. He holds me for probably eight seconds too long. He seems awfully pleased to see me. He mumbles something into my ear. I'm not sure what he's saying, can't make it out, so I just nod my head and laugh.

'SHOTS! SHOTS! SHOTS!' Jason chants. The other two

join in and suddenly I find myself being pulled to the bar by all three of them. I check my phone for the time again as we wait on the barman. 21:19. I definitely won't be home before ten now. Fuck it! Might as well have some fun.

What's the worst that could happen?

6

Number Seven fills her glass with water again. It hasn't gone unnoticed that she uses the facilities more than anyone else. She's bored by proceedings, feels that every argument is dragging on for fifteen minutes more than necessary. Too many jurors are too keen to get the last word in. It means points are getting repeated for emphasis. And emphasis only.

To stop her eyes rolling, Number Seven opts to get up off her seat and make her way to the water dispenser. Number Four follows her – he, too, sick of listening to Brian and Number One re-establishing arguments they've already raised.

'Those two'd do yer head in,' he whispers into Number Seven's ear.

'You do my head in,' she whispers back. He bumps off her, hip-to-hip. Number Six cops it, shakes her head with disdain. She hates these two flirting with each other, yet she can't keep her eyes off them when they're together.

'It's a bit too weird innit… y'know that she was walking around in circles, then just followed them into Coppers,'

Number Four says to Number Seven as he scuttles in front of her to fill his own glass.

'Yeah – but it's just… I can't get away from the fact that she didn't see them go into Coppers. And nobody told her that's where they were going. I really don't know what to make of this argument. Anyway… the most important thing is what happened in the hotel later. If she was or was not pursuing Jason all night… it still didn't call for her being raped, right?'

Number Four shrugs his shoulders, then sucks his lips. He's been baffled by all of the different arguments. His mind seems to be getting swayed depending on who's talking, yet he still remains genuinely undecided on his overall verdict.

'You two shouldn't be talking about the trial away from the conference table,' Number Eight says, raising his voice as he twists his head to look over his shoulder. The room falls silent.

'Oh… no, we were just talking about the water,' Number Four says, holding his glass up to his fellow jurors.

'That's a lie. I heard you mentioning the hotel and whether or not she had been raped by the end of the night.'

'Okay… listen,' Number Four says, looking agitated as he makes his way back to his chair. 'I was just asking Number Seven if she would like a fresh cup of tea instead of a glass of water and then we very briefly just said that it will be interesting when we get to the discussions about what happened at midnight in the hotel room. Honestly.' He holds his hand up in apology, palm out. Number Four is an experienced liar. Is known among his mates as a bit of a bullshitter.

'We should only discussh the trial at the table, that's a very strict rule,' Brian stresses by banging his fist on top of the table.

'Yeah… okay,' says Number Seven as she takes her seat.

'Calm down. We're sorry. It was a five-second conversation. Nothing else was said. I promise.'

There are strict rules when it comes to serving on a jury. The case you are examining can't even be discussed with your loved ones once you go back home. It's a rule that is pretty much broken in almost every circumstance, though. Jurors don't necessarily go into every detail — they keep names out of it for the most part — but they do discuss the trials with their spouses, siblings, parents and friends. Of course they do.

Under Irish law, a former jury member can go to prison for discussing the trial they examined publicly after the fact. But even though the rule is regularly broken, that specific law has never needed to be enforced. It's nigh on impossible for even the most honourable person to keep all of the juicy details bottled up inside. It's tough being a juror overall, more mentally challenging than the majority of people assume it is. Some people detest the thought of being a juror, some revel in it. But nobody can really foretell just what the experience will be like – especially if you are tasked with examining such a high profile case as this one. It's a lottery – not just the trial you are chosen to examine, but whether or not you'll ever be called for jury duty in your lifetime.

Every Irish citizen aged eighteen or upwards, whose name appears on the register of electors within Dail Eireann, is eligible for duty. There are categories of people who are ineligible: lawyers, Gardaí, members of the defence forces. Some are excusable, such as priests, medics, students. Those over the age of sixty-five are excusable too, but Number Six waived her right; was keen to get involved. Anybody, of any adult age, any class and with any range of intelligence can decide the fate of the most complex of cases. And therein lies the biggest problem of the judicial system: everyday people just don't understand law.

Gardaí could spend years piecing together a serious crime, such as murder — for example — only for twelve regular Joes and Josephines to dismiss most of their investigation simply because the nuances of the case went over their heads. The make-up of a jury is a mixed bag — you don't know what you're going to get. It was difficult for the lawyers on both sides to find adequate numbers for this trial. Out of the ninety-eight people summoned for jury duty ahead of selection, seventy-nine confessed to knowing who Jason Kenny was. That meant they couldn't be eligible to serve on this jury. It left both the prosecution and defence lawyers having to narrow to twelve jurors from a tiny pool of nineteen. Still, they ended up with a diverse range of individuals.

The average age of this jury is forty — which happens to be the exact average age of juries in Ireland.

At twenty-two, Number Seven is the youngest juror by some six years over Number Five. Number Six is the oldest at sixty-eight; Number Eight the next eldest — a full decade younger, though he genuinely looks like the oldest in the room. Number Eight's real name is Gerry Considine. He'll be fifty-nine next week. He has never really had a career, just hopped from job-to-job over the course of three decades. At the moment he works as a security guard at Independent House on Talbot Street. He presses a button, lets people in and out of the building. He's huge. Six foot, four inches tall; weighs nineteen stone. The weight is mostly in his belly. He looks unhealthy, as if a heart attack is just around the corner. But his regular check-ups at his local doctors' surgery in East Wall — an inner-city suburb of Dublin —confirm all is good on the inside. Gerry's the other juror – aside from Number Twelve – who lied in order to be selected. He knew who Jason Kenny was prior to being called for jury duty. Is actually quite a big football fan. Number Eight raised his hand as 'undecided' earlier, but has had a strong inkling all the way through the trial the three men are not guilty. Although he feels Sabrina is a very eloquent and attractive girl, there was something about her that he couldn't quite put his finger on. The defence's tactic of painting Sabrina as cunning and untrustworthy had a massive impact on Number Eight. He isn't the only one swayed by their narrative.

'Is it perhaps time for a verdict vote?' Brian offers up.

His suggestion is met with a couple of audible sighs, but he has a point. The jurors have just discussed one of the main arguments of the trial; was or was not Sabrina fixated on sleeping with Jason Kenny that night? Did she seek him out?

Her appearance at Copper Face Jacks — innocent and coincidental as it was — had a huge bearing on most jurors' mindsets. Sabrina, out of respect — not only for her job, but for her client — couldn't bring herself to admit she was following another man to Copper Face Jacks at any stage of the investigation. She didn't divulge this to the Gardaí when they initially questioned her about her claim, nor did she fill her own lawyers in on this key piece of information during any of their multiple meetings over the past eighteen months. She knew she didn't have a good enough reason for turning up at Coppers otherwise, but hoped the jury would believe her insistence that it was an honest coincidence; that she just fancied a dance and by strange synchronicity ended up in the same club as the three men she had been talking to earlier.

It was wise that she never mentioned Niall Stevens during any of the investigation, though. Had Stevens been called as a witness, he would have testified that she blatantly came on to him that night. It would have ruined her case. In fact, the case wouldn't even have made it to court had Stevens been questioned by Gardaí. But the Gardaí weren't looking for him, because nobody mentioned him. The defence lawyers weren't seeking another man as part of their own investigation either. They genuinely believed Sabrina followed Jason, Zach and Li to Copper Face Jacks because the three men themselves remain quite adamant that she had.

Niall Stevens is totally unaware of his involvement in such a fateful evening. He hasn't forgotten about the hot girl in the white jumpsuit who made a pass at him a year and a half ago, but he has no idea whatsoever that she is Ms X – the girl entangled in the major rape trial that has engulfed the nation.

So many details of Sabrina Doyle, even down to what she was wearing on the night in question, have been shared in court, but can't be reported in the media. There are strict rules when it comes to the victim's identity. She can't be named. The professional media never cross this line, but it's impossible to stop anonymous idiots from sharing pictures of her, outing her, on social media.

As for Jason, around half of the country have figured out he's the big-name international footballer on trial, yet he still can't be named by journalists for legal reasons. All defendants, famous or not, have a right to anonymity in major criminal cases; their names will only be reported in the media if the jury find them guilty. If this incident occurred north of the border, all three men would be named in the press. The Irish legal system prefers to protect those accused from public humiliation. In Britain, the accused would be named, the general public even allowed inside the courtroom should they wish to attend the trial.

'Why don't we use the paper slips?' Brian says, stretching to grab the box from the middle of the table.

There are no strict rules on how jurors conduct their verdict votes. But pens and cut-out slips of paper are left in the room for them to conduct secret ballots should they deem it necessary at any point. Using this method, now, contradicts Brian's earlier reasoning for having constant verdict votes. He had said that it would be beneficial for every juror to know where every other juror stood throughout the course of the deliberations. Using the secret ballot method means the jury aren't going to gain that knowledge. Still, nobody questions him. They're all up for a secret ballot; feel it would hurry proceedings, feel they won't necessarily have to explain themselves in detail – they just need to scribble one of three things; guilty, not guilty or undecided on a slip of paper. Brian shuffles around the room behind each juror's chair, tossing a slip of paper and a pen in front of them.

Number One then decides to stand, feeling a need to show awareness of his responsibilities.

'Okay, so this is straightforward,' Number One says, holding his slip of paper and pen up to the jurors, as if he was a teacher about to give instruction.

'Yes, we get it,' says Number Eight.

Number One sits back down, his face slightly brushed with embarrassment. Number Five cups her piece of paper as she writes down her verdict, as if she's doing an exam she doesn't want others to copy from. It's rather pointless – everybody is aware she is firmly in the guilty camp. She has made no secret of that fact.

'Okay, so just fold your paper twice and put it back in the box,' Number One says after scribbling 'guilty' on his. He holds out his piece of paper, the verdict facing him, and genuinely folds it twice as if showing his fellow jurors what folding is. This instruction would be patronising, only nobody glances up at him. They're too busy scribbling. When they're done, they toss their verdict votes into the box; some folded twice, some only folded once, one not folded at all.

Number One glances around the room, notices everybody's slip of paper is now inside, but still asks anyway.

'Is that everybody in?' he says.

'Yep,' rasps Number Twelve. 'Get counting, head boy.'

Number One slides the box onto his lap, out of the sight of everybody except the two jurors seated next to him. He slips the first piece of paper out, looks at it, then places it face down in front of him; then repeats this action another eleven times. When the box is empty, Number One has three small piles of papers on the table. He already knows the result but decides to count again, trying to emphasise to his fellow jurors just how seriously he is taking his role.

'Okay, I have a result,' he finally says after drawing in a large breath for the sake of creating a bit of drama. 'Three guilty… six not guilty… three undecided.'

21:35
Li

Sabrina seems reluctant to join the lads on the dance floor. That suits me; gives me a break without having to stand alone. We watch the other two bounce around to some remix of a shite Drake song and then we smile at each other. She really is beautiful – top to toe. Not my type though. I always assume good-looking girls are hard to live with. They're normally insecure. You just don't know what you're going to get with a looker.

I've seen Jason with quite a few girls who have been plastered on magazine covers and the like and every single one of them proved to be a headache for him. They start off all nicey-nicey, but after a few weeks their true colours come out. They'd moan at him for wanting to watch something on TV rather than paying them attention, or they'd crack up if they ever saw him talking to another girl.

That's why I love Niamh so much. It really is a case of what you see is what you get with her. We've never argued, never had a fight. We're totally open and honest with each other one-hundred per cent of the time. It's quite odd. I always felt inferior to my two best mates. Zach got the looks and the confidence, Jason got the talent and with that, the celebrity. I got nothing. Yet I'm the only one who has ever found true love out of the three of us.

I've no doubt that I'm happier than those two, though they certainly look happy now. They're like two overexcited kids bouncing around a tiny dance floor as if it's the last party they'll ever be at. It's amazing what a few shots of Baby Guinness can do for your mood. I'm glad, because I had a fear when Sabrina showed up in here that it might cause a rift between Zach and Jason. But it hasn't. Not yet anyway.

21:35

Zach's tried to pull Sabrina up for a dance a couple of times, but she ain't budging. My guess is she's too self-conscious to dance, which is odd, given that she told us she only came in here to have a quick dance before she headed home. Though none of us really bought that. She followed us here. She must have.

'Let's play favourites,' she shouts into my ear.

'Favourites?'

'Yeah,' she says, leaning closer. 'It's a good way to get to know each other, especially in this noise. I say something, you tell me what your favourite of that is.'

I look at her and smile. I think I get it.

'Movie?' she shouts.

'Eh... *Goodfellas*.'

She smiles, nods her head.

'You?' I shout back at her.

'The Notebook.'

'Oh – I love that too,' I say back, noting how camp that actually sounds when said so loudly. But I do love it. Me and Niamh. We musta watched it about a dozen times.

'Song?' Sabrina shouts.

I think about it, stew her question over in my mind.

'*Do I Wanna Know* – Arctic Monkeys.'

'Yes!' she says, holding her hand up for me to high five. 'I love the Arctic Monkeys.'

'TV show?'

'Stranger Things. Addicted to it.'

She peels away from me, her mouth slightly ajar, her face folding back into a smile. She high fives me again. Seems like we're into the exact same things. She grabs me in for a hug.

I notice the time on the digital clock behind the bar over her shoulder as we hug. 21:39. Not too bad. We've been out for just over a couple of hours now. Three pints of Heinekens and three Baby Guinness shots down me. Things could have been a lot worse. It's not unlike me to be puking into a toilet bowl after being out with Jason and Zach for a couple of hours. At this rate, I'll be fit and raring to go to Homebase in the morning.

We'll be visiting there quite a lot over the next few months. Me and Niamh have a whole life to plan for. Literally. I woke up a couple of weeks ago, one lazy Sunday morning, to hear her whistling. I'd never heard her whistle before. Didn't know what the hell was going on. I staggered downstairs, watched her frying up some sausages and rashers and knew instantly that she was in a great mood.

'What's up with you?' I asked her.

She just turned to me, beamed a huge smile and continued whistling.

'Niamh?'

'Just take a seat, sweetheart,' she said. 'Breakfast's nearly ready.'

I sat on our coach, in just my boxer shorts, and turned on the TV. There's normally a whole load of politics shite on every Sunday, so I switched over to the sports channel, hoping to see Jason in a bit of action. Though it's rare that the highlights of his games make broadcast anymore. Sunderland were rock bottom of the Championship at this stage, their relegation to League One all but confirmed. They're just not significant anymore.

'Hey, turn off the tele,' Niamh said as she entered the living room. She handed me a tray with a mountain of breakfast on it, then retreated to the kitchen and came back with a tray of her own.

'You woke up hungry, I gather?'

'I woke up happy,' she said. 'Now eat up!'

I did as I was told; Niamh and I staring at each other as we stuffed our faces. She couldn't stop the smile from beaming on her face. I knew she was excited, assumed it had something to do with buying something in Homebase later that day. When we'd finished breakfast, she took my tray from my lap, placed both my tray and hers on the carpet and then pulled a white stick from the pocket of her dressing-gown. I took it off her, stared at the blue cross on it, then beamed a smile right back into her face. I'm still as giddy about that now as I was in that moment.

'Book?' she shouts.

I gurn my face, hold my hand up.

'Eh, don't really read that much,' I say to her. She frowns; looks disappointed in that answer. Such a shame. We'd just learned we had so much in common. I can't believe a girl can be this down to earth *and* this good looking.

She leans towards my ear, is about to tell me what her favourite book is when Zach arrives between us. Instead of trying to drag her to the dance floor this time, he drags her aside. Shit! I've a feeling the awkwardness I was dreading is about to erupt.

'Fancy another drink?' Jason asks me as Sabrina and Zach stroll away.

'Sure.'

We both walk towards the bar in silence. It was only after he ordered two pints of Heineken that I posed the question.

'You not worried he's gonna fuck things up with her?'

'Nah. She followed us here for me,' Jason says.

'Yeah, but he'll get pissed off, won't he? I'm more worried about him fucking our night up, than anything.'

Jason shrugs his shoulders, hands the barman his debit card and then clinks my glass.

'We'll see how he handles it,' Jason says as we stare over at both of them on the other side of the club. Zach places his hand on the small of Sabrina's back and leads her up the stairs. I take Jason in, out of the corner of my eye.

'Where the hell they going?' I ask. He doesn't answer. He

just stares at the stairs until they're out of sight. I take him in again. I know Jason. I know every single look he can possibly adopt on his face. He looks worried.

Bollocks.

I've got a bad feeling about this.

21:40
Zach

I love that I'm a better dancer than Jason. I've always had better rhythm than him, better balance. It's why I was a more natural footballer than he'll ever be.

But I know that people are only dancin' round us because of him. Celebrity really does fascinate the regular Joe. But I'm not gonna let his celebrity beat me to that Sabrina bird. She's amazin'. My eyes nearly popped out of me head when I saw her come over to us again. I'm delighted she followed us here. I guess she came for Jason, but she'll be leavin' with me. She's playing hard to get at the moment, though. Won't get on the dance floor with me. Maybe I should take her aside, have a chat with her; let her know I'm interested. I'm sure I can charm that jumpsuit right off her by the end of the night.

'C'mere for a sec,' I say into her ear as I grab her hand. I don't even look back at Jason; assume he'll be all right with it. He can score any bird in this club he wants.

I walk her over to the stairs, away from the blast of the speakers.

'So... what brought you here; wasn't me was it?' I say.

'Sorry?' she shouts back at me, turning her face so that her ear inches towards my face.

'Did you come here lookin' for me?' I shout.

She looks confused. I don't think she caught the humour in my question.

'We can't really talk here,' I say. 'Let's pop outside for a minute.'

I don't even think of Tina when I'm chattin' up other birds. I think all the guilt I could ever feel was used up on The Secret. Even when it comes to sellin' drugs, helping fund gangland crime, I feel no guilt whatsoever. I just get the impression that life is too damn short for feeling that way.

Alan Keating first asked me to sell drugs for him when I bumped into him in the toilets in my local boozer. I'd been hanging around him and his associates for a couple of months, keen for company more than anything else. He broke it down for me really easily; said if I could shift fifty grams of coke for him every week, I'd end up pocketing a grand for myself. I couldn't say no to that. The most I'd ever earned in a week was four hundred euros, and that was doing shitty security shifts. Selling drugs is an easy gig. All I had to do was pick up the merch from Keating's associate out in Blanchardstown, build up some leads and literally swap small bags of coke for large wads of cash.

For the first few weeks I only brought in about two grand, my cut being fifteen per cent. But I pretty soon got the hang of it and within two months I was earning the grand a week Keating had promised I would. He's alright Keating, if you're on the good side of him. But I know things about him that would keep most people up at night.

It's funny. Most of the tabloids know exactly what Keating gets up to, but he always keeps his nose clean. The cops have nothin' on him. He's been one of Ireland's most notorious gangsters for a couple of decades, yet he hasn't spent any time behind bars. I sorta respect him. I don't envy him, not like I envy Jason. But I respect him.

Though getting involved with him was not how I'd hoped my life would go. Word started to get around that I was entangled in the Keating gang, but I denied it to anyone who brought it up with me. Li must've asked me about it a hundred times. He kept catching wind that I was hangin' around with that lot. I just told him that we all happened to drink in the same pub and that was that.

I was initially worried he'd tell Jason. And if Jason found

out, he'd freak out. He was always adamant that we'd steer clear of the gangs in Drimnagh. It was driven into him by his parents. I agreed; promised him a thousand times I wouldn't get involved. But it's difficult when you have fuck all else to do. Especially when your best mate is away in England livin' out your dream.

I started to do a bit of coke myself, just to pass the time. I began skimming off the top of the stuff I was supposed to be sellin' for Keating; assumed I wouldn't get caught. But I couldn't have been more wrong. When it comes to shifting cocaine, every single granule is practically accounted for.

'You've been stealing from me,' Keating said, staring through me one evening. I stuttered some awful excuse back at him.

'Don't worry about it, kid,' he said. 'I'll let you away with it... on one condition. You're mates with Jason Kenny, right? I wanna meet him.'

I take all of her in after we've stepped outside. She really is a fuckin' cracker. A proper ten. Definitely out of my league. But I don't give a shit. I'll try it on with whoever I happen to think is the hottest bird in the place. And nobody's gonna be hotter than Sabrina — not tonight anyway.

'So, what were you saying?' she says, making me refocus after we step outside.

'I was just askin' if you came to Coppers lookin' for me?'

She makes a gurning face. My fault. The line didn't come out the way I intended it to. It was supposed to be banter. Comedy is all in the timing; I didn't get the timing right with that one.

'I just fancied a dance,' she says, filling the silence. 'I didn't know you guys were in here.'

'No... I'm... eh... I was just eh... kiddin',' I say. Jesus. A girl's never had me this tongue-tied before.

'So... are you good friends with Jason?' she asks.

21:40

Bollocks! She's too into him. This is gonna take a whole lotta charm to win her over to my side.

'Yeah – we're best mates. Have been since we were kids. He eh… he could have any woman he wants in there,' I say, nodding back to the club.

'I'm sure he could,' she says, putting her hands on her hips and nodding. I swallow hard; think about giving up the ghost until I notice two rickshaws parked up at the footpath a few yards down from the club entrance.

'Hey… ever taken a rickshaw ride around Dublin?' I ask.

She looks over her shoulder. Laughs.

'Can't say I have, no.'

'C'mon then.'

I grab her hand and begin to run down the few steps towards the footpath.

'What? No… I… I—'

'C'mon, it'll be fun!'

21:45
Sabrina

He's just bought me two drinks; a shot of Baby Guinness that all three of us downed before I'd barely said hello to each of them, and then a glass of red, which I'm still holding as he throws himself around the dance floor in front of me.

It seems quite bizarre that he can't dance. I would have thought a professional sportsman would have had at least some sort of natural rhythm. He seems to miss the beat every time he jumps... or claps... or does any type of movement. It'd probably be embarrassing if it wasn't for the fact that everybody is surrounding him, as if he's brilliant – as if he's Justin Timberlake or something. His moves look awkward, but they're kind of endearing in a way. He's not taking himself too seriously, has a smile practically tattooed across his face.

I just stand at the edge of the dance floor, trying to get to know Li a little better. Perhaps if you want to impress a guy, it's good to impress his mates first. I drift away in the Drake song that's booming out, imagine myself as a footballer's wife. A WAG. I picture the lifestyle: the cars, the swimming pool, the big house. I've never wanted much, am not that interested in money, really. But my thoughts are floating away, like a loose buoy in the ocean. Maybe I deserve all those luxuries, to compensate for all the shit I've been though over the years. That'd certainly infuriate Eddie... if he knew I was dating a footballer. It'd sting like hell. I'd love it.

He wasn't all bad, Eddie. Just at the end. We started off like any other couple, dating in restaurants, bars, clubs. We used to come here a lot actually. But that all died off after about six months. Suddenly, we were just sitting in, watching crap on TV, barely talking. We had nothing to say anyway;

we were bored of each other. He started going out himself, leaving me to watch the crap TV alone. I should have known then; should have known he wasn't for me. But I stayed with him – just because I didn't want to be single. Not again. I can understand why women stay in bad relationships. A bad relationship is only bad to them. But being single looks bad to everybody. I'd probably still be with Eddie if I hadn't, by chance, bumped into Lorna a couple of years ago. I wonder how much better Jason is compared to Eddie. Maybe all blokes are the same. And he's a footballer after all... that probably makes things even worse. He can score any girl, any night. The thought of this stops my buoy from drifting any further out to sea. Suddenly the big house, the swimming pool and the fancy cars disappear from my mind. Why was I even thinking that far ahead in the first place? I had barely introduced myself to him when he had his tongue down my throat, opening his jeans so I could wank him off. I sigh. A deep loud sigh; disappointed in myself for getting carried away. Then I turn to Li, realise I've gone quiet on him, that I have forgotten we were in the middle of getting to know each other.

'Book?' I ask him.

'Eh, don't really read that much,' he says, disappointing me. I read constantly, sometimes consuming three books at the same time. I look at him with mock disappointment etched on my face.

'C'mere for a sec,' Zach says, butting in between me and my new best buddy.

He leads me towards the stairs. It's quieter here, but not much. He tries to say something else to me, but I can barely hear him.

'We can't really talk here. Let's pop outside for a minute,' he shouts while pointing up the stairs. I look over my shoulder, towards Jason. He's just followed Li to the bar, barely noticing me walking off with his mate. I silently tut, then follow Zach up the steps, playing over in my mind whether or not I should just go home.

'So, what were you saying?' I ask when we get outside.

'I was just asking if you came to Coppers lookin for me?'

What the hell is he talking about? He can't be serious…

'I just fancied a dance,' I say. 'I didn't know you guys were in here.'

'No… I'm…eh… I was just eh… kidding,' he says. Wow. If that was him kidding, this guy ain't gonna make it as a stand-up comedian, that's for sure.

'So… are you good friends with Jason?' I ask, trying to suss whether or not Jason is actually into me.

'Yeah – we're best mates. Have been since we were kids. He eh… he could have any woman he wants in there,' he tells me. My heart sinks. I know what he's trying to allude to. Jason's not interested. Maybe this guy's just trying to get his famous mate's cast offs. I'm sure that happens all the time. I check the time on my phone again. 21:54. I should probably get a taxi — call it a night.

'Hey… ever taken a rickshaw ride around Dublin?' he asks, his face beaming like a kid at Christmas.

'Can't say I have, no.'

He grabs my hand, jumps down the three concrete steps onto the footpath and leads me towards one of the rickshaws lined up on the pavement.

'What? No… I… I.'

'C'mon, it'll be fun!'

I remain silent, hop on the back of the rickshaw, then laugh at him when I notice his big grin. You'd swear he was a ten-year-old after being allowed on his first roller coaster.

'Where d'yis wanna go?' the guy cycling the rickshaw asks us.

Zach looks at me. I'd like to say, 'My house in Drumcondra if your legs can take you that far'. But I don't. I remain silent as I try to figure out in my head what the hell I'm doing.

'Just around town,' Zach says. 'About fifteen minutes' worth. How much is it?'

'Fifteen minutes around town, eh... twenty quid.'

'Cool – let's go, mate!'

I've never been on one of these before; don't know why the hell I'm on one now. But here I am, sitting on an uncomfortable wooden bench while some poor young fella cycles as fast as he can to bring us nowhere in particular. I don't wanna be here. Not just because it's uncomfortable on my ass, but because it's uncomfortable in general. I'm pretty sure Zach is about to come on to me. How can I tell him I'm not interested, that I was only hanging around because I liked his best mate? His famous mate. Though maybe he's used to it. Maybe he won't mind being told that.

'Are you a magician?' he asks, turning to face me.

'Huh?'

'Are you a magician? Because every time I look at you everybody else disappears.'

I laugh. Properly laugh. Not because his line is funny. But because it's so *not* funny. I've had guys come on to me before, but not as if they're reading Christmas cracker jokes.

'Was your da a boxer?' he says, 'because damn! You're a knockout.'

I laugh again, almost snorting into my hand as I hold it to my face out of embarrassment for him. Zach sure is funny; just not in the way he thinks he is.

21:50
Jason

I love these tunes; could bounce around the dance floor to this shit all night. Though in truth, I'd love to be doing nothing more than kissing Sabrina right now. But I'm trying to play it cool with her; feel I probably pushed things a little too far when we first met in the Hairy Lemon earlier. Perhaps I don't need to be this stand off-ish given that she's followed me here, but I'll just refrain from being all over her a little more; give her the impression I'm not desperate. She is cute. *Very* cute. But it's not just that. There's a connection. I can't quite put my finger on it. But I have a feeling – or probably a hope more than anything – that something could come of this. And I need this. I need a bit of fortune back in my life. Maybe I'll give it another couple of songs, then I'll drag her aside, try to have a quiet word with her. Try to get to know her.

Bollocks.

I watch as Zach acts before me, taking her aside, walking her towards the stairs. He can be such a selfish cunt sometimes. I stop dancing, walk towards Li and ask him if he fancies another drink.

'You not worried he's gonna fuck things up with her?' he asks me.

'Nah. She followed me here,' I say. I'm trying to remain calm. But I am a little pissed off. Sabrina's way out of Zach's league but I wouldn't put it past him pulling her. He's pulled out of his league loadsa times before.

'Yeah, but he'll get antsy won't he, if she tells him she's already been with you? I'm more worried for him fucking our night up than anything,' Li says.

'We'll see how he handles it,' I reply as I watch them head up the stairs, hoping that she stares back at me. She doesn't.

'Where the hell are they going?' Li asks. I don't answer.

'Two Heineken,' I say turning to the barman.

Tonight's the first night I've drank alcohol in almost a year. I stayed off it all season. Was doing my best to have my contract renewed. I'm not sure anyone at the club noticed, to be honest. The club's a fucking mess. Top to bottom.

I only enjoyed my first season at Sunderland, after that it turned into a cluster fuck. We've been relegated in each of the last two years, from the glamour of the Premier League down to the averageness of League One. I miss my days at Everton; miss the thrill of a proper Merseyside Derby, the excitement of being on the television almost every week.

Sunderland offered Everton eighteen million for me in the summer of 2014. I had another offer; could have gone to Crystal Palace. I wish now that I had. But at the time, Sunderland looked in better shape than them… felt I was going to a club with aspirations. I was thirty-one at the time, had a feeling it would be my last major contract. They were paying me twenty grand a week, until we were relegated to the Championship and that was halved. I know things could have been worse – a lot worse. But it's difficult to transition from significance into insignificance.

If I had never made it, never played in the Premier League, I wouldn't be depressed now. But because I did make it, because I was somebody, the crash back to reality has been hard to take in. Such is life, I suppose. There's not much I'd change looking back. Maybe a few things. I'd have signed for Palace over Sunderland for one, would definitely have worked harder at keeping Jessica. Oh yeah – and I certainly wouldn't have let Li drive the car that night. I never forgot her face, never forgot her name.

I've searched for that name all over the internet, but I

haven't found her. I'd say I think about Caitlin Tyrell as much as I think about my own dad. Practically every day. Certainly every time I'm praying.

'Cheers,' Li says as we clink glasses again. 'She'll be back in looking for you in a few minutes — don't worry about it.'

We stay at the bar, in the quiet, staring out at the crowds of people. This place is starting to get pretty packed. I think of a technique my therapist often recommends to me – 'think of the positive'. I don't really have much positivity going on in my own life, but Li's news is reason enough for me to be upbeat. I should be really happy for him. I guess he's the only one out of the three of us who's truly happy, who has managed to get practically everything he's ever wanted.

'I'm so proud of you, Li,' I say, nudging his shoulder.

'You're gonna be a great husband. Niamh's a lucky girl to have you, and you're lucky to have her.'

He smiles; a big wide grin that has a ripple effect on me. Suddenly I'm smiling — even if it is someone else's happiness that's doing it for me. I play over the possibility in my head of opening up to Li; finally telling him I've been depressed for two years... that I'm really unhappy... that I have no contract for next season... that my career is over. But I don't want to ruin his excitement. Instead, I grab him in for a hug.

'I love you, man.'

'I love you too.'

I can see tears form in his eyes when I release him.

'I eh... nah,' he shakes his head.

'What?'

'I can't.'

'Ye can't what?' I ask.

'I can't tell you... well I really shouldn't tell you...'

'You can tell me anything,' I say, grabbing onto his shoulder.

'Niamh will kill me. It's early. She's only two months—'

'Yesss!' I say, picking him up and spinning him around. 'Oh man – whatever about being a great husband, you're definitely going to be a great father!'

And I mean it. He will be.

He's been such a great older brother to Jinny. Nobody cares more about other people than Li. If anyone had've pointed out the nerdy Korean kid in Primary School and told me he'd be the person I'd be most envious of in the whole world in thirty years' time I would have thought they were fucking insane.

But it's true. Li is living a life I could only wish for.

7

The ambience in the room heightened somewhat after the secret ballot result was revealed; most of the jurors beginning to feel eerily optimistic that a final verdict is just around the corner. The pace of discussions has picked up somewhat. Everyone – even Brian and Number One – seem to be giving their opinions in bullet-point bursts, keen to move the debates on as swiftly as possible. Though in truth, the secret ballot vote hasn't made as massive an adjustment from their initial vote as they feel it has.

There was certainly a shift towards not guilty, especially in comparison to the earlier vote. But had they taken the time to think through the latest vote in more detail, rather than rush into the next discussion, they would have realised they weren't really speeding towards a final decision at all. Three undecided out of twelve is still a lot of votes to play for — exactly one-quarter in fact. And if those undecided were persuaded into the *guilty* camp, then all matters would be tied: six each. The old adage of 'it ain't over till the fat lady sings' is a well-worn saying in legal circles. It has even been known that eleven:one ratios have been overturned by jurors, albeit very rare. So the six not guilty, three guilty and three undecided result of the secret ballot means relatively little in terms of reaching conclusion.

The judge set these twelve off to find a unanimous decision; that is *all* twelve jurors must agree on the same verdict, as is the norm in every case of this magnitude. Some judges may call jurors back, as early as five or six hours into deliberations — though most likely after a couple of days — to let them know he or she will take an eleven:one vote ratio, maybe even a ten:two.

Judge Delia McCormick — who presided over the Sabrina Doyle versus Jason Kenny, Zach Brophy and Li Xiang trial — has a reputation for being quite patient with her jurors. She's likely to not want to see them for at least another few days. Though this is certainly the most high profile case she has ever presided over and it's conceivable that she, too, is feeling pressure like she's never felt it before.

She did, to her credit, handle the whole trial particularly well. She was fair, yet stern, with both sides of the courtroom. The defence may have received a slightly harsher time of it — more of her raised eyebrows, more of her quick, snappy retorts — than the prosecution, but that was only because they were more experienced lawyers when dealing with cases of this magnitude. They knew just how far to push a judge.

Still, Sabrina's lawyer — Joseph Ryan — didn't have a free ride of it. McCormick kept him in check, was as short and snappy with the young buck as she was with the more experienced lawyers on occasion. Ryan tried all the original tricks everybody would recommend to a victim. He insisted Sabrina dressed demurely in the courtroom. Most days her hair was tied back into a simple ponytail. She always wore a skirted suit, all of them a dark shade. No make up. Ryan told her to try to look as vacant as she possibly could in the courtroom when witnesses were giving evidence. He wanted her to look like the everygirl as much as possible.

'Don't react. To anything.'

He said that to her over and over again, stressing the point on days he felt she may get particularly emotional.

He was delighted with her performance on the stand, though that was a self-congratulatory pat on the back more than anything. He coached her. His predictions about what questions would arrive from the defence were on the money. Her rehearsed answers were delivered with the expressionless face and tone he had drilled into her.

Judge McCormick would have been aware that Sabrina's answers were rehearsed. Three jurors — Number Twelve, Number Ten and Number Nine — clocked that some answers came across as scripted too, but most jurors just didn't even consider the possibility.

Truth is, these rehearsed answers paint no sign of guilt on her part. Both Jason's and Li's testimonies were rehearsed to some extent too. Though there was one real moment from Li when he broke down on the stand having informed the court that he had lost his fiancée, Niamh, and full access to his ten-month-old daughter, Sally, because of these accusations. Aside from that, he was always on script. A lawyer wouldn't be doing their job properly if they didn't pre-script answers for any questions they could foresee coming their client's way. It's part and parcel of the system. For lawyers, each case is like a game – a game they are intent on winning. And in order to win that game, they'll take *any* advantage they can get.

Sabrina was – understandably – stressed about her cross-examination. In rape trials, it can often seem as if it is the victim who's on trial. She felt her whole life was being examined. Sabrina was accused of stalking Jason Kenny on the night in question, accused of heavy drinking, accused of being fame hungry and accused of being a nude glamour model desperate for attention. One tabloid ran with the headline 'Ms X is Ms XXX' after Patrick Clavin's testimony. And yet Sabrina is supposed to be the victim in this case. No wonder a large number of rape victims are reluctant to report their attackers.

Jason, Zach and Li's defence lawyers did all they could to paint Sabrina in a negative light. They also aimed to make her appear hesitant on the stand. If defence lawyers are successful in making a complainant seem hesitant, then it can go a long way to breathing a feeling of reasonable doubt in the jurors' minds.

Although the defence team are considered to be among the best in their field, they were disappointed overall with their cross examination of Sabrina Doyle. Perhaps they thought she would be an easy target, but she somehow, from somewhere, found an inner-strength when she was on the stand.

When Gerd Bracken — the defence team's lead lawyer — ended his interrogation of Sabrina by whipping off his glasses and moving intimidatingly towards the stand, raising his voice: 'I suggest to you, Sabrina Doyle, that this is *not* a case of non-consensual sexual relations, but a case of consensual sexual relations with three men that you subsequently regretted, isn't that right?' she looked him square in the eye and replied 'I said no, I said no, I said no — not subsequently, but *while* I was being raped.'

Although she gripped a handful of tissues throughout the two days the defence lawyers cross-examined her, she didn't have to use them to wipe away any tears. She was impressive up there; had a steely determination to get through the test without giving the three defendants — or indeed their legal team who she had grown to despise — any satisfaction whatsoever. She wanted to portray herself as a strong woman when she was up there. And she did.

'Well that's true,' Number Ten says, 'you can look at it both ways.' She was agreeing with a point Number One had just raised about Jason's character. Discussions were heating up; the secret ballot result changing the gears of the conversation. 'Jason Kenny is far from squeaky clean. He may have made a success of himself, but he's no saint.'

The jurors had moved on, were now at the beginning stages of a discussion about the three character witnesses that were called to give testimony about Jason Kenny.

Clara Groves, a sixty-three-year-old founder of a charity called YouKnight — set up in in Dublin in 1978 to support disabled people — testified that Jason was not only generous with his money, but with his time too.

'For the purposes of this trial, I actually went through all of my notes and counted up the hours Jason has given to us over the years,' she testified. 'He became an ambassador for YouKnight in December 2009, still is to this day. He has, according to my calculations, given up almost six hundred hours to help us. He's over and back to Dublin as much as he can be to offer support. Has travelled to America with us too, just to see some of our beneficiaries live out their dreams. And that's on top of the seventy-eight thousand pounds he has personally donated within that time frame too. He's an amazing, caring man. We have a couple of celebrities who are ambassadors of YouKnight, but nobody gives more than Jason.'

Former Ireland international coach Mick Dempsey also backed up Jason's character on the stand, the highlight of his testimony suggesting 'Jason is the kindest footballer of all of the footballers I've worked with — over three hundred of them. He's deeply religious, and it shows in his character. He's very humble, very caring.'

It had been reported in the newspapers that former Ireland captains Robbie Keane and Richard Dunne would also act as character witnesses for the high-profile accused, but while the defence did certainly make initial plans to contact these famous names, this route was never going to be taken. It wouldn't have been wise for Keane and Dunne to put themselves on display like that. Their reputations would have been damaged by a guilty verdict had they testified.

The truth is, they were never officially approached. The newspapers caught wind of something small and blew it all out of proportion. They splashed with 'Keane and Dunne to give evidence' headlines. It was sensationalised bullshit. And the journalists who reported it knew it.

Despite Clara Groves's and Mick Dempsey's positive accounts of their dealings with Jason Kenny, it was the testimony of a prosecution witness — a Mr Frank Keville — that made the biggest impact on the jury.

Keville is a freelance crime journalist, courted by all major newspapers in Ireland. He never considers any of the contracts offered to him though, preferring freelancing. He makes much more money that way, selling to the highest bidder. His bravery as a journalist and a photographer has been lauded by those in the Dail on occasions. He's been in a wheelchair for six years after one gang's assassination attempt on him failed. And even since then, he has proven he has no fear inside his bones. Keville makes his money trying to expose Dublin gangland criminals, stalking them in an attempt to catch them in precarious situations. The tabloids love to run a story about criminals partying it up; living a luxurious life on money made underground. These stories both intrigue and disgust readers in equal measure. Keville knows what the mass population wants; certainly knows what editors want.

'I have no doubt whatsoever that Jason Kenny and indeed

Zach Brophy are good friends —associates, I would say — of Alan Keating,' Keville said on the stand.

Alan Keating is one of — if not *the* — most notorious gangsters in Ireland. It was fully explained to the jurors who Keating is, not that they needed telling or reminding.

Keville had photographed Jason and Zach with Keating and other members of his gang on five separate occasions. These pictures appeared in both the *Irish Daily Star* and *Sunday World* over a four-year period. Not much was made of them at the time. Jason was from Drimnagh; same place a lot of gangland members are from. Painting Jason as a criminal, or as a criminal by proxy, didn't ring true with the population of Ireland. They just figured Jason and Keating had friends in common, that the newspapers were just sensationalising. But Keville's testimony didn't seem sensationalised at all. The jury hung on his every word.

'Jason and Zach have not only been good friends with Keating for a few years, they both knew this man from a very young age. They grew up in Keating's shadow. Some in Drimnagh say Jason would have been a gangster had it not been for football. I don't believe being a footballer took him away from gangland crime — it's still a part of his life.'

Keville wasn't making things up for the sake of it. He genuinely believed Jason was involved with Keating's racketing and smuggling; had been told this by a few insiders. It was the insiders feeding him the information who were wrong. They sensationalised the story. They said Jason was part of Keating's gang because they knew it would make a good article, and that — as a result — they would get more money from Keville for passing on such juicy information.

'Frank Keville is a very decent man,' says Number One. 'Somebody we should believe. He has nothing to lose; is hardly making stories up for the sake of it. And look, he has photographs to prove his testimony.'

'Yep, this guy has evidence,' Number Five follows up.

'Hold on,' says Brian. 'A photograph is not evidensh that Jason Kenny is a gangster. And it certainly isn't evidensh that he is a rapist.'

'No, but it proves that he hangs around with gangsters, that he probably hangs around with rapists,' Number Five retorts.

'Ah for crying out loud! Who said Keating and these gangland criminal are rapists? Surely they're just into trafficking drugs, laundering money,' Number Twelve argues, his face turning red.

'Criminals are criminals. Probably into every sort of crime,' Number Five says.

'That makes no fuckin' sense—'

'Hold on, hold on,' Number One says, standing up. 'Can we calm things a bit?' He sits back down, bumps his paperwork off the table again.

'Frank Keville is a character witness,' he says, steadying his tone. 'His job on the stand was to give us an understanding of Jason Kenny and Zach Brophy's personalities. I think it's fair that we can deduce Jason and Zach are no saints, given Keville's testimony. No, it doesn't confirm to us that Jason and Zach and Li raped Sabrina, but it does confirm to us that Jason and Zach can't be fully trusted. Remember... the police statements say that Jason denied all involvement with Keating, yet Keville was able to provide us with proof that they — at the very least — socialise with each other.'

One photograph that appeared on the front page of the *Sunday World* in 2011 — when Jason Kenny was at the peak of his career — portrayed Jason laughing with his left arm wrapped around Alan Keating in an inner-city Dublin pub. Zach was also in the photo. It had a huge impact on some jurors, particularly those who felt the three men were guilty of rape. It gave their verdict validation; painting Jason and Zach as scumbags. Not even Clara Groves' or Mick Dempsey's glowing testimonies about Jason — which followed Keville's testimony — could smooth over that massive bump.

'I, one hundred per cent, believe Frank Keville,' says Number Five.

'Me too,' Number Six follows up.

'And me,' Number Three says, readjusting her wheelchair so she can be more face on with Number One — the juror she was aiming her feelings at. Number Three was now being swung back towards a guilty verdict having changed her initial 'guilty' call in the first vote to 'undecided' in the secret ballot.

'I believe him too,' says Number Four, speaking on this subject for the first time. 'And I know he's just a character witness; he wasn't talking about the rape or anything like that, just giving us details on Jason and Zach's background... what sort of shit they're into. But... I don't know how to say this without sounding a bit stupid. I kinda forgot about his testimony a bit until we brought it up in this room. Now that we're talking about it, it seems like one of the most intriguing parts of the trial, yet twenty minutes ago, it barely registered with me.'

'Well that's why we are given this time in the jury room — to thrash out everything we heard, to highlight it all,' says Number Ten. 'And I agree with you. Keville's testimony has rung more true in this jury room, on reflection. I guess reading it in black and white has had a bit more impact. It's really making me question Jason Kenny's character.'

'Agreed. I have to admit, I don't like Zach and I'm not really sure about Jason,' says Number Four. Maybe there's something really dark about him. He's holding secrets. Probably feels entitled because he's both a footballer and a gangster. He might even think he's invincible, certainly will if he's found not guilty by us.'

Number Four's mind was racing. He was never quite sure what way he was leaning, every new discussion pulling him in a different direction.

Number Four's real name is Clive Suttie, a thirty-nine-year-old from Donabate in north Dublin. He's a manger for a finance and insurance firm called Fullams. He's likable, but has the maturity levels of somebody ten years his junior. It's why he keeps following Number Seven to the water dispenser; still has a tendency to believe that stalking a girl is the best way to get her into bed. He is really starting to get bored by the deliberations, but is still intrigued and is enjoying the responsibility he has been handed. Though he is slightly growing annoyed by the fact that his mind seems to be changing on a whim. Overall, he's undecided; is not sure how this is all going to pan out. He has an inkling the jury may be hung after a few days of deliberating. He can't see how Brian and Number One, for starters, are ever going to agree on a verdict, let alone everyone else in the room.

And if he's right — if the jury are still hung after the judge's patience wears thin — the case will be dismissed. Jason, Zach and Li will walk out of the court free men. Even if the vast majority of jurors think they're guilty.

22:10
Zach

She's still laughing – hasn't stopped – as the rickshaw guy races off Grafton Street, turning right at Stephen's Green to make his way back towards Coppers.

I've used a couple of cheesy lines – not my normal approach – but they seemed to have worked. Though I'm still not sure if she's into me or into Jason more. I decide to stop with the cheesiness; cut to the chase.

'Your eyes are amazin',' I say. She doesn't answer. Just stares at me, purses her lips in mock embarrassment before turning away. I'm sure she's heard that line a million times before.

'I've a feelin' me and you are gonna hook up tonight,' I say.

'What?' she says, turning to me again.

'Yeah… I'm not saying that we're gonna hook up right now, but at some stage tonight.'

I smile. Her mouth just falls open. Then she looks the other way again.

I'm not sure how to take that. Maybe she's thinkin' about telling me that my prediction is not gonna happen in any way shape or form. Or maybe she's contemplating it; wondering if she should be pursuing me now, not Jason.

I allow the silence to remain between us. I've done most of the talkin' anyway for the past ten or fifteen minutes. All she's done is laugh. We're about five minutes away from the club. I needed to let her know what I was thinking. Needed to do it before we got back, before she ran into Jason's arms. I did the right thing, no matter how awkward I feel right now.

Tina's face threatens to pop into my head but I don't let it.

Fuck that. She bores me. We're just set in our ways. Our relationship is a necessity, because we have two kids, but it's boring. I know it and she knows it. She doesn't mind me going to the pub all the time, doesn't mind me going to clubs. She's probably aware I cheat on her, but she's willing to turn a blind eye, just to keep the family together.

I don't like being a parent. Have never been afraid to admit that. Once the kids came along, all the doors to my life closed. It meant I could never follow my brothers to other corners of the world; could never make life choices that I'd like to have had the option to make. Freedom becomes a thing of the past once you become a parent. It sucks. Plus, kids are annoying as hell. Who the fuck wants a poxy little six-year-old snotty-nosed high-pitched idiot running around their house anyway?

I'm pretty certain that lads only have kids because women talk them into it. And women only have kids because they feel that's what they're supposed to do. If anyone thinks it through properly, like *really* thinks the whole thing through, the world's population would be a helluva lot smaller.

'You got any kids?' I ask. The silence has been going on too long.

'Me? No!' she says. 'You?'

I shake my head. Stare up at the night sky as our rickshaw guy approaches Harcourt Street.

'Y'know what… you can leave us here,' I say, handing a twenty euro note to him over his shoulder. Poor fella. I can't believe he cycled around town with us two on his back for a quarter of an hour for the sake of a bloody score. I help Sabrina off the rickshaw by taking her hand. I almost pull her into me as she gets off, but I'm not quite getting the vibe that that's what she wants. She's hard to read. Maybe I came on too strong by suggesting we were gonna get it on tonight.

I should have just continued with the cheesy lines. She was enjoying them.

It's starting to get cold. If I had a jacket I'd take it off, throw it around her shoulders, start playing the gentleman card. I can change my game up depending on the circumstances. I initially thought this bird was just up for a laugh, but maybe she needs a bit more maturity.

'My eh… my mam's unwell,' I say as we slowly walk towards Coppers.

'Oh, I'm so sorry to hear that,' she says.

'Yeah – Alzheimer's. Barely knows who I am anymore. Sometimes she thinks I'm her husband… once she thought I was her father.'

I notice her stare at me as I slump my hands into my jeans pocket. I probably should have been an actor. My ma's fine. Nothing wrong with her. Has the sharpest mind I know.

'Once… when I visited her in the hospital, she jumped out of the bed, wrapped her arms around me and tried to kiss me on the mouth. Started calling me Frank – my dad's name. I had to leave the room, didn't stop crying for about half-an-hour. It's tough going. I'm all she has. And I'm there every day for her. I go up to have lunch with her in the hospital and stay for about three hours at a time.'

'That's so sweet,' she says. 'And is your boss okay with that? What is it you do for work?'

'I eh… I run my own business. A digital tech company. We're doin' very well. Well, we were doin' very well. With me taking time off work, the business has suffered. But family before profit right?'

She purses her lips at me again but this time in a sweet way, not in the pitiful way she pursed her lips at me ten minutes ago. I pause when we get to the entrance of Coppers, swirling my foot in a circular motion around the pathway.

'It's tough, y'know. It was always me and Mam. The two of us together. Now I just feel like I'm on my own. I'd never known what loneliness was until my mam started to forget who I was.'

She reaches out with both her hands, grabs me in for a hug. I can feel her tits press against my chest. I'm a fuckin' genius. I always know how to play it with birds. Always know how to read the game. Just like I did as a footballer.

'I'm really sorry you're going through this,' she says. 'But… y'know what? It doesn't mean you have to stop living your own life, right? Your mother would want you to get on with it; would want you to be happy.' She leans off me. Stares into my eyes. 'C'mon, let's go back inside. Let's get you back on that dance floor.'

I can't help it. I lean in. Lips first.

22:10
Jason

'Bottle of champagne,' I shout to the barman. 'Most expensive one you have.'

'No, will ye bleeding stop,' says Li. 'Stop buying champagne, man — none of us enjoy it. What are you like?'

I just laugh. Out loud. Then I drag him in for another hug. A long one. So long, I even have time to wave the barman away from us over Li's shoulder as he shows me another black bottle of champers. Probably the exact same piss I spent a grand on earlier.

'That kid is going to be one lucky little shit having a dad like you,' I say. And I mean it. I never lie. I may hold the truth back a lot. But I never lie.

'Thanks,' Li says, pulling back from the hug, staring into my face.

He can tell I'm tearing up.

'Jeez... I'm not the only one to have a kid. Zach's got two you know? Why the tears?'

'I just... I'm just so happy for you,' I say, as I wipe my eyes. 'And...' I pause. I'm not sure what to say. I can't pour it all out. Not here. Not when Li can barely hear what I'm saying anyway over the loud music. I just hold a finger to each temple and let everything sink in. 'I'm just not having a good time of it lately,' I spit out. 'But fuck it, your news has perked me right up. So... you're gonna be a husband *and* a dad next year huh... unbelievable!'

'Yeah — but keep it a secret, okay? Niamh doesn't want anyone to know. Not until she's past the three-month mark. Start of August, that's when we're telling everyone. 'Sure you'll be back in Newcastle by then, right? What date does the new season kick off?'

I pinch at my temples again. Close my eyes.

'Jason... Jason, what's wrong, mate?'

'I've no contract, Li. I'm done. It's over.'

I've been dreading telling anyone this. Mainly because I have no idea what I'm going to do. My agent has tried to pimp me around to other League One clubs, even League Two clubs. The consensus seems to be that I'm past it. The only way I can make money now is through celebrity appearances. But fuck that! Or I could do what Zach does – sell drugs. He thinks I don't know. But of course I do. I've known for years. He came to me one day, palms up in apology.

'Don't overreact, but I've been.... I've been hanging around Alan Keating and that lot for the past while,' he said. It wasn't a surprise to me. Li had filled me in, told me those were the rumours doing the rounds in Drimnagh. 'I kinda got myself into a bit of trouble... it's fine. Nothing's gonna happen to me. But eh... Alan, he eh... he wants to meet you. Just to have drinks with you. That's it.'

I could have punched him in the face. It was one thing getting himself caught up in that sort of mess, but dragging me into it was close to unforgiveable. But there's a bond between the three of us that means we never fall out, never fight. We're devoted to each other, no matter how much of a prick Zach can be at times. I guess it all stems back to The Secret. We'll always have each other's backs no matter the circumstances.

'He's just a fan of yours. Would like to hang out, that's all.'

So I did. I hung out with Alan Keating and his cronies. I still kinda do, every now and then. Just to keep the peace. I'm in no danger. They just enjoy the fact that they can hang out with a professional footballer. It makes them all feel a bit more significant. I have a couple of pints with them when I'm back in Dublin and have arranged a few match tickets for them every now and then. They've always been cool with me.

Treat me well. But didn't the newspapers get hold of pictures that were taken of us hanging out; splashed them across the front pages of their fucking papers.

'Kenny And Keating: Best Buddies' was the headline in one. I wanted to sue the arse off them but there was nothing to sue for. The article didn't libel me, it didn't really say anything, other than insinuate I was hanging around with Ireland's most notorious crime lord. Which is exactly what I *was* doing.

I didn't react, didn't even release a statement acknowledging the article. I just let it slide. It was the talk of the town for a few days before the nation moved on to talking about something else. I'm sure it's damaged my reputation somewhat. But it's a good job I scored that jammy goal against Holland all those years back. It's kept me relevant. If it wasn't for that goal, I'd just be another washed up footballer nobody gives two shits about.

'What do you mean no contract? Sunderland are letting you go? You're their best player for fuck sake.'

Li looks shocked. His mouth is practically hanging open.

'New manager, new ideas,' I say, still holding my temples.

'What are you gonna do?'

I shake my head. I don't know the answer to Li's question. I've played that question over and over in my head almost every hour for the past couple of months, but I genuinely haven't come to a conclusion.

'I'm just... I'm falling apart,' I say, almost crying.

Li grabs a hold of me. Steadies me.

'Jason, tell me what I can do to help. Anything. I'd do anything for you, mate.'

'You're all I have.'

'You need somebody else, Jason. You need to find someone to settle down with. Hey — what about this Sabrina girl, you seem into her. And she's lovely. I get on great with her. Why not give it a proper go? Not just a one-night thing, ask her out… see what can come of it.'

I shrug my shoulders. I get his line of thinking. It aligns with mine. That's exactly what I've been stewing on for most of the night. Well, from the moment I first saw her. She could be the one for me, could be exactly what my life is missing.

'Y'know what? Let's fuck off to Newcastle,' Li says. 'You're always at your most comfortable in your own home. C'mon, fuck it, Jason. The four of us. Me, you, Zach, Sabrina. Show her what you're all about.'

'Newcastle? Tonight? Sure I only came home yesterday.'

'Yeah – but to hell with it. Look around you. Fuck this shit. Let's go on an adventure. I'm with you. Show Sabrina your gaff, show her what she could have if she was to hook up with you.'

He's talking shite. Must be the Baby Guinness. But without even thinking it through I find myself taking my phone from my jeans pocket and clicking into the Ryanair app.

22:15
Li

I've only ever seen Jason cry at his dad's funeral. I know these are supposed to be happy tears. But I sense he's not just crying because I told him I'm going to be a dad. There's something else going on. I can always tell with Jason. I know he's depressed, has been for the last couple of years.

'I've no contract, Li. I'm done. It's over.'

Wow. I didn't see that coming. I can't believe Sunderland don't want to keep him on. He's been the only one trying over the past couple of seasons. He gives his all to that club.

'New manager, new ideas,' he tells me as he stares down at his feet. He's embarrassed telling me this. Feels as if he's letting us all down. He's so sensitive. He wears the weight of our expectation on his shoulders. Always has done.

'What are you gonna do?' I ask him.

He continues to stare at his feet – pinching his temples as if he's trying to massage his troubles away.

'I'm just… I'm falling apart,' he says as the tears begin to fall down his face. I hold him in to me, so nobody else can see him crying.

'Jason, tell me what I can do to help. Anything. I'd do *anything* for you, mate.'

'You're all I have,' he sobs.

'You need somebody else Jason, you need to find someone to settle down with… Hey – what about this Sabrina girl, you seem into her. And she's lovely. I get on great with her. Why not y'know… give it a proper go. Not just a one-night thing, ask her out… see what can come of it.'

I'm not just feeding him this line to help him feel instantly better. Jason needs somebody. He needs a partner; a reason to get up every morning. He needs his Niamh.

22:15

Maybe this Sabrina girl is it. I know he could have any other girl in this nightclub, but I've seen the way he looks at Sabrina. I sensed his frustration when she walked up the stairs with Zach. I knew his heart was cracking bit.

'Y'know what? Let's fuck off to Newcastle. You're always at your happiest in the comfort of your own home. C'mon, fuck it, Jason. The four of us. Me, you, Zach, Sabrina. Show her what you're all about.'

I don't know why I offer that as a remedy. I'm trying to think of ways he can impress the girl he's into.

'Newcastle? Tonight? Sure I only came home yesterday.'

'Yeah – but to hell with it. Look around you. Fuck this shit. Let's go on an adventure. I'm with you. Show Sabrina your gaff, show her what she could have if she was to hook up with you.'

He shakes his head, but I watch as he takes his phone out of his pocket and clicks into the Ryanair app.

'There's a flight at eleven thirty-five,' he says, sucking up his tears. 'What's that… an hour and a half from now? Think we could make it?'

I nod my head and smile, but I'm not that enthused at all. I'm supposed to go to bloody Homebase with Niamh in the morning. She won't be happy if I tell her I'm in Newcastle. But she'll understand in time. She knows I'd do anything for Jason and Zach. Has actually mentioned to me a few times that she adores how loyal I am to my two best mates. It's one of the reasons she fell in love with me. It makes her feel certain that I'd never hurt her. She trusts me and I trust her. One hundred per cent. She's the only one I've ever told about The Secret. I couldn't help it. Couldn't bear to keep anything from her. I guess that's true love.

'Sweetie, I have something to tell you that I'm ashamed of — but no matter what, you have to promise you'll keep it a secret,' I said to her as we were lying in bed one night.

She took it well, just as I imagined she would. She kept repeating that we were young and dumb and didn't know any better. She held me close, wiped my tears; made me a big fry up the next morning. We haven't mentioned it since.

I'd already known I wanted to spend my life with her, but her handling of the biggest secret I will ever have confirmed it for me. I started to look for engagement rings online the next day. I had no idea how expensive they were. I thought of asking Jason for a loan but knew deep in my heart that there was nothing romantic about that. So I saved; put a hundred euro aside every month for a whole year until I could afford the ring I had picked out. I hope she likes it. I can't wait to ask her to marry me; can't wait to be a dad.

I'm the luckiest mother fucker alive. If only I could help Jason and Zach to be as happy as I am. But maybe none of us deserve to be happy. After all, we did ruin a young girl's life. Perhaps karma already caught up with them, and is just around the corner waiting to pounce on me.

'Fuck it!' Jason says. 'It's booked. Four flights. She's gonna think I'm a fuckin' psycho, isn't she?'

I laugh, not knowing what to make of it all. But I know I must be positive. This was my suggestion after all.

'I think she'll think it's romantic,' I say. But I don't know what to believe. 'Won't we need our passports though?' I say, sipping from my beer.

Jason shakes his head.

'Nah.. just once you have photo ID you can catch a flight from Ireland to UK, right?'

I shrug my shoulders.

'Think so, yeah. We'll see what she says when they get back. So what exactly happened between you two at the Hairy Lemon anyway?' I ask.

'I asked her to go outside, couldn't help myself. I pushed her up against the wall, started snogging the face off her.

Then I bloody unzipped my jeans, asked her to stick her hand inside.'

I cringe. I've known Jason to be this up front before, but only with girls who give off the impression that that's exactly what they're after – Jason's dick.

'And…?'

'Well she did, started jerking me for a while. But I felt guilty immediately. Couldn't understand why I was being so disrespectful to a girl I actually liked.'

I blow out my lips, almost making a fart sound. Jason just laughs. At least I've cheered him up a bit.

Then I notice the eyes almost pop out of his head. I turn around to see what he's staring at and catch her walking back down the steps, Zach lagging behind.

'How the fuck are you gonna tell her you've just booked her a flight to Newcastle?'

I laugh as I ask this.

Jason repeats what I'd just done moments ago – blows out his lips and shrugs his shoulders.

'I've no fuckin' idea, mate.'

22:25
Sabrina

He's a nice guy — I'm sure of it — but he didn't half make me cringe throughout the entirety of that rickshaw ride. It was a cute attempt at trying to chat me up; certainly a new experience for me. Nobody's ever tried to charm me that way before. But I did want to get off the rickshaw as soon as I got on it. It was blatant what was happening. He used every trick in the book. He started off with some God-awful cheesy lines I'm sure he read somewhere in a list online, and then opted to be all confident and cocky as if that's what would win me over. When none of that worked, he gave me the sob story about his mother. It's endearing that he looks after her, that he has a big heart. But I'm just not into him. Even if I wasn't into Jason, there's not a chance I'd hook up with Zach. He's just not my type in any way. He's too laddish, too immature, too short.

I'm beginning to feel the discomfort dissipating as if we both agree that nothing's going to happen, that we can both just be friends. But that's the moment he decides to lean in for a kiss.

'Oi,' I say laughing, trying to lighten the tension so he doesn't get offended. But I feel I owe it to be straight with him; to be honest with him after he just opened up to me. 'I'm sorry, Zach but… y'know. I'm kinda… I'm into Jason.'

I watch his chin fall to his chest. I reach out my finger and pick his chin back up so that he's looking at me.

'I'm sure you'll make a wonderful girl happy some day,' I say. 'But it's not me. I'm sorry.'

He smiles back, then motions that we should just head back inside.

22:25

I've no idea whether Jason is into me or not, so it's a bit of a gamble going back in here. I'm half tempted to go home, but intrigue has a hold of me. I'll probably walk in to see Jason pinning another girl up against the wall, his tongue circling her mouth just like it was circling mine a few hours ago. He probably has no intentions of getting to know me any further, but fuck it — I'll give it a go. I keep reminding myself that I need to lighten up, that I need more fun in my life. Let's see what Jason's intentions really are. If he isn't interested, I can just head home, which is what I was about to do anyway until he dragged me over for a drink with his mates. It'll be no loss either way. In half-an-hours' time I'm either gonna be hooking back up with a celebrity or I'll be on my way home in a taxi. Win-win either way. Though I certainly know which win I'd prefer. Which is exactly why I find myself walking back down the stairs of Copper Face Jacks.

Any other time I've come in here, I've been with Eddie. I never quite understood why he used to bring me to this place. We'd spend most of our time standing at the edge of the dance floor, drink in hand, watching everybody else have a good time. He took himself way too seriously to dance. And that's actually part of the reason I've chanced coming back in. I watched Jason dance earlier on — or attempting to dance. I love that he doesn't take himself too seriously. I love that he's the total opposite of Eddie in that respect. Though maybe he's just as much as an untrustworthy bastard. I don't know for certain how many times Eddie cheated on me, but I do know he would have fucked Lorna one night when she came on to him. She reported to me that his exact words were 'fuck yeah!' when she suggested bringing him back to her place. I wasn't surprised when she told me. I just packed up my stuff, wrote him a note and closed the door behind me. He tried ringing me about ten times a day over the next week; even called up to my parents' house with a bunch of flowers. My dad told him where to go. I haven't seen or heard from him since.

I stare at his face, just to gauge his reaction as he notices me and Zach walking towards him and Li. His smile makes my stomach flip. I need to calm down. I shouldn't be getting this excited, this carried away. But then again, love – or lust as it most probably is – isn't really an emotion you can control.

'Drink?' Jason asks.

'Sure. Red wine please,' I reply. Zach doesn't say anything. He just scratches his head, looking awkward, almost embarrassed. I wonder if Jason knew what Zach was about to do and it makes my heart race again. Maybe they're all in it together. But as Jason grabs my hand and leads me towards the bar, my paranoia subsides. I can't believe he is having such an effect on me. My emotions have been up and down all night.

'Where've you two been then?' he asks, as he rests his forearms on the bar.

'Oh, lovely Zach took me out for a rickshaw ride.'

'A fuckin' rickshaw ride? — the old romantic.'

I squint at him, trying to understand what the fuck is going on. He pulls me in close, talks into my ear.

'Don't mind Zach. He just tries it on with any girl he thinks is pretty. I haven't told him you and I had kissed.'

He leans back to gauge my reaction. I just squint again.

'Listen, I like you. I do. Really like you. Don't let Zach's cheesiness put you off me. I'm nothing like him. We're best mates, but total opposites.'

I bite my bottom lip, just to stop my mouth from smiling as wide as it wants to.

'I hope your lines are better than his,' I say.

Jason laughs out loud, then leans back into to my ear.

'You gotta tell me one of the lines he said to you.'

I try to think back. I remember them being explicitly cheesy, yet can't remember any of them word-for-word.

'Oh something like 'Is your dad a boxer, because you are a knockout'.'

We both burst out laughing; so loud that the couple standing next to us at the bar stop talking just to stare.

'Ah Jason Kenny,' the fella says, holding his hand out. 'Ye bloody legend!'

I play with my hair, try to keep calm. But I'm excited. I've always wondered what it would be like to go out with someone famous; someone other people look up to. I just stand back and watch as the fella stands with his arm wrapped around Jason while his girlfriend takes a photo of them together. When they're done, I lean in to Jason – just to let everyone know he's with me. Jee… I am changing. I am lightening up. Maybe Jason is Mr Right for me. I've never felt this comfortable in any man's company before. It's so strange — we've only known each other for about ten minutes.

'So… can you beat that?' I ask him as he leans back on the bar.

'Beat what?'

'Is your dad a boxer?'

We laugh again. Almost in sync.

'I think I can,' he says.

I raise my eyebrows, signal to him that I'm ready to hear what he has to offer.

'Well, let me ask you this first: what are your plans tomorrow?'

Wow; now that is a good opening line. He's already talking about the future. Our future.

'I eh… I say,' swiping strands of my hair away from my eyes. 'I don't have any plans tomorrow.'

'And eh.. do you have any photo ID on you tonight?'

'Huh?' I say, wrinkling my brow.

'Do you have photo ID with you?'

'Yeah... why?' I ask, really slowly.

'Good,' he says. 'We're flying to Newcastle tonight and you're coming with us.'

8

A light knock rattles the door. Number Nine — being nearest to the door — stands up, takes three steps and opens it. The other jurors can't see the face on the other side of the door, just the paperwork being handed over to their peer.

'Thanks a mill,' Number Nine says, offering the young man dressed in black a polite smile.

She strolls back over to the table and stretches across it to hand Number One the notes.

'Okay, here we go,' he says, licking his finger and then flicking through the three sheets.

'It was about half-way through his testimony,' says Number Twelve, trying to be helpful.

'Hang on,' Number One says, before humming to himself as he tries to speed-read through the pages. 'Got it.'

He sits more upright, both elbows now resting on the table. '"They were laughing and joking all the time,"' he reads. '"They looked like boyfriend and girlfriend" – and then Mr Ryan asks: "Yes, but that was just your assumption, right? That they were boyfriend and girlfriend?" – Scott answers,

"Yes, of course — my assumption. That's what I even told police when they interviewed me. I thought they were boyfriend and girlfriend, found out much later — when the investigation was going on — that they weren't." Ryan then asks: "You told Gardaí that even though you assumed they were boyfriend and girlfriend you thought she — and I quote — "wore the trousers", yes?" Okay – and this is the sentence we're looking for… Scott then answered: "she was in control, laughing, joking. I can't remember what they were saying, but I got the impression she was having more fun than him. She was doing all the laughing."'

'Ah, so – "*she was having more fun than him, she was doing all the laughing*" – I knew it was something like that,' Number Twelve says. 'So… what does this tell us?'

'Well, it contradicts her testimony, doesn't it?' Brian says. 'Sabrina said she was trying to get Zach away from her, that he kinda made her go onto the rickshaw; that all she wanted to do was go back to the club.'

The jury room falls silent. Each juror trying to soak in the opposing testimonies of Sabrina and an eye-witness called by the defence – a Mr Donagh Scott. Scott was only eighteen when he pulled up in his rickshaw outside Copper Face Jacks at ten-forty on the night in question, to be met by Sabrina and Zach running towards him.

Scott testified on the stand that it was indeed Zach who called to him first, that he didn't notice whether Sabrina was reluctant to get on the rickshaw or not. But he did testify that she seemed more than comfortable when she was taking the ride.

'She wasn't just comfortable, she was enjoying herself, I thought,' Scott said on the stand. 'I remember her laughing and joking.'

He admitted he remembered Zach and Sabrina clearly from that night, because he thought the girl was 'particularly attractive'. He remembered thinking Zach had 'done well for himself'.

'This Donagh guy isn't the first witness to contradict statements made by Sabrina. The photographer Patrick Clavin, Donagh now — and obviously the other two; Jason and Zach — they *all* contradict almost everything she has said. She is the common denominator here... perhaps she is just a consistent liar?'

'Well of course Jason and Li would contradict what Sabrina is saying. She believes she was raped, they don't believe they raped her. Of course they have opposite views — that's bleedin obvious,' Number Five says.

'Yesh, but Patrick Clavin the photographer and Donagh Scott — they're both independent witnesses. I mean they don't need to lie, do they? They don't gain anything,' Brian says, offering up his opinion for the first time in two minutes, an unusually quiet break for him.

'Well, we could say the same about the journalist guy that testified against Jason and Zach — what's his name again?

'Frank Keville,' says Number One.

'Yes, Mr Keville — he is an independent witness too and he has differences of opinions to Jason Kenny and Zach Brophy. Does that make them consistent liars too? And... for the record, this Donagh Scott guy — nice as he is — his testimony is kinda pointless, isn't it? It's all assumption. If he *assumed* Sabrina and Zach were boyfriend and girlfriend — and we know for a fact that that assumption was wrong — then maybe all of his assumptions are wrong. Maybe his assumption that Sabrina was enjoying the rickshaw ride has been wrong all along too.'

'Yeah — that is a point Sabrina's lawyer raised in court. How valid is this guy's testimony anyway?' asks Number Six.

'Well, if the judge allowed it, it's valid. He was an eye-witness in the middle of the night in question. We have to take on board what he said.'

Scott's testimony didn't do the prosecution any favours. It painted Sabrina in a bad light, suggesting she was flirting up a storm with Zach. If any jury member felt it was accurate that she was flirting with both Zach and Jason during the night in question, then it enhances the argument that the intercourse that took place later in the hotel room was consensual.

'I just… I can't,' Number Four rubs his face with his palm. 'My mind keeps changing. I keep feeling sorry for Sabrina, thinking these men raped her, then the next minute I think she's just a liar.'

'Everybody,' Brian says, rotating both his arms as if he is a preacher addressing his congregation, 'we keep falling into the trap of making ashumptions, opinions. It's not about what we feel. We can't pass judgement based on how we feel. We need to go by the evidensh.'

'Change the record, Brian,' Number Five says.

'It needs re-emphasi—'

'Hold on,' Number Twelve says, interrupting Brian's comeback. 'Brian is right. We take each piece of evidence at its merit. Here,' he says pointing at the sheets of paper in Number One's grasp, 'we have an eye-witness testifying that Sabrina wasn't uncomfortable on that rickshaw, okay? We have to put that in our pocket and move on. It is evidence that perhaps suggests Sabrina isn't always truthful.'

'Well, we could put it in our pocket — as you say — as evidence that doesn't paint Sabrina in a good light. But I will put it in my pocket as evidence I won't consider too strongly,' Number Eleven says.

It's been a while since Number Eleven voluntarily offered her thoughts.

'Donagh Scott's testimony is all based on assumption,' she

continues. 'He doesn't know how Sabrina was feeling. He can't have known. Yes, we should all put it in our pocket as evidence, but not necessarily how you see it, Number Twelve. How we individually see it — and that may be differently. We all have our own perception on this.'

Number Eleven's starting to grow in confidence as deliberations drag on. She, too, sick of listening to the same voices over and over again.

Number Eleven has had a strong feeling that the three men raped Sabrina. She was particularly disturbed by the doctor's evidence towards the end of the trial.

Doctor Dermot Johnson examined Sabrina two days after the alleged rape, testifying on the stand that Sabrina had suffered an internal cut on the night in question. But he also emphasised that this type of cut can appear as a result of consensual sex, not just forced sex.

Even so, Number Eleven was appalled by his testimony. The images Sabrina's lawyer showed in court of similar internal cuts, tattooed Number Eleven's mind. From the moment Doctor Johnson left the stand, Number Eleven was convinced Jason, Zach and Li raped Sabrina.

Number Eleven is a forty-one-year-old mother of three from Tallaght called Magdelena Andris. She's been a resident in Dublin her whole life after her parents emigrated from their home city of Saldus in Latvia back in 1973. She is highly creative — works as a graphic designer for a popular digital company called ebow in the centre of Dublin — but lacks in other areas. She can't piece all of the evidence together bit-by-bit like some jurors do. She can only see the bigger picture. It's the way most creative brains work. The doctor's testimony, although not supposed to be taken as any proof of rape whatsoever, has been making her decision for her. She is firmly in the guilty camp. Hasn't wavered.

'Let's move on,' says Number One. We can all take

Donagh Scott's evidence as we see fit. There are differences of opinions, but that's why we're here — to argue this case. We are getting to the key part of the night — the decision to go to the airport. What do we make of this?'

Number One turns to his nemesis, Brian, as he asks this. It's a gesture of goodwill. He is beginning to feel their spat needs mending if he is to eventually persuade everybody to agree with him and find the three men guilty.

'Oh me?' asks Brian a little taken aback. 'I think it'sh quite telling that Sabrina was up for something. She was certainly up for flying to Newcastle, right?'

'Doesn't mean she was up for sex with all three men?' Number Three says, tapping her fingers against the armrest of her wheelchair.

'True,' replies Brian. 'But I'm just stating a fact. Sabrina admitting she was keen to go to Newcastle with the three men does shay a lot, don't you think? She was certainly comfortable in their company at that stage.'

Sabrina *had* admitted to police during their investigation, as well as on the stand during the trial, that she had fallen for Jason in Copper Face Jacks and hoped a relationship might form between the two of them. When Jason suggested all four of them fly to Newcastle, and back to his house for the night, she felt accepting this invitation would help her get to know him more. She said she liked Li, thought he was a nice man: "harmless" was an adjective she used. But admitted that Zach "kinda unnerved me a little bit". She said she wished at the time that it was just her and Jason who were flying back to Newcastle. Either way, she felt comfortable enough in all three men's company to take them up on their offer; felt she had got to know them somewhat. The possibility of being raped never entered her mind.

It's estimated by the Rape Crisis Network that in eighty-five per cent of rape cases, the victim is known to the accused. This particular case is a grey area when it comes to that statistic. Sabrina barely knew each of the three men she was accusing of rape; had met them only five hours previous to the incident. Although she admits to being "comfortable enough" in their presence, this case would be added to the statistic of the fifteen per cent of rape cases where the victim does not know the accused. It's unusual that random rapes occur. Most sex crimes are premeditated, normally by a family member or a friend of the victim. In fact, most rapes aren't necessarily motivated by attraction, but more so by opportunity and a lust for power men crave over women. This case was slightly more unusual than a regular rape trial. Especially so, given that there was a major celebrity involved.

'So, Sabrina admitted that she fancied Jason by this point and was quite intrigued when he suggested they all fly to Newcastle, back to his house for a party,' says Number One. 'What was she thinking?'

'Eh... that she was going back to a footballer's house for a party,' replies Brian.

'And would that be a decision most women would take? I mean, I find that hard to believe—'

'I can't speak on behalf of 'most women' but I do think a lot of women would be interested in an invite back to a celebrity's house,' Number Eleven says, interrupting Brian.

A ripple of argument races around the table. Most jurors feel Sabrina's position here was justifiable; that it certainly didn't point to any agreement to having sex with all three men. Her lawyer justified her statements on this when he cross-examined Jason and Li; made sure both men admitted on the stand that no talk of sex had occurred at this stage of the evening and that everybody was in agreement that they would just fly to Newcastle to have some fun. Despite this, Number One was adamant that Sabrina's actions at this point in the night were incredibly suspicious.

'I think she knew what she was up to here,' he says. 'She knew something kinky was going on. She meets a guy one night and a few hours later she decides to go back to his house? C'mon guys... what sensible girl would do that?'

'I would,' Number Eleven admits. 'In fact, I have done that.'

'Me too,' says Number Five.

The jury room falls silent, except for the sound of some jurors shuffling in their chairs.

22:50
Sabrina

I take a peek at my phone as Li turns to face us, arguing that there is no way we can make the flight. And if we do, photo ID may not be enough to get us on board.

'It's ten to eleven,' I say. 'The flight's taking off in just over half-an-hour, right?'

Jason nods his head.

'Yeah – we should be boarding now,' Li says.

'Shut up, Li, relax will ya — we'll get there,' groans Zach.

I turn my head, just to look out the window as we speed up the N1. If I got out of the taxi now, I'd only have about a twenty-minute walk to the comfort of my own bed.

'Guys we're supposed to be boarding around now, and we're a fifteen minute drive from the airport, we still have to go through security, walk to the gate.... I don't think we'll make it,' Li says, still staring over his shoulder at the three of us in the back seat. I'm on the left side of Jason, Zach to his right.

'Let's just see...' Jason says. Then the taxi falls silent.

I try to soak in what's going on. I'm practically by-passing my neighbourhood to head to the airport, in order to catch a flight to Newcastle — what am I doing? I have no plans for the weekend, won't be letting anybody down — but this is a little crazy, especially for me. Maybe I'm coming across as desperate. I've observed girls being desperate before and it's really cringeworthy. I've seen models practically sell their souls to get ahead in life. I never thought I'd be one of them. Not in a million years.

I close my eyes, rest my head back on the chair and think my actions through again. I'm trying to comprehend whether going to Newcastle or not will make Jason fall for me. If I go,

I've got his attention. But if I ask the taxi man to pull over now, to let me out, that's it, isn't it? I'll never see Jason again. He assured me we'd get time alone once we got to his place, that his house was so big that the other lads would most likely just crash out in the cinema room while we got to know each other a little better. I assume sex is on his mind. Why wouldn't it be? I've already tugged at his penis. I think I will have sex with him. It could be my first step on the ladder of me trying to lighten up. I've only ever had sex with two men before. That's quite disappointing, especially for someone who looks like me. I have men come on to me all the time, but barely give any of them more than a polite smile and a shrug of my shoulders. I don't intend on being slutty, but maybe I should adopt a bit more of a personality. Become more outgoing. More fun. Begin to live the life I want to live, not the one that I live in fear of other people judging me. When am I ever gonna get a chance to have sex with a celebrity anyway?

My head starts to spin. The angel on my shoulder is urging me to retreat into the quiet little hermit I've always been — the person I don't want to be anymore. The devil on my shoulder is telling me I am the complete opposite of that; young, free, single. Up for fun. Up for the craic. I'm pretty sure nine out of ten girls in this situation would have sex with Jason Kenny. Why can't I be one of those nine? For once. But mostly I want to be with Jason Kenny because… well, I want to be with Jason Kenny. Not just tonight, but beyond tonight. I know I'm attracted to his fame, to his lifestyle, but why shouldn't I be? If that is part of who he is then I'm entitled to be attracted to it. But if I want Jason Kenny long-term, what should I do short-term? What should I do tonight? Play hard to get? Doesn't that make me that one out of ten who doesn't have sex with the celebrity… the frigid?

Doesn't that just make me the Sabrina bloody Doyle I don't want to be?

I open my eyes, lift my head from the back of the chair and look at him. He stares back, smiles then rests his hand on my knee. A wave of warmth washes through my stomach. That's made my mind up for me. I'm really into this guy. Fuck it. I check my phone again, then sit more upright.

'Okay, it's almost eleven. We'll probably get to the airport at a quarter past. If there are no queues at security, which there probably won't be this time of night, we could get to the departure gate around half-past, twenty-to twelve at the latest. If the flight is slightly delayed, we can make it.'

'That's the girl,' says Zach, holding a hand up for me to high five. 'You really are up for this, huh?' he says. 'Ye know Jason has a swimming pool? Ye like to swim?'

I just laugh, probably because I'm excited by the notion that my next boyfriend could genuinely have a bloody swimming pool in his own home.

'I do like to swim, yeah,' I reply. 'Pity you didn't give me time to go home and get my swimming gear.'

'Ah, we don't use swimming gear. It's all skinny dipping in Jason's gaff,' says Zach. 'It's a strict rule.'

I try to imagine what Jason's house is like. I remember actually being impressed by Eddie's house, and that was because it was a three-bed semi-detached. I bet Jason's is ten times bigger.

Eddie would have liked me to have been his house slave. He was happy for me to give up modelling. Happy for me to clean his kitchen, hoover his floors, iron his shirts. It was never going to happen. I think that's why we started to have rows actually. I was never going to fit in with his idea of a picture-perfect girlfriend. He courted that old-fashioned, traditional relationship. I was way past that. I wanted my own independence. He tried to downplay my career, insisted

I wasn't a model — just a marketing puppet. He knew how to hurt me; knew what buttons to push. I still maintain that I only went out with him because I was desperate. Before him, I only ever had one boyfriend. And perhaps labelling Stuart a 'boyfriend' is pushing it. We only hooked up a few times over the course of about a month when I was nineteen.

Stu was a model, too. We met on a shoot, decided to go out for lunch together during a break in our day. I lost my virginity to him a week later. Never told him he was popping my cherry. I was too embarrassed to admit that I was a virgin at that age. We had sex another three times before his phone calls stalled. He never explained to me that he was dumping me, we just never saw each other again. I didn't have sex with anyone else until I met Eddie two-and-a-half years later. I didn't miss it, certainly didn't pine for intercourse. Stuart's penis was quite big, quite painful. It wasn't until I met Eddie that I actually enjoyed sex for the first time. He was a lot smaller than Stu. A lot more comfortable inside me. But after doing it non-stop for the first four months, our sex life took a nose-dive. I didn't realise until about two years later that he must have been getting it elsewhere during all that time. I started to miss the sex and genuinely only started to masturbate for the first time when I was twenty-three. Still do so on a regular basis. I'm often envious of people who have great sex lives. When you look at porn on the Internet, people are into all sorts of quirky stuff. I've never quite worked out what gives me my kicks. When I lie back and play with myself, I'm normally thinking of a rugged, handsome man lying on top of me. I'm sure that's boring to most other people — straight missionary sex — but it's kind of all I know. Maybe it's not just my mind that needs opening, maybe my legs need it too. I begin to wonder what positions me and Jason will do it in tonight.

23:00
Zach

This was a great idea. There's only one chick. But what a fuckin' chick she is.

Normally when we go back to Jason's gaff, there's a gaggle of birds with us. He's probably not up for sharin' Sabrina, but I'll see what I can do.

We've never shared the same bird on the same night, but I know Jason's well aware of a bit of roasting. It's ripe in football. I've read about it countless times in the tabloids — four or five players sharing the same bird at the same time. Jason's always maintained his innocence in that regard; claims he's never been a part of any gang banging. But let's see if I can change his mind tonight. It'll be a bit weird fuckin' a bird in front of me mate, but things could be worse. I could be at home, lying beside Tina with a limp dick — which is practically what I do six nights a week anyway.

I don't hate Tina. I just hate the boredom of our relationship. It's tedious. I'm no good with routine — and a wife and kids is all about routine, especially if you want it to work perfectly. It's not as if I don't want to remain with Tina for the rest of my life, or that I don't want to be a great dad. I do. I just don't want that to be my entire life.

Li turns around from the passenger seat, but I don't give him time to moan again.

'Relax will ya? For crying out loud. Just turn around and keep your fingers crossed.'

He does. He stares out the windscreen as we turn onto the airport road. I think we'll make the flight. They're always running a bit behind. My problem is — though I haven't said it out loud — that I think you now need a passport to fly from Ireland to the UK. I don't think any old photo ID works these days. It used to. But I think they stopped that a couple of years ago. Fuck it. It'll be an adventure anyway.

'Have you rung Niamh yet?' I ask Li. I'm guessin' he's secretly hoping we don't make the flight so he can have a lie in with his bird in the morning. So much has happened tonight, I almost forgot he's told us she's going to be his fiancée soon.

'No, I'll call her once we get to the airport,' he says. 'What about you? You let Tina know?'

I stare at him, crease my brow. He doesn't get it.

'Who's Tina?' Sabrina asks. The taxi falls silent. Jason turns to me, knows I must have been feeding Sabrina's head full of shit when I took her for that rickshaw ride.

'Me eh… me wife,' I admit.

'You're married? Wow!' Sabrina laughs. 'Wedding ring in the pocket is it?'

'I don't wear one,' I tell her. 'Never have.'

'That's interesting. I could have sworn you were trying to come on to me earlier… remember… on the rickshaw… You eh… asked if my dad was a boxer?'

Jason giggles.

Fuckin' bitch. She's trying to embarrass me in front of my mates. I'm gonna hurt her when I fuck her later. She'll be walkin' funny in the morning. I'll make sure of it.

I actually haven't had a bit of strange pussy in a few weeks. That can happen. I can go a while without pickin' some bird up. But hangin around with Keating and his lot can normally clean up any dry spells for me.

They're all mad into prostitutes. Keating even has a few on his payroll. Sex with prostitutes is a bit of a last resort for me though. I don't enjoy it as much. Not sure how anyone can get satisfaction from having sex with someone who doesn't necessarily want to have sex with them. If a girl is fuckin' you for the pay, not for the enjoyment, then where's the thrill in that?

I hooked up with a tiny little Scottish hooker last summer who made me wash my dick in front of her before we had sex. That was a load of me bollix. I couldn't enjoy the session we had. Not after that. Even when I came, I produced a retarded amount of cum. Just a spit that dribbled down my shaft. It looked a bit pathetic; almost embarrassing.

Hookers just don't do it for me. I can never quite figure out why they do it for anyone. Same as rapists. Where is the fun in having sex with someone who doesn't want it as much as you? If the pussy is dry, how is a man supposed to enjoy it? And trust me, I've fucked dry pussy lotsa times. Tina's. She just seems incapable of getting wet these days.

Our sex life is shit. When I get horny, I jump on board. It's either that or have a wank. Sometimes I opt for the wank, but more often than not I call Tina upstairs, ask her to lie on the bed and do her duty. But it's not that enjoyable. The best part of sex is convincing somebody to have sex with you. Talking them into it. That's how I get my kicks — that moment when they finally give in, finally give me the go-ahead to fuck them. That's the real thrill of sex for me. Pulling birds is the main event. I'll have my work cut out for me pulling tonight. But I'm up for the challenge.

I look over at her. She winks at me. I'm not sure if that's finally a sign that she's up for it with me or whether or not she's just cooling tensions because she knows she just tried to embarrass me.

The driver takes us up the ramp of the airport slip road, over the speed bumps and finally comes to a stop.

'Forty-two euro,' the taxi man says. Jason looks at me. I look at Li.

'Do you take card?' Jason says, breaking the silence.

'Course I don't take card,' the taxi man says, his foreign accent thick and condescending. 'It is a taxi.'

'I've no cash,' Jason says.

'Nobody has cash these days,' I say, just before I notice Sabrina reach inside her bag.

'Here's fifty,' keep the change,' she says to the taxi man, before opening her door. We all follow her out.

'Don't worry about it, Jason can pay me back,' she says as all four of us run towards the entrance.

'It's almost twenty-past,' Li cries racing inside, heading straight towards the security gates. 'Bollocks!'

We look at what he's pointing at. There's quite a queue at security. It's not huge, but this'll take at least ten minutes to get through.

'Fuck it,' says Jason. 'Let's try it anyway. We might get lucky; certainly if the flight is delayed.

He scrolls through his phone, walks towards the first security gate and swipes his way through. Then he hands the phone back to Sabrina.

'Scan this here, sweetie,' he says, 'then pass the phone back to the lads.'

23:15
Li

There are only two security gates open. Both of them have a queue of maybe twenty people. We won't be getting through here in a hurry. I check the Dublin airport app on my phone, it informs me the flight is due to leave on time. We're not going to make it.

'Don't mind that shit,' Zach says to me when I share the bad news. 'Those apps are bollocks. They don't update them often enough. We'll be fine.'

I don't share his optimism but I decide to call Niamh anyway, let her know I won't be home tonight. She's used to me spending some time in Newcastle with Jason, has even been over with me once or twice to his place. But I've never rung her on a whim and told her I'm imminently taking a flight.

I step away from the queue as the tone rings.

'Hello,' she says, sounding groggy. She must have already crashed out.

'Hey babe,' I tell her. 'Listen, Jason isn't having a good time of it. Remember I told you I thought he was suffering a bit of depression?'

'Huh huh,' she says. I can hear the rustling of our duvet. She must be sitting up in the bed, anticipating bad news.

'Well… it's true. He opened up to me tonight. I suggested he head home, back to Newcastle, back to his house where he's most comfortable. And eh… I'm going with him. Me and Zach. We're just going to stay with him for the night.'

'You're flying out to Newcastle tonight?'

'Yeah. He needs us, Niamh. I don't know everything, but when I find out exactly what the cause of his depression is,

I'll let you know. Either way, I'll be back with you tomorrow. Probably tomorrow evening sometime.'

She pauses. I know she's thinking of our plans to spend some of our hard-earned dough in Homebase in the morning. But she won't mention that. I know she won't. She's way too selfless.

'Okay, hun. What has he said so far… what's wrong?'

'Well… I think it's his career. I think Sunderland are letting him go. No other club seem that interested in signing him. That, coupled with Jessica finishing things with him last year, he's just… he's just… he cried on my shoulder tonight, Niamh. Haven't seen him cry apart from the day of his dad's funeral.'

'Oooh,' she says, 'give him a big hug from me, won't ya, hun?'

'Course I will. And… we'll do Homebase maybe on Sunday instead, is that okay?'

'Don't worry about that. You get Jason smiling again.'

That's why I'm marrying this girl. She's so understanding. I can imagine Zach trying to make the same phone call to Tina… letting her know he's queuing up for a flight to Newcastle on a whim. She'd go ape shit. She just doesn't trust him. And I don't blame her.

I hang up the call and re-join the lads and Sabrina in the queue. It's moving slowly. I can't understand how people get this so wrong. Why do they have to be repeatedly told that liquids must go in a clear plastic bag? Why do they have to be retold that laptops and iPads have to go in separate trays? It's all sign-posted around this place, yet some travellers only realise what they're supposed to do once they get to the top of the queue. I love that scene in *Up in the Air* where George Clooney's character is teaching Anna Kendrick's character how to travel. He suggests queuing behind Asian people at security checks because they always travel light, and always pay attention to the rules. It's one sure-fire way to get through security quicker, but we don't have that luxury here. We just have two queue options, and both are filled with half-drunk Irish people. I guess we're half-drunk Irish people too, but we've no baggage; no liquids to put in plastic bags, no laptops or iPads that need placing in separate trays. As soon as it's our turn, we'll fly through security – but it's the waiting that's paining me. I check my phone again. 11:25. We're supposed to have boarded by now. I don't think there's a chance in hell we'll make this flight. But I don't want to say that to the lads. Not again. I've been moaning about our chances of catching this flight all through the taxi journey here. I could sense they were all getting irritated by me.

I stand behind the three of them and keep my mouth shut. I'm kind of miffed that Jason is playing it so coolly with Sabrina. The whole idea of this trip is to get him excited about her. She's so open and genuine — would be a good steady influence on him if it worked out. But he seems to be treating her like another mate of his. The three of them are just laughing and joking. He should be all over her, letting her know that he's really into her. Maybe he's playing it cool on purpose — trying to treat her differently to how he treats any other girl he picks up on a Friday night.

At least he's laughing. He seems to be a far cry from the Jason who was crying on my shoulder an hour ago. I let out a big sigh as another passenger at the front of the queue has to be called back to take his bloody belt off. What the fuck am I doing here? I just want to be at home. Would love to be curled up, spooning my girlfriend right now.

I take my phone from my pocket again, flick through my pictures. I bring up a photo of Niamh and pinch at my screen so I can zoom right into her face, to catch her beauty. I know most men wouldn't find her attractive, but I can make out every perfection on her face when I do this. I fancy her as much now as I did when I first fell in love with her three years ago.

I flick to the image of the engagement ring I've ordered for her and it sends a spark of excitement through my stomach. I can't wait to make her mine forever.

23:20
Jason

I can tell Li is agitated. I'm not sure if it's because he thinks we're going to miss the flight or whether it's down to the fact that he's going to miss Niamh tonight. He's the last one through. Typical that the alarm would go off as he walks under the security gate. Myself, Zach and Sabrina stand back, watch him get patted down and when the security guard finally waves him on, the four of us race as quickly as we can through Duty Free, slaloming around the aisles as we go.

We all come to a stop at a large screen when we reach the other side. I spot the flight we're on first.

'There,' I say. 'The 690 flight. Gate 117.'

'It says 'closing',' Li screeches, before we all sprint off again.

'We'll be fine.'

It's a good job we've got no baggage with us. The airport is fairly empty, but I can sense everybody in here staring at us as we leap over cases and seats, pelting through the departure lounges as if our lives depend on it.

If somebody caught this on video, I'm pretty sure it would make the news. 'Kenny Races Through Airport'. It's a nothing story. But I've been part of nothing stories plenty of times. I think the most needless headline I've ever read about myself was 'Kenny Queues For Burger'. Somebody spotted me ordering at a food truck in Newcastle's city centre during a random mid-week lunch time. And that was it. That was the story. A man ordering lunch. That's modern media. Everybody and anybody can be a journalist. They just need to use that little mobile device they have in their pocket and if they get an image of a celebrity doing anything, the media will lap it up. Journalism well and truly has gone to the dogs. Anything can be posted as news these days, passed off as fact when it isn't true whatsoever. It's how Donald Trump got into the White House, how fuckwits like Boris Johnson, Michael Gove and Nigel Farage managed to persuade people in Britain to leave the EU. All lies. And the main problem is that most people are just too fucking dumb to see through the lies. I'm definitely depressed about not having my contract renewed at Sunderland. But the one shining light about no longer being a pro footballer will be the fact that I'm no longer newsworthy. Knowing that I can queue up for a burger without being paranoid that I might be making a headline will be a nice little victory for me.

'Down here,' Li says, pointing at steps. The bloody Ryanair flights always take off from the back arse of every airport. That company are too miserable with their money to spend on the nearer gates to depart from.

The four of us shuffle down the steps and when we arrive at gate 117 we're met by nobody. It's empty. Totally derelict. The only thing left here is a wheelchair that somebody must have taken to the departure gate. I hate seeing wheelchairs or disabled signs. They make me think of Caitlin Tyrell.

When I couldn't find any trace of Caitlin online, I decided to pay a visit to a charity who dealt with people who had been left disabled by car accidents. YouKnight they were called. I visited their headquarters without invitation one day. Just so it would remove some guilt from my mindset. The charity is run by a bunch of saints; folk who give up their time for those in need. Nobody earns a cent for the work they do with people in need. I walked in, had no meeting booked or anything, just strolled towards a woman sitting at a random desk at the front of the dilapidated building.

'I'm eh… here to just take a look around,' I said. 'I'm interested in maybe helping out if I can.'

'Sure, we'd love that,' the woman said. 'I'll call down Clara and she'd be happy to have a word with you.'

I sat on a chair as she made a phone call and took in my surroundings. It looked like a community centre, slightly run down, but with a lot of love attempting to cover over the cracks. There were paintings and drawings from patients dotted across the walls. Photographs of their faces, too. I wanted to believe one of the patients was called Caitlin. But I never found her.

'Hi, can I help you?' a woman said to my back.

'Oh – hi,' I replied turning around. 'You must be Clara…'

I saw her face light up.

'Jason Kenny. Wow – what are you doing here?' she said, holding her hand out for me to shake.

'I eh… I read about what you guys do and I want to help out.' I put my hand inside my jacket, pulled out an envelope from my pocket.

'I'm hoping you might take this for starters.'

I watched Clara's face as she opened the envelope and pulled out the cheque. She lit up.

'Are we late… did we miss the flight to Newcastle?' I ask the first person we come across.

'Eh…' she scratches her head. 'I can get you on. Quickly though.'

She holds her hand towards me.

'Passport,' she says.

'We eh.. don't have passports, but you take regular ID, right?' I say.

She shakes her head.

'We haven't done that for a few years now. You need a passport to travel by air, even to Britain.'

Bollocks!

I sigh. A deep loud sigh, muffled by my hands spread across my face.

Then we all look to our feet and hobble off to sit on the horribly uncomfortable steel chairs.

'I need to go to the loo,' I say after a while.

I peel my back up, vertebrae by vertebrae, and head for the stairs.

'Hold up,' Zach shouts, jogging after me. 'I need a piss meself.'

We both plod up the steps and when we reach the top, Zach holds a hand across my chest.

'Hey, let's book a hotel room across the way,' he says.

'Okay...' I reply without really thinking it through. 'Eh... what do we need a hotel for?'

'C'mon man.' Zach steps in front of me.

'We're both banging that bird tonight. I don't care if it's in your gaff in Newcastle or the Airport B&B. She's too hot to not bang. We're not letting this opportunity go.'

I squint my eyes at him. Try to make out whether he's being serious or not. I don't say a word. I just study his face.

'C'mon man, you're a fuckin' footballer. This is what footballers do. They play football and fuck hot birds. How many times have I talked to you about a roasting, huh? Here's the perfect opportunity. She's mad for it.'

'She's not mad for it, she's—'

'She's willing to take a flight with three strange blokes to Newcastle for fuck sake. She's practically got her tits out all night... her nipples are fighting to stay inside that jumpsuit she's wearing. She followed us to Coppers. She has 'mad for it' written all over her.'

I'm still staring at Zach's face, still squinting.

'She's already kissed you, right?' he says, not relenting. 'Already kissed me. She's probably down there sucking the face off Li as we speak.'

'Hold on. She *kissed* you?'

'Course she did. Was all over me on that rickshaw. She's up for it, man. I'm tellin' ye. C'mon – we owe each other this, Jason. You're a pro footballer. I've always had a hard on for roasting some young one. I get mad jealous when I read about footballers doing this all the time. You know all I wanted was to be a footballer… I've missed out on all these opportunities. C'mon man… ye know what this would mean to me.'

I lean my head back against the wall. What Zach is saying is just noise. I'm barely listening to his bullshit anyway. I'm used to zoning out on him. He doesn't see women as human beings… just as sex toys. It's nothing new. It's not the first time he's mentioned roasting to me. And it won't be the first time I turn down his offer either. But all I'm playing over and over in my head is an image of Sabrina kissing him. My heart feels heavy. I thought she was different; thought she was genuinely into me. I was even thinking I wouldn't have sex with her tonight. That it'd be more romantic if I just got to know her. I was hoping we would just curl up, watch a movie together in my cinema room. Maybe have a few snogs under a blanket. But that's all out the window now. She has no intentions of getting to know me. Zach's right. She's only after one thing. I fuckin' hate being a celebrity.

I let out a sigh, zone back in to hear Zach still talking about fucking roastings.

'Here mate, give us your phone,' he says. 'You go have a piss, I'll book a hotel room nearby.'

I let out a loud sigh, clench both of my fists until my knuckles turn white. Then I release them slowly, finger by finger.

'It's okay,' I say grabbing at my phone. 'I'll book it.'

9

Number Five's silently hoping her face isn't turning red as she coughs into her hand, aware all eyes are on her.

She sits more upright, eyeballs Number One and repeats what she'd said for emphasis.

'Yeah – I have gone home with guys after meeting them that night. I think most women — definitely of my age or whatever — they would say the same. It doesn't always lead to sex and I certainly wasn't just going home with them for sex. But y'know... y'know...' She begins to stutter.

'Absolutely,' Number Eleven says, backing Number Five up. 'Socialising in these days is a lot different to what it was a generation ago. Both myself and Number Five have admitted to going back to guys' houses after meeting them that night, and that's just two girls out of seven in this room. I don't—'

Number Seven holds her hand up, stopping Number Eleven in her tracks.

All jurors turn towards her.

'Listen, I wouldn't say this to most people... but I feel I need to say it here. I've done the same; have gone back to a man's apartment after meeting him that night. Like Number

Five said, it wasn't necessarily for sex… I just… I just wanted the night to continue. I have a feeling Sabrina did the same thing here. I don't think we should judge her just for wanting to go to Jason's home. Agreeing to go to his house is not an agreement for sex.'

The jury room falls silent, save for the sound of a couple of jurors swallowing hard. The arguments are not only getting heated, they are getting personal too.

Brian tap claps his hands, in appreciation of the three jury members speaking their truth, though most view it as him seeking attention again.

'Okay…' Number One says, killing the silence. He shuffles his paperwork, wondering where they should go next with their deliberations. 'Ah yes,' he says, 'the taxi driver who drove them to the airport… what did we make of his testimo—?'

'Inshignificant,' Brian spits out before Number One has finished the question. 'Well, inshignificant in terms of he didn't really add much, did he? He jusht said that he drove them to the airport.'

'I agree with Brian,' Number Five says, generating stares from around the table. It was the first time Number Five had agreed with anything Brian had said. 'All this fella said was that Li sat in the front, Jason, Zach and Sabrina in the back and that there were no signals of discomfort or anything. I didn't see his testimony as helpful in any way.'

'Yeah — I'm surprised the judge allowed it,' says Number One. 'I mean what did it do for either side?'

'Well, the defence tried their best to make him say Sabrina was comfortable, right?' Number Seven says. 'But yeah… it doesn't add anything to the case because Sabrina admits herself that she was quite comfortable at this stage.'

'I guess the judge just wanted the testimony of all those who interacted with the four of them throughout the night;

thought it would benefit us. The rickshaw guy testified, the taxi man who brought them to the airport… the taxi man who then dropped them from the airport to the hotel… I guess his testimony was kinda insignificant too, huh?'

A nod of heads circulates the table.

Trevor Coyne — a fifty-two-year-old taxi driver for over two decades — also testified, despite only driving the three men and Sabrina for less than five minutes from one side of the airport to the other. He described Zach as being 'snappy' and 'a little hostile' but aside from that offered nothing of significance during his time on the stand. In rape cases — especially ones like this where there is an admission of sex from both sides, but a discrepancy over whether or not it was consensual — evidence is hard to come by. Judge McCormick was trying to give the jurors an overall picture of the night in question, by allowing the rickshaw driver and taxi drivers to give accounts of their time spent with all four players.

Delia McCormick has thirteen years' experience of presiding over trials. This has been her tenth rape trial to judge. In eight of those trials, the defendant — or defendants — were found to be not guilty. Rape is one of the most difficult crimes to earn a conviction in. In fact rape is one of the most difficult crimes to even make it to trial. This trial barely made it because evidence is practically non-existent. This whole case relies heavily on the statements of witnesses. And even at that, there are zero witnesses to the actual crime itself. Except, of course, for the four people involved; three of whom offer almost the exact same account of the specific half-an-hour — between midnight and half-past midnight on the night in question during which the claimant claims she was raped — while her account is, obviously, in stark contrast to theirs. 'The odd one out' as defence lawyer Gerd Bracken suggested during his closing argument.

The only hard evidence offered to the court was that delivered by Dr Dermot Johnson – the doctor Sabrina visited two days after the incident. He professed that the internal cut Sabrina suffered was 'certainly as a result of rough intercourse', backing Sabrina's claim. Though under cross examination, Dr Johnson was forced to admit that cuts like the one found inside Sabrina can occur as a result of consensual sex. He did suggest on the stand that this type of cut wouldn't occur if intercourse was being enjoyed by the claimant, but this vital piece of expert evidence washed over the jurors.

'If Ms Doyle,' he said on the stand, 'was a full participant in the intercourse and — as a result — was producing cervical fluid, this cut would likely not have occurred.' He was trying to state, in his opinion, that this cut was the result of non-consensual sex; that Sabrina's vagina must have been dry in order to be cut. But every time Number Eleven — the only juror affected by the doctor's testimony — tried to bring this up, she was shut down.

'If the cut can happen in consensual sex then it's insignificant isn't it?' Number Twelve had said, his arms out almost in apology. All of the other jurors agreed with him on this. They agreed to wash over Dr Johnson's testimony; felt the defence lawyer's counter argument overshadowed it.

'So, given your expertise, Doctor Johnson, can you inform the jury that these cuts can — and indeed *do* — occur from consensual intercourse?' Gerd Bracken asked.

Dr Johnson, being the noble and honest man he is, nodded his head, moved closer to the microphone and said 'yes'.

That was enough for the jurors to forget the main point he was trying to make; that Sabrina mustn't have been producing 'cervical fluid' during the intercourse. Had he not been so technical with his phraseology, this argument might have rung more true with more jurors than just Number

Eleven. Had Sabrina's lawyer highlighted this part of the doctor's testimony by describing it in layman's terms, using words such as 'cum', or 'wet' or 'moist' then the jurors would have considered it more readily. As it was, Dr Johnson's testimony — which Judge McCormick felt was pivotal in the trial — was far from pivotal in the minds of eleven of the twelve jurors.

'It seems it's all we have to go on, innit?' says Number Three. Just random people's words. How are we supposed to convict these three men when we have such little evidence to use against them?'

'It'sh what I've been saying all along,' Brian says, his face gurning into a smug grin. 'There jusht isn't enough evidensh to convict.'

Number Three taps her fingers against her wheelchair armrest again, then takes in a loud breath through her nostrils.

'But how do prosecutors provide evidence in a case like this? How is a girl who has been raped supposed to get a conviction against those who raped her when they all agree that sex did indeed take place? The argument is consensual or not consensual isn't it? But how are we supposed to know?'

The room falls silent again. Some jurors shake their heads. The speed in which their discussion turned once they felt they were on their way to a verdict has stalled. There's been more silences in the past fifteen minutes than there had been for the entirety of the three-hours of deliberating before that.

'I just… I just,' Number Three says, pushing a finger to her eyeball, forcing the tear that threatened to fall from it back inside. 'I know we're not supposed to let our own personal feelings dictate our argument, but I can't help but think that if Sabrina was raped — and I think she was — we can't let these men get away with it. It's our job to deliver justice.'

'That'sh not true,' says Brian. 'It's the judge's job to deliver jushtice. Our job is to weigh up the arguments. That's all.'

Number Three snorts in an attempt to suck back up the tear that has now begun to fall down her cheek.

'I think I have to change my mind,' she says. 'I have to go from guilty to not guilty. I thought all along that I'd decide guilty, because I believe in my heart that Sabrina was raped. Well...' she says, holding up her palm before steadying her breathing, 'I believe that Sabrina feels she was raped. That, I genuinely believe. The three men might not think it was rape, but she certainly does.'

Then the tears come quicker. She holds her entire face in the palms of her hands and begins to sob.

Number Three's emotions reverberate around the table. She wasn't supposed to be the one to crack. She had proven to other jurors that she was strong minded, probably because she was weak in body.

Number Three's real name is Caitlin Tyrell. She's just turned thirty. She's been in a wheelchair since three months before her tenth birthday when she was run over by a car a mere ninety-metres from her home in Howth, County Dublin. It was a hit and run; the driver never caught. She underwent almost three years of rehab before she was allowed home full-time. Since then she has gone on to live a happy life. She works as a receptionist at a health club in Dublin's city centre and recently got engaged to a man who suffered a similar tragedy to herself; he too wheelchair bound for life. She had felt, from the very outset, that all three men in this case were guilty; she just damned the lack of evidence, so much so that she was now beginning to change her mind.

The tears currently rolling down her face have nothing to

do with Sabrina – as most jurors assume they do. She is crying because she has just — in the past few moments — realised that she *has* to find all three men not guilty of this charge, even though she doesn't want to. Her head is overruling her heart. And that's exactly how it should be when you sit on a jury.

Despite Number Three's realisation, she is hopeful that an argument can be raised that will help her change her mind once more. But she's not confident of that. She's been through everything in her head countless times... she doesn't think such an argument exists. Her tears are tears of frustration, tears of guilt almost. She wants to see Jason, Zach and Li go down.

Number Eleven rubs Number Three's back and offers a sympathetic turning down of her lips.

'I know how you feel,' she whispers into her ear.

'This is difficult for all of us,' Number One says, standing up. 'None of us could have predicted just how emotional this would be. I almost feel like crying myself sometimes. In fact I've found myself wiping my eyes when I'm in bed at night these past few days as the trial culminated... but I guess we need to try to push emotion aside for now and give full focus to our mission: debating the arguments raised in this case and eventually coming to a verdict.'

Number Three sniffs and nods frantically at the same time, to agree with Number One's sentiment. She sweeps the palm of her right hand across her face, removing any moisture left and then smiles up at the Head Juror.

'I guess,' he says to her, 'when this is all finished, we'll all be crying. This will bear a heavy scar on all of us.'

A succession of tuts are heard around the table; not tuts of irritation, but tuts of sorrow.

'The hotel,' Number One then says before sitting down and re-adjusting his glasses.

Brian interrupts him.

'Yesh... the hotel. It's one thing that Sabrina wanted to go to Newcashtle, to maybe see how the other half lived, to witness the luxuries a professional footballer possesses... but why go to a hotel room with three strangers, a hotel room that ish only twenty minutes from her own home?'

Number One coughs, then answers Brian's point.

'It's interesting that that is your take from the whole hotel room thingy,' he says. 'My take on it is different. As the prosecution lawyer mentioned a few times in court, why the hell did Jason only book one hotel room, when all three men were coming back to it with Sabrina? Talk about evidence, there's evidence right there that there was collusion from the three men about group sex.'

'That's not evidensh,' Brian says raising his voice, dissipating the emotional sentiment that existed in the room moments prior. The arguments were well and truly back underway. 'There is no evidensh of collusion there at all.'

'If he only booked one hotel room, what does that say?'

'That he booked one hotel room,' Brian says, his voice still louder than it needs to be. It was almost as if he was taking Number One's point as a personal attack.

'Listen,' Number One says, rising from his seat again, looking down at Brian. 'It is reasonable for us to believe that there were discussions in the airport by the three men that alluded to them all having sex with Sabrina. If there wasn't... why did he only book the one room?'

'He booked a suite. The defence lawyers showed us the picturesh of the suite. There was more than enough room for four people to shleep there that night.'

'There was only one fuckin' bed, Brian!' Number One snaps back, shouting louder than his nemesis had just moments ago.

'Calm down!' Number Three says. 'We are arguing the

case, not arguing egos here.' The rest of the jurors look to her, not at Brian nor Number One, to continue the debate.

'This was an argument raised by Sabrina's lawyer because he felt it was significant,' she says. 'It is certainly worth us arguing, but not in these tones. I suggest you sit down, Number One — and I suggest both of you refrain from raising your voices so much.'

Number Three pats down the shoulders of her blazer, readjusts her lapels and then places both of her hands, palms down, on to the armrests of her wheelchair.

'At the airport, Jason booked the Merchant Penthouse Suite for all four of them. The prosecution and defence raise different arguments for this... it's our job to straighten out those arguments. Let's do this sensibly and maturely. It might change people's minds in here... my mind has already been changed and it may even change again, so this is really important. Let's calm down and ask the very obvious question here.' She looks around the table, her head swivelling right, then left. 'Number Four, let's start with you. Do you believe Jason booked the hotel suite so that all three of the men could have sex with Sabrina?'

Number Four sucks in some air, then twists his bum into a more comfortable seating position.

'My opinion on that is...' he pauses, staring into space to consider his answer. 'My opinion on that is—'

A knock at the door interrupts him. Number Nine rises from her seat and pulls at the door. The jurors look at her as she nods her head at the young man dressed in black before turning to them.

'Lunch is ready,' she says.

23:25
Li

All that bloody running and we didn't even have the right ID.

I don't know whether I'm happy about this or not. The whole trip was supposed to be about Jason anyway — a mission to get him to cheer up. But maybe it's just best that he asks Sabrina for her phone number and they try to get to know each other another time. There's no need to try and get her to fall in love with him tonight. I was just trying to think of ways to keep him feeling positive. It almost broke my heart, hearing him sob on my shoulder in Coppers earlier.

I glance over at him. I don't know whether he's back to feeling down or whether or not he's just jaded after we ran here. Each of the four of us are sprawled out on a steel chair in the departure lounge opposite the gate we were supposed to depart from. He shouldn't be jaded, I guess. He is a professional athlete after all. Maybe he *is* feeling down again... depressed. He's awfully quiet for someone who's supposed to be trying to impress this girl. I'll get into his ear in a minute. If anyone can cheer him up, it's me. I'll tell him to play it cool with Sabrina, that I was wrong to suggest he should rush things tonight with her.

'I need to go to the loo,' Jason says.

Zach gets up almost immediately after him. I wouldn't mind joining them, wouldn't mind having a go at trying to alleviate the tension in Jason. But I'm too tired. I need a couple of minutes to get my breath back. I haven't run that far or that fast in... actually I don't think I've ever run that far or that fast. And all for nothing.

'Tired?' Sabrina asks, turning her head to face me as the

other two ramble up the steps. She's slouched just as much as I am in her chair.

'Bollixed,' I reply while letting out a deep breath.

'Me too. Who would have thought I'd ever be in such a rush to go to bloody Newcastle?'

I laugh. It's not the first time she's made me laugh tonight. She's strangely funny for someone so attractive. That combination rarely marries. I assume that if you're good looking you must be a bit more reserved. More self-conscious. Sabrina was certainly quieter in the first part of the night when we met her, but she's opened up since. Maybe it's the wine. She seems to have come out of her shell as she's got to know us. And I think she likes me; she's comfortable with me.

She stood joking and laughing with me at the edge of the dance floor when we were in Coppers and snapped at both of the lads when they were taking the piss out of me on the taxi ride here. She's lovely. I can certainly see what Jason sees in her. She seems to have it all. I hope it works out between her and Jason. Would like Sabrina to be a part of our lives. I know I've only known her for a few hours, but I think I'd actually miss her if I never saw her again.

'Well, you were right all along,' she says to me.

'Huh?'

'You kept telling everyone that we wouldn't get on that flight.'

'Oh yeah,' I say letting a sniffle of laughter come out of my nose. I finally sit more upright. Sabrina does the same. But we both just stare ahead. Too tired to move any more than sitting up.

'I'm so happy for you.'

'For me?' I say, turning to face her.

'Yeah. Getting engaged. That's such amazing news. Niamh's a lucky girl. You're gonna make her so happy.'

'Thank you,' I say, studying her face, wondering why she's so perfect in every possible way. She must have flaws. Can't be this ideal. Surely perfect women don't actually exist. You can't have it all. You can't have the personality to match the looks.

'How you going to do it — how are you going to ask her?' she asks.

'Well,' I pause before letting another laugh sniffle out from my nose. 'I was originally going to ask her when we go on holiday next month. We're going to Lanzarote.'

Sabrina lets a little squeal seep from the back of her throat.

'That would be so romantic. Over dinner, when the sun is going down or something like that?' she says smiling at me.

'Yeah... that's... that's *exactly* how I was imaging it,' I say. 'It's just eh... Zach thought that was a bit cheesy.'

'Zach?' she says, resting her forearms on her knees. She turns her face to look at me. 'Zach who does nothing but cheat on his poor wife is trying to tell you how to treat yours?'

I laugh and begin to play with my fingers out of discomfort. I don't know why Sabrina is making me feel this way. I'm starting to think I might actually fancy her. That's nuts. I haven't fancied anyone since I met Niamh. I haven't even had a celebrity crush.

'You're right, I suppose,' I say.

'No – *you're* right. You do it whatever way you want. Just make sure it's a special memory for Niamh. That should be your main aim.'

I smile at her, soak in her beauty. Then shake my thoughts away. I imagine Niamh curled up in our bed at home. Our baby growing inside her. Maybe it's time I joined her back there.

I check the time on my iPhone. 11:31. If I get a taxi from

outside the airport I could be home by midnight. I won't wake Niamh or anything. But I can just squeeze up against her. Spoon her. Place my hand on her swelling belly.

Sabrina takes me out of my thought by placing her hand on my knee.

'You're a good man, Li. You've got it all. Guys wanna look like Zach or maybe they wanna have the celebrity like Jason, but ye know what? All a girl really wants is somebody who's nice. Who's trustworthy. Who's genuine. I kinda... I envy Niamh.'

She's staring into my eyes as she's saying this. I feel my dick wake up. It removes itself from slouching on my balls, as if its alarm clock has just gone off. I stand up immediately, turn my back on her and pace across the floor.

'Thank you,' I say back over my shoulder before I shake my head again, removing the guilty thoughts from my mind. I pace towards the window, see my reflection staring back at me.

'Where are those two?' I ask, trying to change the subject.

'Hmmm,' Sabrina mumbles before walking towards the edge of the steps. She stares up them. The airport is eerily quiet. 'Wonder what they're up to?'

She begins to walk up the steps, but just as she rests her hand on the bannister we can hear them. Well, not necessarily both of them. Zach more so.

'Whoop,' he calls out, running down the steps. He rushes at Sabrina, almost pulling her over in a sort of wrestling move. I think it's his idea of a hug. 'C'mon, you two, we're going over to the Merchant Hotel for drinks. Jason's sorted it.'

I walk closer to my reflection, then let out a big sigh that fogs up the window. Balls. I really don't wanna do that. I just wanna go home.

23:30
Sabrina

He's so adorable. I bet he's totally devoted to Niamh; wouldn't even dream of cheating on her. She's lucky. I tell him that. I'm glad I can open up to him, that I can pay people compliments without feeling self-conscious. I'm starting to come out of my shell tonight. Being around these three has really helped me. They're a good remedy for somebody with a slice of depression.

I lean over to Li, just to let him know how proud I am of him, even though I've only known him for a few hours. It's almost as if he feels like a little brother to me.

'You're a good man, Li,' I say, honestly as I can. 'You've got it all. Guys wanna look like Zach or maybe they wanna have the celebrity like Jason, but ye know what? All a girl wants is somebody like you. Somebody's who's nice. Who's trustworthy. Who's genuine. I kinda... I envy Niamh.'

I think my straightforwardness has unnerved him a little. I'm not sure he's used to compliments. He gets up from his chair, paces towards the other side of the room. He's probably wishing he was back home with his soon-to-be fiancée.

The entire departure lounge falls silent again. Just the sound of Li's footsteps brushing off the shiny floor producing hardly any noise at all.

'Where are those two?' I ask before getting up off my chair and heading towards the steps. I'm about to climb them in search of Jason when I hear the two of them coming towards me. When Zach sees me, he runs down the steps, yelling. He practically lands on top of me as if we're celebrating a lottery win or something.

'C'mon, you two, we're going over to the Merchant Hotel for drinks. Jason's sorted it.'

23:30

I stare at Jason over Zach's shoulder as he plods down the stairs. He doesn't seem to be as excited about this as Zach is. In fact, he barely looks at me, he just offers me a strained smile without our eyes meeting.

'Yeah – c'mon, we'll go over for a few drinks. I have this deadly suite we can all crash in,' he says.

I swallow hard. Not sure how to take it. Is that just confirmation that I'm going to have sex with him? Shouldn't I be a little upset that he booked a hotel room without even asking me? I'm not sure how I'm supposed to feel; how I'm supposed to play this.

I think Zach notices my hesitation more than Jason.

'Fuck it, Sabrina, c'mon. They do some lovely cocktails over there. Let's have a few of them, let's make a night of it, huh?'

I just nod my head. But I'm still a bit hesitant. Unsure.

'Ye know what… I think I might just go home,' Li says as he walks towards us.

'Well, if you're going home, I'm going home too,' I say. And I mean it. I need Li to come with us to the hotel. Somebody needs to keep Zach company if me and Jason are to get down to business.

'Whoa, whoa, whoa,' says Zach, holding his arms out. 'You're both coming over. We're having a few drinks each… if you all wanna go home after that, I'll order you a taxi each, but c'mon — were having fun, right?'

He grins wide. I'm not sure why he's so excited about a couple of extra drinks.

I look at Jason, wondering why he's quiet in comparison. Maybe he's wondering if he's coming on too strong by booking a hotel room. I bet that's why he's asked Zach to reveal the news… as if it was all Zach's decision, not his. That's kinda cute. I think. I walk over to Jason, just to let him know he shouldn't be feeling guilty. I'll let him know I'm up for it. That I want to have sex with him.

'Come on, Li, we'll both go over, have a cocktail and a bit more of a laugh. It's early days, right? Not even midnight,' I say.

I smile at Jason. He smiles back. Then I wrap both my arms around his waist and lean in to him.

'Relax,' I whisper into his ear. 'Everything's going to be okay. You don't have to feel any guilt. I'm up for this. I'm eh... actually quite horny.'

It's the naughtiest thing I've ever whispered to anyone. But I feel like I'm a different person tonight. It's probably the excitement of hooking up with a celebrity. I hope that's not too strong; hope Jason is up for sex just as much as I am. He must be. He practically had me pulling him off after meeting him for two minutes earlier on.

'You really are a filthy little bitch, aren't you?' he says, cupping my ear.

I giggle. I feel so happy. In about an hour's time I'm going to be having sex with somebody who people have posters of in their bedrooms. This is going to be one of the best nights of my life. It already is. I genuinely think I've found not just a future boyfriend, but two new best friends too.

I've never really had male friends before. I've always assumed any guy who wants to talk to me is talking to me because I'm attractive. I certainly didn't have any male friends when I went out with Eddie. He wouldn't even let me talk to *his* friends. That's how jealous he was. His paranoia must've rubbed off on me. After about six months of being convinced he was cheating on me, I found a company online who would confirm it for me: Honest Entrapment. For two thousand euro they would have an attractive girl come on to my boyfriend and send a full report of his reaction to me. I met with Lorna one Tuesday morning and by Friday she was all dressed up, ready to coincidentally bump into Eddie when he was out with his mates in Tallaght. I called to her small offices in Rathfarnham the following Monday for my report. I wasn't surprised. Not one bit. Lorna is gorgeous. She may not be as naturally pretty as I am, but she's definitely sexy. Long blonde hair, bright green eyes. She always wears roaring red lipstick. It makes her look like a magazine model. But like me, she never made it into the magazine pages as a model. She had just as much of a stressful time of it in that industry as I had.

'I flirted with him from the outset, played it a little cool, then turned up the heat. When I suggested he come back to my place, his exact words were "fuck yeah",' she told me. She reached out a hand to mine. Held it. I didn't need the comforting she was offering. I knew there was no chance in hell he would turn down an offer of sex from another woman. I just wanted clarification. A definite reason to dump him. Which is what I did later that day.

'Go on then, I'll go over for an hour or two,' Li says. I beam a big smile, then walk towards him and offer him a hug of his own.

'Okay then, boys — let's go,' I say as I lead them all up the steps. I really am starting to like the new me.

23:35
Jason

She walks towards me, smiles, then wraps both of her arms around my waist —seconds after she did the exact same thing to Zach.

'Relax,' she whispers into my ear. 'Everything's going to be okay. Lighten up. I'm up for this. I'm eh...' she leans in closer to my ear, 'actually quite horny.'

Wow. I really thought she was a genuinely nice girl. I can't believe I had almost fallen for her; almost visualising a future for the two of us. I'm such a fucking idiot. I should know this by now. No hot girl wants a future with me. They just want a night. A thrill. A story for their friends.

'You really are a filthy little bitch, aren't you?' I whisper back. And I mean it. She is. It's such a shame. She really doesn't need to be like this. I wasn't even planning on having sex with her. I wanted to play it cool. Play it slow.

I stare down at her as she snuggles into my shoulder, then my eyes gaze down the length of the V in her jumpsuit and decide I can't turn this offer down, no matter how hurt I'm feeling right now. This'll be nothing new for me — fucking a hot girl while depressed. It's what I've been doing every weekend for the past year, ever since Jessica left me.

I look over at Zach as Sabrina releases her bear hug. He winks at me. He's such a little shite. But I love him. I don't know what I'd be like if it wasn't for Zach and Li. I'd probably be suicidal. They are the only two blokes on the planet who make me genuinely laugh. I mean, I laugh all the time in the dressing-room. But I'm not genuinely laughing. I'm just laughing because that's what I'm supposed to do.

Dressing-rooms are full of men who have never really

grown up. Millionaires who think it's funny to put glue in their mate's shampoo, or who think it's funny to cut the toes out of a mate's socks. I probably thought those things were funny the first time they happened. But it's been the same shit jokes for the past fifteen years now. I'm bored by it all.

I'm devastated by the fact that my time as a footballer is at an end, but I'll only miss the buzz of playing in front of tens of thousands of fans every week. I won't miss the dressing-room, won't miss the ladishness.

I took my first coaching badges a couple of years ago, but I didn't progress further than that. I knew even then that I didn't want to be involved in football once I retired from playing. Punditry is an option. I do talk a good game; have been on the RTÉ panel a couple of times. But punditry is genuinely full of bullshit. The truth is, there are no experts looking in from the outside of football. No observer of the game can ever truly know what a manager's intention is when he sets out his team. And that's why every opinion a pundit throws out there is literally nonsensical. Players talk about this all the time in the dressing-room; we cringe listening to pundits pretend to know what they're talking about.

I want out of the sport altogether; think I might work in charities. It's probably my calling. It's probably what God wants me to do. Maybe we were meant to hit Caitlin that night.

I watch Sabrina laugh and joke with Li as the four of us stroll up the steps, in search of the exit. I am disappointed, but I think I'm mostly annoyed; annoyed at myself for falling for her. I should have known. Then I notice Zach looking at me. He winks again. Little shite! His cheeky winking is starting to turn a light bulb on over my head. Why the fuck do I believe him? Why have I bought the line that she snogged him? *Yes*, I know she hugged him as soon as he ran down the stairs, and *yes* she did go missing from Coppers with him for about twenty minutes or so. But she told me he came on to her and she denied his advances. Why do I believe him over her? He fucking lies on a regular basis.

But he wouldn't lie to me. Would he? Not his best mate. Surely.

As the four of us stroll through the deserted airport I begin to play all of my time spent with Sabrina over in my head. I'm trying to work her out. Then I let out a sigh. If she hadn't made it so blatantly clear to me that she wanted sex, I could have bought the nice-girl persona.

I rub my face with the palm of my hand. This is always the way my body informs me that I'm feeling depressed. Maybe I should cancel this whole hotel room thing; ask Sabrina out on a date next week. Get to really know her.

I take my phone out of my pocket, log into my Facebook account and search for Sabrina Doyle, hoping I might get some insight on her. There are dozens of Sabrina Doyles. None of them look like her.

'Ah, here we are, here's a way out,' she says. I watch as she wraps her arm around Li and leads him through the door. What the fuck is she playing at? Is she up for fucking all of us? Is this what she's after? Three dicks? It couldn't be. She just likes Li as a friend, surely.

'Hey,' I say, calling after her. 'My phone's just died. Can I have a quick look at yours? Just want to check in on my emails to make sure the hotel reservation came through.'

She goes into her handbag and takes out her phone.

'Sure,' she says thumbing in her passcode. 'Here you go.'

I haven't really thought this through. I'm just trying to get a sense of who she is. She doesn't have the Facebook app. Doesn't seem to have any social media apps at all. So I check her text messages; bring up the last one she sent.

23:35

Asked Niall out straight if he would be interested in going home with me tonight. Red light on this one, Lorna. He genuinely wasn't interested. I'll give you a full run down in the morning.

That was two hours ago. Who the fuck is this chick?

23:40
Zach

We pace out of the departure lounge lookin' like the oddest gang of misfits on the planet.

I've no idea how this is going to go down. She's defo more into Jason than me, but when we get her into that hotel room, we'll get her up for it. No better man than me to convince a girl to let me inside her.

I've never had a threesome before. Have often fantasised about having one, but there's normally two pussies and one dick in those fantasies, not the other way around. But this is what life should be like for a footballer. Jason should be well up for this. I'm not sure why he's gone all quiet and mopey since they wouldn't let us on the flight. Maybe he's just nervous at the thought of having sex while I'm in the room. But we'll be fine. It's not like we're gonna force her into sex or anything like that. We'll just talk her into it. She probably won't need much talkin' into it anyway — she's going to have sex with two blokes; one of them a professional footballer, it should be every girl's fantasy for fuck sake.

We spot a short line of taxis as soon as we get outside and hop in the first one. Li, as usual, gets in the front. This time Sabrina sits in the middle of the back seat, between me and Jason. It seems exciting to me, but everything falls kinda quiet after we tell the taxi man where we're going. The Merchant Hotel is only a two or three-minute drive, the opposite side of the car park.

'Are you eh… Jason Kenny?' the taxi man asks, staring into his rear-view mirror.

'That's me,' Jason replies.

'Jaysus, Sunderland are gone to the dogs, aren't they?'

23:40

Most people who meet Jason like to mention the goal he scored against Holland, but the odd one or two can be ignorant bastards.

'They're still a professional football club, mate,' I reply. 'Playing ball for them sure as hell beats driving around in a taxi.'

'Ah jaysus, I was just sayin—'

'It's alright,' Jason says, relieving the tension. 'And you're right, they have gone to the dogs.'

'Can you not get a move? Back up to the Championship again, or even the Premier League. You were never the fastest, maybe you can still play Premier League,' the taxi man says.

Jason forces out a laugh.

'My Premier League days are long gone.'

'Sorry,' the taxi man says again. 'I didn't mean anything bad by that... it's just y'know yourself. Two relegations in two years for Sunderland. They used to be such a great club. I'm a big footie fan meself... You eh... you don't play for Ireland anymore, no?'

'No, retired from international ball there about three years ago,' Jason says. 'Thought it might prolong the club game for me... not sure it worked.'

They're still ping-ponging football talk to one another when the car comes to a halt.

'Here y'are, lads... there's seven euro on the meter, but it's on me,' the taxi man says. 'If you can sign this for me.'

Jason leans over to sign a small slip of paper the taxi man pulled from somewhere while the rest of us climb out of the car. I stare at Sabrina's ass as she shuffles out ahead of me. I can't believe I'm gonna fuck her later. She'll defo be the most attractive bird I've ever pulled.

Jason follows us into the lobby and then heads straight for

the reception desk. I stand back with Li and Sabrina, wondering how all of this is going to play out. It probably would've been better if we'd just let Li go home when he said he wanted to. It'd be beneficial if he was out of the way for this.

I let a loud breath seep out of my nostrils. I'm not sure whether I'm more excited or nervous for what's about to happen. I'll be mortified if it turns out Jason has a bigger dick than me. But God couldn't have been that kind to him. Surely he didn't get the breaks in football and the bigger cock. Not that I believe in God. Jason's the only deluded one out of us in that regard. But I don't even think he does believe in that bullshit. He's just been conditioned to follow through with his faith. His whole family are religious. His ma and his younger brother still go to mass every Sunday. I often say it's quite the coincidence that they all ended up believing in the same God. Out of the three thousand or so Gods that humans have invented, it's quite the coincidence that every member of the same family believes in the same one. It has to be conditioning. People only believe in Gods for one of two reasons, one; conditioning – their faith is decided by their family before they're even born or two; they're desperate. Only desperate people who are looking for direction in life, looking for friends, end up believing in that type of bullshit. I can't wrap my head around why anybody would want to lie to themselves. It's all a bit nuts to me. All I know is that I've got one life to live, then I'll be worm food. Which is why I'm gonna make the most of the time I have. It's why I don't mind hangin' out with Keating and his cronies. And it's why I don't mind fuckin as many women as I can.

'Alright guys, the Merchant suite, top floor,' Jason says, swingin' a key card at us. We all walk slowly towards the lift. I pick up a menu from the reception desk as we go.

23:40

'Here, what cocktails do you wanna order?' I say, handing it to Sabrina.

Li practically rests his chin on her shoulder as he looks at the menu. Jason presses the number twelve on the elevator and suddenly we are rising high.

'Oh, that has loads of ice in it, must be like a Slush Puppie. I'll have one of them; a Mango Margarita,' Li says. 'That'll go down well.'

'Yer ma goes down well,' I say, holding my fist out. Li and Jason bump me, Sabrina just eyeballs me and mocks a head shake.

'Me too. I'll have one of those as well,' she says.

'Fuck it,' I say, 'we'll order four. Jason... you up for one, yeah?'

Silence.

'Jason?'

'Huh?' he says, snapping out of his daydream. He must be feeling the same way I am. Half excited, half shittin' himself. He's probably wondering if my dick is gonna be bigger than his.

'Do you want a Mango Margarita like the rest of us?'

He nods his head, laughs a little. Then he walks out of the lift, leading us down a wide corridor towards the suite. Li makes a phone call to the reception as we stroll along the corridor and orders the four cocktails.

'Here we are,' Jason says, swiping his key over the reader by the door.

I allow the three of them to go in ahead of me. I wanna see Sabrina's face when she notices we've only booked one room.

'Oh wow,' she says, entering. 'This really is stunning.'

I watch as she takes in the lounge, follow her as she makes her way to the tiny kitchenette and then towards the flowers before she takes a sniff of them.

Then she walks through the double doors that lead to the large bedroom. She doesn't react. Doesn't say anything apart from purring at how amazing the suite is. She isn't put out at all by the fact that there's only one bed. My palms begin to moisten. Fuckin' deadly! This bitch really is up for this.

10

There's not much of an aesthetic difference between this room and the one they'd spent the previous three and a half hours in.

This one's slightly larger, and certainly more dimly lit. They don't have that big bright lamp shining down on them — just a regular bulb that doesn't offer as much of an unflattering glare. It's a more hollow room, too — the voices almost echo around it. The walls are still painted a clean white and the carpet is the same bright red that seems to lie behind every door in this building.

The young man dressed in all black paces quietly around the table, stopping at each juror to stretch over them and fill their glass with ice water. The table is more rectangular than the one in the jury room; five seats on each side, one then at each end. Brian, of course, sat in one of these as if he was the head of the family. Number Ten, who sat in the other, offered her chair to Number One – as Head Juror – but he waved away her invite, insisting it didn't matter where he was seated during lunch.

The young man dressed in all black pauses in the doorway after he's finished filling each of their glasses, then asks the jurors if they have any questions. Each of them shake their heads.

'Lunch will be served in the next few minutes,' the young man dressed in black then tells them before he opens the door and walks out, shutting it tight behind him. The turning of the latch echoes off the walls, almost like the clanging sound of a prison cell being locked. The room falls silent, save for the subtle sound of a few jurors sipping on their water.

'Okay,' Number One finally says, 'the judge said it is dependent on us whether or not we'd like to continue deliberations over lunch. I propose we do, but if the majority feels as if they'd like to take a break for the next hour, I totally understand.'

His fellow jurors all look around the room, most nodding their head in unison.

'So will we do a vote?' Brian asks.

Number Five tuts — loudly — but nobody responds to her, they just stare at their Head Juror for instruction.

'Hands up,' he says, 'if you would like to continue deliberations over lunch?'

Eight hands fly up, followed by another hesitant two. Only Number Four and Number Five keep their hands down. They both fancy taking a legitimate break; Number Five because she is lazy, Number Four because he knows that if deliberations are to continue, he will be called on first. After all, the jurors were seeking his opinion on the fact that Jason only booked one hotel room when they were interrupted by the lunch call.

'Ten:two,' Number One says, calling out the result. 'Majority rules. We *will* continue deliberations. So… we were discussing the hotel, right? Number Four, you were about to give your opinion on why Jason only booked one room. Would you like to begin the discussion?'

Number Four rubs one of his eyes, buying himself another couple of seconds to think through his opinion. It didn't help that he had the two-minute walk through a maze of corridors to consider his answer before he found himself in this position, because his mind kept changing. His answer to this question didn't match with his verdict overall. He was now beginning to feel that the men should be acquitted, that they didn't rape Sabrina Doyle. But he couldn't justify the booking of only one hotel room based on this verdict.

'I eh… I think Jason ordered one hotel room because they all felt as if group sex was what was gonna happen,' he says really slowly, as if he didn't want to say it at all. When the room stays silent and all eyes remain fixed on him, he feels pressured into elaborating. 'I eh… just don't see any other reason for it. One bed? They must have known what was going to happen at this stage. But…' he says, sitting more upright, 'maybe Sabrina knew at this stage, too. Maybe they discussed group sex, all four of them, at the airport.'

'That's total speculation,' Number Five says. 'Nobody, not Jason or Li or Zach or Sabrina mentioned group sex was discussed at the airport. So you've just made that up.'

'I'm just—' Number Four was about to answer but his words were being drowned out by arguments reverberating around the whole table. Almost everybody was talking, nobody listening.

'Hold on!' Number One says loudly, slamming the palm of his hand onto the table, causing the cutlery to zing with vibration. 'Can we all just settle down?' The room falls into line immediately. 'It's a good point Number Five has raised. Nobody has testified that group sex was ever mentioned at the airport, yet only one bedroom was booked. I mean... this seems really iffy.'

Another ripple of murmurings arise, but Number One holds his hand up to stop it and then stretches his index finger out, pointing it at Number Ten. 'Sorry guys, one at a time. Number Ten — you speak up.'

'I just wonder if at this particular time in the night Jason was just booking the room for him and Sabrina to spend the night in, that the other two just went along for the cocktails but were supposed to leave when the party died down or whatever. I find it hard to believe that he just booked one bed for all four of them to sleep in. I don't think the room was booked for all of them to spend the night there. They failed to get to Newcastle, so they decided to continue the party in the Merchant Suite... maybe the idea was that Zach and Li would get a taxi home or whatever at some point in the night. And y'know... one thing led to another and...'

'And what?' Number Five asks.

'And all three men had sex with Sabrina.'

'Yeah but with her consent or not?' Number Twelve poses.

'Well that's the big question isn't it?' Number Ten says. 'Sabrina insists she said "no", the boys insist that word never came out of her mouth.'

This whole trial boils down to whether or not the jurors believed Sabrina tried to stop the men from having intercourse with her. The defence team tried to argue that everybody consented to group sex; probably agreed upon because of the amount of alcohol that had been consumed by all involved. Gerd Bracken said that Jason, Zach and Li had drunk five or six pints of Heineken each, had three shots of Baby Guinness and then sipped on a cocktail when they got to the Merchant Hotel. He held both his hands up in the court, right in front of the jury and said, 'Yes, my clients are willing to admit they were intoxicated to some extent that evening, they are honest, hard-working men. They want to tell you the truth... and yes, they consumed a lot of alcohol during the night in question. Unlike Sabrina Doyle,' he said, turning to face the claimant. 'She says she wasn't really intoxicated because she mostly drank non-alcoholic wine throughout the evening. But it is a fact that Jason bought Sabrina four glasses of red wine — *alcoholic* red wine — two Baby Guinness shots and a Mango Margarita cocktail. Sabrina Doyle wasn't as sober during the night in question as she would try to lead you to believe,' he continued. 'She consumed, that we know of — there could have been more — twelve units of alcohol. The men also consumed twelve units of alcohol. Each of them were relatively as intoxicated as each other. Sabrina Doyle was not as sober as she would like to lead you to believe.'

Bracken was telling the truth. Given that wine contains more alcohol than lager, even though Sabrina had fewer drinks, she consumed just as much alcohol. Though he did sensationalise Sabrina's testimony. She didn't argue that she was sober during her time on the stand, she just insisted that she drank a mixture of non-alcoholic wine and alcoholic wine. She testified she "may have been drunk, but didn't necessarily feel drunk," during the night in question.

It was an argument Bracken spent too much time on; the jury weren't swayed by it at all.

'So...' Number One says, 'we had a strong movement towards not guilty in our last vote. Are we saying that this argument, about there being only one bed, will lean us back the other way?'

'Doesn't change my mind,' says Number Twelve.

'Me neither,' says Brian. 'There just ishn't enough evidensh.'

Number Six coughs into her wrinkled hand. It's the only

noise she's made in about an hour. It makes everybody turn to her; interpreting her cough as her preparation to finally speak. She picks up her glass of water as everybody looks at her, takes a long sip, swirls the water around her mouth and then lets out a gasp.

'I just would like to know... eh... how does the topic of group sex come up? I know I am from a different generation, but is group sex something that is a regular occurrence these days?'

She turns to face Number Seven, not because she is aware that Number Seven is a bit slutty, but because there are only two people in the room who are particularly young looking, and she opted for Number Seven over Number Five, simply because she doesn't fully trust the latter.

'Well... no. I agree that our generation is a little more forthcoming when it comes to sex, but I agree with you, Number Six — I don't know how the topic of group sex would ever raise its head,' Number Seven says. 'How does a guy ask a girl if she would like to have sex, not just with him, but with his two friends, too?'

The jury stew on this notion, each of them playing it over in their heads when they are interrupted by the door unlocking and then re-opening. The young man dressed in all black wheels in a large trolley, then stands to attention.

'These are the chicken dishes,' he says. 'Can you raise your hand if you ordered chicken?'

He then places a dish in front of those whose hands are stretched towards the dim light bulb, before leaving the room again.

'Has anyone, for inshtance...' Brian says before hesitating. He knows he is heading into controversial territory. 'Eh... I know some of you have been very kind to be forthright with your own experienshes, but has anybody here ever... y'know... eh.' Brian blushes, scratches the side of his head before continuing, 'anyone ever participated in group sex?'

The door opens again.

'These are the beef dishes. Can anyone who ordered beef now raise their hand?'

The young man dressed in all black then rounds the table, placing plates in front of those who now have their hand in the air. He then tilts his head forward in a bow as he stands at the top of the table before wheeling his trolley back out and closing the door behind him.

'Can you pass the salt?' Number Five says to Number Eleven. Number Eleven reaches across the table, grabs at the shaker and then passes it along the line.

'The chicken's nice today,' Number Three says.

'Yeah… nicer than it was yesterday, isn't it? Sauce is more sweet or something, isn't it?' says Number Seven.

'I have,' says Number Nine.

Number One stares at her and raises his eyebrows as he takes a bite of his lunch.

'I mean, I have eh… I have had group sex,' she says.

The sound of forks being placed back down on plates clangs around the room.

All eyes turn to Number Nine. She just stares down at her lap, her fork still holding a bite-sized chunk of beef in its prongs.

'And… for the record, we did discuss it beforehand. My eh… husband and his friend eh… Mike… we just…'

Number Nine's real name is Valerie Kinsella, a thirty-six-year-old factory operative who lived most of her life in Co Wexford before moving up to Clondalkin in Dublin two years ago to find employment. She dyes her hair platinum, packs her face with make-up. Her whole look screams insecurity, because that's exactly what she is: insecure. But she's nice; doesn't wallow in self pity; is happy to concede that she's not perfect and never will be. Though she does try to look as perfect as she can; or certainly what she perceives to be 'perfect'. She's actually had threesomes quite a number of times; but is only recalling the first time she did it to her fellow jurors. She doesn't want to come across as too slutty. Though she doesn't regard herself as a slut at all; she and her husband just have a more exciting sex life than most. However, she feels she owes the jury some sort of truth here. Is aware that consensual group sex is a real possibility with regards to the night in question. She believes Sabrina did have sex with all three and then perhaps regretted it the next morning upon reflection. She's believed this from quite an early stage during the trial because she has seen it happen before. She once had sex with a friend of hers and her husband, only for her friend to never speak to her again out of sheer guilt. She genuinely believes Sabrina may have suffered the same — or similar — post-sex shame.

'My husband and I got talking and we discussed what we'd like in the bedroom and so he asked his friend and...' she sighs, stops talking, feels she has shared enough. She wants to get across the fact that – in her experience – threesomes *are* discussed before they occur. They don't just happen by chance.

'Thank you so much for sharing your truth with us,' Number Twelve says. Number One's mouth is slightly ajar, others just eyeball each other or look down at their dinner.

'So... you feel as if the idea of everybody having sex during the night in question would have been discussed, it didn't just happen?' Number Twelve says directly to Number Nine.

She nods her head, then finally bites beef she'd been holding on her fork for the past two minutes.

'From my experience, yes,' she says, her mouth full.

'I always assumed she was having sex with Jason and then

the others just walked into the room, took it upon themselves to get involved,' Number Seven says, 'but its just my own theory. I can't imagine a discussion where Sabrina is asked if she would have sex with all three men and she just agreed to it. I think she was having sex with Jason, then either got caught up in the moment and had sex with the other two... or...'

'Or what?' Number Four asks.

'Or they all took advantage of her, raped her.'

'Why didn't she scream the house down?' Number Four asks, putting his fork aside. 'If she was raped, why wasn't she screaming "no"? That's one thing I can't get right in my head.'

'When girls are being raped, they go numb,' Number Five says.

'And do you know that for a fact?' Number Four asks.

'No!' she snaps back. 'I think I read that somewhere,' she says.

'You *think* you read it shomewhere?' Brian rhetorically asks in a condescending tone, almost huffing out a laugh.

Not many around the table were buying Number Five's argument. But she was right. Studies have found that victims of rape are more likely to fall silent during the ordeal rather than fight against their attackers. They can fall limp, waiting on the ordeal to be over and done with. This reaction, albeit quite sensible in a way, goes a long way to blurring the lines between consensual and non-consensual sex. If a victim isn't saying 'no', how is the attacker supposed to understand their reluctance? Of course, another argument can — and often does — ignite from this: if a victim hasn't given consent, why is an attacker having sex with them in the first place?

This is just another element that makes rape cases as convoluted as any criminal case can be. Except, in this trial specifically, the claimant insists she said "no". She admits she didn't scream the hotel room down, admits she didn't fight strongly against her attackers, but is adamant that she said "no". Sabrina claims she said it "at least three times" when one of the three men was penetrating her from behind "while the others looked on". All three men deny this. They say the word "no" never came out of her mouth.

The reporting of this specific part of the trial has led to one of the hashtags that has gone viral over the past couple of weeks via social media: #SheSaidNo. In fact both #MeToo and #SheSaidNo have trended every day of the past fortnight on Twitter in Ireland. Women's voices are echoing around the hills and valleys of the entire nation as this trial dominates the media. The jury aren't aware of this; they all agreed not to check any news during the entirety of their service. But they were made aware of some of the protestors who swamped the entry to Dublin's Criminal Courts over the past two days as both sides delivered their final argument and it become apparent that the jury would soon be deliberating their verdict. Each of the jurors heard the chant 'She Said No' as they were escorted through the back door of the courts earlier this morning. Judge McCormick informed them that they needed to blank out any protests they had overheard, and re-established to them that they were the only ones who could make a proper judgement; that those protesting were not privy to the facts of this case like they were.

'Uuuugh,' Number One says as he rubs at his face. '*No*. Such a simple word. Two letters. I guess this is what it all boils down to, isn't it? We've been arguing for...' he hesitates, twists his left wrist, 'almost four hours now. Arguments over who approached who first; did Sabrina give Jason a handjob; did Sabrina follow the men to Copper Face Jacks; why decide to go to Newcastle; why book one hotel room; who looked uncomfortable in the taxis... lots of different arguments. And while all those arguments and points are important in us understanding what happened that night, our judgement essentially boils down to what happened in that hotel room, doesn't it?'

'Yep,' Number Seven says, the 'p' of the word popping out of her mouth. 'What I wouldn't give to have been a fly on the wall in the hotel suite that night.'

23:50
Sabrina

Jason swipes the keycard over the reader of the door and it instantly unlocks. He pushes at it, walks in ahead of me.

Wow.

I guess this is how the other half live. When I stay in hotels, I barely have enough space in the rooms to walk either side of the bed. But I can't even see the bed in this place yet. There's a huge plasma screen on the wall, facing two lush grey sofas. A bar area. A kitchen. The smell of the fresh tulips is subtle, yet it's the overpowering scent. The hotel rooms I normally stay in are damp, musty. I walk towards the tulips standing in a gorgeous Waterford crystal vase on a desk on the far side of the room near the big window, take in all of their freshness through my nose, then read the message attached.

'Welcome to the Merchant Penthouse Suite. Enjoy your stay.'

I watch as Jason walks towards a huge wooden door, almost the entire width of the room before he slides it open. The bedroom. It looks so cosy, densely lit. Almost romantic. I walk towards the room and as I do, I can feel Zach staring at me. He's still into me, there's no doubt about that. He probably envisages getting into this bed with me, but that's not going to happen. This room is for me and Jason. Zach and Li can sort themselves out.

There is such a peaceful presence in the whole suite; the quiet, the subtle lighting, the smell of the flowers. An excited twinge twists in my stomach. I'm not excited about the sex, I'm excited about the prospective lifestyle I could be living if

I become Jason's girlfriend. Jaysus, even Jason's wife. Imagine. Mrs Sabrina Kenny.

I shake my head. I can't get too far ahead of myself. In fact I'm still trying to figure out if he's on the same page as me tonight, let alone years down the line. I thought he was a while ago, but he keeps turning from hot to cold. I strain my eyes towards him, trying to read his thoughts without making it obvious I'm checking him out. I watch as he runs his hand over the bed sheets, watch as he walks out of the bedroom towards the sofas, watch as he lounges down into one of them and grabs at the TV remote control. Only then does he look at me. He winks. Then turns away. I'm pretty sure his coldness is calculated. He's trying to play it cool, trying to not come on to me too heavily, too eagerly. He intrigues me. His cold isn't like Eddie's cold. When Eddie was in bad humour, it was transparent. He didn't hide it. He held no intrigue for me whatsoever. I didn't feel any sort of loss after I'd dumped him. I only felt excited. Not just because I was starting a new life without him, but because I was starting a new professional life. My new job took up all of my time. Eddie was pretty much forgotten within a week of me telling him it was all over. Once Lorna filled me in on her entrapment of Eddie, she offered me a job.

'I need a hot brunette,' she told me. 'I've got to know you well over the past few weeks and genuinely feel you could be an asset to the business.'

I didn't know what to say. I didn't think I'd have the nerve to carry out the work. But I accepted her offer later that day for the simple reason that I felt it would be more exciting than handing out discount vouchers which was all my work seemed to consist of those days. Besides, the money on offer was too good to turn down. I've made thirty-eight thousand euro since starting with Lorna in the space of fifteen months. I'd never come even close to earning that amount as a model or in marketing. It's not a life-changing amount, but it's consistent and it's fulfilling.

I've carried out seventeen entrapment cases for her, including Niall tonight, and my statistics lie at ten green lights, seven red lights. I've had to break ten women's hearts with my findings. I, rather pretentiously, assumed no man would turn down the advances of somebody who looked like me, or indeed Lorna. But that's not the case at all; some men are genuinely faithful to their other halves. And I think that's what gives me the most fulfilment in my job. The knowledge that great men do exist. Somewhere.

It's weird – I get my kicks out of being turned down, rejected. I almost fist pumped the air earlier when Niall told me he was 'loved up'. I'm actually looking forward to writing up my report for Lorna tomorrow, ahead of meeting his fiancée on Monday evening to pass on the positive news. She'll be delighted. And I'll be delighted for her. She's a lucky girl.

Li motions over to Jason to turn down the volume on the TV as he walks to the door.

'Just in here,' he says to the waiter, 'leave them on the table.'

The waiter places a large circular tray — on which sits four yellow-coloured iced Margaritas — on top of the coffee table in front of Jason and then stands up, staring straight ahead.

'Oh,' Jason says, patting down the pockets of his trousers. 'We eh… don't carry cash on us, can you add a tip to the bill?'

I intervene, pulling my purse out of my bag, retrieving a tenner from it.

'Here you are… forget adding it to the bill.'

The young man smiles at me, folds the ten euro note neatly into his waistcoat pocket and leaves us to it. As soon as he's gone, Jason re-highers the volume on the TV, then picks up one of the glasses.

'To the boys,' he says.

Both Li and Zach reach for glasses of their own, before I move between them and pick up mine.

'And Sabrina,' Li says as we all clink.

'Yeah, and Sabrina,' Jason says, before staring over the rim of his glass at me while he downs his first sip. He looks menacingly at me. Maybe he's trying to be sexy; trying to motion to me that he's ready for action. He's not being presumptuous. I have told him, after all, that I'm horny, that I'm up for this.

I look behind me, eyeball the bedroom and then look back at him. He smiles at me; gets the gist. A wave of excitement runs itself down my spine. I can't believe I'm going to have sex with a celebrity.

23:50
Li

I stroll into the room, and head straight for one of the big grey couches in front of me. I could actually spread out on it at this stage, lift me legs up, lie my head down, fall asleep. But I'm actually looking forward to the cocktails we ordered. That was the only reason I came here. I think.

I watch Sabrina as she walks around the room, taking it all in. She's probably never been in a suite this impressive before. I wonder what her life has been like; her family, her upbringing, her career. She's really cool, really attractive. It'd be quite unfortunate if she hasn't had these type of luxuries before, but I get the impression she hasn't. She's practically purring as she takes in the entire suite. I guess just because you've got the looks, doesn't mean you also get the luck.

Which is quite funny. It seems as if she has everything, yet I bet she's not as happy in life as my Niamh. And poor Niamh, even I have to admit it, didn't get the luck when it comes to looks. But that just goes to show. All these things we worry about as kids such as what we look like to other people it means sweet fuck all in the grand scheme of things. The main goal of life should be maintaining a level of happiness. But we seem to relate happiness in a bizarre way. If you looked at Jason from a distance, you would assume he has everything: fame, wealth, adoration — yet he's the most miserable man I know. Sabrina looks as if God personally designed her, yet there's a sadness behind her eyes. Then take me and Niamh; we've no money at all — just a very basic income that affords us a small flat in Drimnagh — and we certainly weren't personally designed by any God, yet we are as giddy and as happy as any people we know. I don't think there is any correlation with the things we equate to happiness with actual happiness.

There's a knock on the door. I swing my legs off the couch and go to answer it. A young man in a white shirt enters and places the tray with four cocktails on it onto the glass coffee table. Jason tells him he should add the tip to the entire bill, but Sabrina intervenes, handing him a tenner. Before the young man leaves I already have my cocktail in my hand. It looks just like I'd hoped it would — a large glass of slushed ice.

'To the boys,' Jason says holding out his glass.

'And Sabrina,' I say, before clinking. I stare at her, wait on her to acknowledge the fact that I included her in our little gang, but she's too busy eyeballing Jason. Now that we're in the hotel room, I get the impression she's ready to forget the fact that me and Zach are even here. That's fine by me. If they want to go into the bedroom and fuck, I'm okay sipping on my cocktail out here.

I pick up the TV remote and turn the volume even higher than Jason did on the music channels. I assume this will distract me. Yet I can't help but turn my eyes to Sabrina every now and then. I'm beginning to feel really guilty. I haven't fancied anyone else since I met Niamh. Yet here I am, weeks after finding out the love of my life is pregnant and just weeks before I'm about to ask her to marry me, getting distracted by a hot brunette in a white jumpsuit.

I decide to pick up my phone and flick through pictures of my girlfriend while I sip on my cocktail. This'll help ease the guilt.

Niamh's got the same colour hair as Sabrina. Only Niamh's isn't natural. She dyes her hair dark brown because she hates her mousy natural colour. But hair colour is the only thing they share in common. Niamh's a lot shorter than Sabrina. She's certainly a lot wider. I'm pretty sure a hundred out of a hundred blokes would pick Sabrina over Niamh. But as I stare at pictures of my soon-to-be fiancée I know just who I'd pick. Sabrina might have the tight waistline, the perfect skin and a sheen of light running right down her cleavage. But I bet she's not as easy to live with as my Niamh is. Niamh never argues, never creates any sort of rifts between us. There is no such thing as drama in my life.

As I flick through my photos, the guilt seems to be dissipating. My body begins to fill with relief. I was genuinely getting worried how much I was beginning to fancy this girl. I almost felt as if I was going behind Niamh's back just looking at her. It was a weird, dark feeling that I don't ever want to creep up on me again. When I ask Niamh to marry me next month; that's it. I want one of those marriages where the man doesn't even look at another woman. I'm going to be faithful to her for the rest of our lives.

I begin to cheer up and start singing along to the Little Mix song playing on the TV as I throw the straw out of my glass and begin to swig down my cocktail. Jesus, I wish I had been drinking these all night. They are a million times more refreshing than a pint of bloody beer. I begin to rock my hips back and forth wondering whether it's the alcohol in this Margarita that's making me feel so good or the release of the guilt I had been feeling for fancying Sabrina. Then I watch as Jason takes Sabrina by the hand and walks her towards the bedroom. Suddenly I stop dancing, stop singing. The good feeling engulfing me suddenly dies and I find myself back on the couch, placing my straw back in my glass and stretching out my feet so I can fall back into a slouched position. Jesus… I think I feel jealous.

23:55
Jason

Zach has been trying to create a party atmosphere. As soon as we got in, he paced around the room, looking for signs of whether or not Sabrina is interested in a threesome and then decided to turn on MTV. Maybe he wants to get us all up dancing, hoping that will lead into the bedroom.

I'm not sure how I'm feeling. It's unusual I would read a girl wrong like this. I'm not sure why I assumed Sabrina was different to the rest of them. Perhaps it was Li. He seemed to oversell her to me; telling me that if I showed her my house in Newcastle that she'd eventually fall for me. I'm beginning to think that Li is more fixated on Sabrina than me and Zach are. At this stage, all Zach and I want from her is a bit of pleasure. Li seems to want to befriend her, to make her part of our lives. After the text I just read on her phone, I've no interest in ever seeing Sabrina again. She's here for one reason and one reason only. It's such a shame she's a slut, she really doesn't need to be.

I watch her as she sips on her cocktail. Jesus, she really is gorgeous. Perfect looking I would say; head-to-toe perfect. I can't find a flaw in her appearance. The only flaw I found was in her phone. If she hadn't whispered that into my ear about half-an-hour ago when we were back in the airport, I wouldn't be feeling so low right now. It's hugely frustrating but I find myself in a position no different to any other night out. Some hot girl wants to bang me, and I ain't gonna say no. I've have this assumption in my head for the past year or so that sex will relieve me of my pain. But I'm not sure I even enjoy sex anymore. I don't think I've enjoyed sex since I last made love to Jessica.

I know I felt down — depressed — long before she and I

finished, but it wasn't really strong in those days. I didn't mope around like I do now. I was only down because the football I was playing was quite shite and the club I was playing for seemed to lack any ambition. If Jessica had stayed with me, had have supported me through it, I think I'd be fine by now. But we finished things around about the same time Sunderland were refusing to negotiate a new contract with me. I knew I was losing my girlfriend and my career at the same time.

I tried to make up for my miserableness by donating more to YouKnight and hanging around with some of their patrons. But it didn't really fix my head. I have no idea how I feel. Or why I feel. I don't know whether the guilt of us hitting Caitlin all those years ago is the reason my head is fucked up.

Bizarrely, my life didn't become any worse for almost killing her. In fact it rapidly improved in the years straight after. I lived out my dreams, became a rich man in the process. Only now, as my life is slowing down and I am waking from that dream, am I starting to suffer from all of the guilt football had steered me away from. I always thanked God for looking after me following The Secret, but I'm beginning to think now that God barely even knows I exist. He has seven billion people to look after on earth. Why was I ever so arrogant to believe he was looking down on me? I was arrogant to genuinely believe that he not only let me get away with almost killing Caitlin and running away, but also allowed me to become a professional footballer thereafter.

I pick up the crucifix from my chest, stare at it and then sneer. I genuinely don't know what to believe anymore. I've never been more confused in my entire life. I swig at my cocktail, then place the glass back down and gurn at its bitterness. Sabrina catches my eye. I play the words she whispered into my ear back at the airport.

I'm up for this. I'm horny.

I feel my dick twitch a bit. Fuck it. There's no way I'm turning my back on her. I'm not going to deny myself the chance to have sex with a perfect looking girl just because she didn't turn out to be as innocent as I first assumed she was. I'm going to peel that jumpsuit off her, have her bounce up and down on me until I shoot a load. I know I'll feel like shit straight after it, as I do every time I have a one-night stand, but I'll enjoy it while it lasts. I think I will anyway. Though I'm wary of Zach. I want to have Sabrina to myself, at least until I'm done. If she's up for having sex with him after she's had sex with me, fine. I genuinely won't care. But I'm not interested in the whole threesome thing.

I fake-laugh at Zach and Li jumping around the hotel room, attempting to get some sort of party started. While they're distracted, I walk towards Sabrina, take her by the hand and lead her to the bedroom.

'You said you were horny, right?' I say as I turn around and sweep the doors shut.

00:00
Zach

Yes! I thought I was the only one in partyin' mood. But Li lifts his lazy ass from the couch and begins to sing and dance; shouting out the wrong lyrics as he normally does when he's in good humour.

Jason's barely said a word since we got here. I think he's nervous about the threesome. I wonder if he's nervous about the actual act of the threesome or whether it's because he doesn't know how to raise the subject with Sabrina. I often wonder how these roasting sessions normally play out among footballers. Do they ask girls straight out if they want as many dicks as they can fit in, or does it all happen naturally? Does one guy start having sex with a girl and the rest just join in when they feel like it?

Jason's probably playing the same shit out in his head. But you'd think he'd know more about this than I do. He hangs around footballers on a regular basis. He has to know how these things go down. I'm well aware he hasn't taken part on any roastings before, but he must have heard a hundred stories in the dressing-room.

I don't take my eyes off him as he walks towards Sabrina, takes her by the hand and leads her into the bedroom. Then I stare over at Li, assume we'll just keep the party going while Jason fills Sabrina in on what's gonna happen. But Li's already given up.

He plonks himself back down on the sofa, staring through the television, not necessarily at it.

'C'mon Li,' I scream over at him. 'Give me more of them dance moves!'

He doesn't answer me, he just continues to stare into space.

00:00

I pick up the remote, turn the volume down on the TV and then plonk myself beside him. I'll play it cool; give Sabrina and Jason a few minutes before I go in.

'Penny for 'em,' I say to Li.

'Huh?' he says,

'Penny for your thoughts, mate.'

'Ah,' he says while trying to sit back upright. 'I don't know. Bit of a weird night, isn't it?'

I just nod my head; half-wondering what's going on behind those closed doors, half-wondering what the hell Li is going on about. He can be quite innocent and naïve, can Li. I bet he doesn't know what's going on.

'It was supposed to be a night where the three of us catch up, but it seems as if the whole night became about her,' he says, nodding his head towards the bedroom door.

'Our nights out always become about women,' I say, elbowing his shoulder.

'Aren't we all a bit old for that shit now, though?' he says. 'I mean you're married, I'm getting married. We're all in our mid-thirties now... it just seems a little... I don't know, juvenile. I really wanted to have a good night with my two best mates, share my good news. I feel like my news has just been sorta... I don't know... almost forgotten about.'

Jesus. I've never known Li to be the self-pitying type. I don't recall him ever making the conversation about him. This is the sort of deep shite Jason normally comes out with. Me, me, me. Sad, sad, sad. Li is normally the one that shakes this sort of shite from Jason. Maybe I got it wrong. Maybe Li understands exactly what's going on here. And maybe he doesn't agree with it – thinks we're pushing things a bit too far.

'I'm going to be a daddy,' he says looking up at me.

'*What?*'

'Yeah, Niamh's only two months in. She's due in the new year.'

'Man!' I say as I get to my feet. I hold out my hand for him to shake, then I fall back on top of him, squeezing him as hard as I can.

'I'm so happy for you, Li. You're going to be a great dad.' And I mean it. He will be. There's no doubt about that. 'So, you're gonna be a married man with a kid next year huh?'

He smiles at me. But it's a weak smile.

'What's up with you the last hour or so... why ye so glum, Li?'

He sighs, then shrugs his shoulders.

'Maybe I'm just tired. Maybe I should just go home to Niamh. I should have gone home straight from the airport. Probably shouldn't have even gone to the airport, that was a shite idea. How did I get so drunk to even think we could get to England using our bloody driving licenses?'

He puffs out a fake-laugh.

'Hold on, it was *your* idea to go to Newcastle?' I ask.

'I was just tryna cheer Jason up. He said he wanted to impress Sabrina, so I suggested going back to his place, showing her everything he has to offer.'

I stare at Li, then scratch at the stubble under my chin.

'But... she's not that into him.'

'Huh?' he says, twisting his head to stare at the closed bedroom door. 'Looks to me as if she's pretty into him right now.'

'Nah man, she's just interested in sex. She's gaggin' for it. I'm gonna fuck her meself.'

Li looks at me, then refocuses his eyes as if he can't believe quite what he's looking at.

'Yeah, she's up for it,' I say. 'She told me, told Jason. That's why Jason booked the room, she's up for a threesome.'

'Bollocks,' he says, his jaw slightly open.

00:00

'Honestly,' I say as I get up from the sofa again.

'Doesn't make any sense. Why did she insist I come back to the hotel room too, then? She said she wouldn't come here if I didn't.'

I walk towards the bedroom door, as if I'm desperate to prove Li wrong.

'Maybe she wants your little Korean dick too,' I say before I slide the bedroom doors open and step inside.

00:00
Sabrina

Jason grabs at my hand without even looking at me and leads me towards the bedroom. My stomach turns itself over. I know that's down to nerves, but there's also some excitement wrapped up in there somewhere. I'm about to have sex with a celebrity.

'You said you were horny, right?' he whispers to me as he sweeps the doors shut. The noise of Li and Zach singing along to Little Mix is instantly drowned out.

'Eh… yeah,' I say, biting at my bottom lip in an attempt to look sexy. Then I swallow. Hard. That's particularly unsexy, I'm sure. But I couldn't help it. The nerves are getting the better of me.

'Let's get it done then,' Jason says.

'Done?' I ask.

'Yeah… lets have sex,' he says as he moves closer to me, placing a hand around the back of my neck and pulling me in for a kiss. And I do kiss him, take his tongue into my mouth as I stew over what he's just said. Then I pull away from him.

'Get it *done*… as in get it done and over with?'

He stares at me, then squints his eyes to look past me.

'I eh… didn't mean it like that, but you eh… you said you were horny, that you wanted to have sex with me… so, here I am, here you are and here,' he says patting at the duvet cover, 'is a bed.'

Then he kisses me again. I don't pull away. I let his tongue circle my mouth again as it dawns on me that I'm nothing special to Jason Kenny whatsoever. I'm just his Friday night girl for this week. I should have known all along. What was I thinking? Why the hell did I think I'd mean anything to him?

I swing him around, then release from the kiss and push

him onto the bed. I genuinely flick my thoughts between jumping on top of him and turning around and opening the door to leave. His smile makes my mind up for me. I deserve a bit of fun. I need to stop being a prude. A celebrity is lying on a bed waiting on me to have sex with him. Why am I even hesitating? I owe myself this. I owe the devil on my shoulder this little victory. Only two dicks in my twenty-five years? That's quite sad. In fact, it's worse than quite sad. It's pathetic.

I place a knee either side of Jason's hips and straddle him, bending down to take his tongue back into my mouth. Suddenly, he's tugging at the zip on the back of my jumpsuit. The shoulders of my suit release and I actually feel a bit of relief as my boobs pop out. They'd be threatening to do that all night. I no longer have to pull at the V to make sure they're tucked in. They're out there now. Free. And they're all yours, Jason Kenny. He doesn't hesitate. He snuggles his face in between them, proving no man, not even one who must get it on a regular basis, has any patience when it comes to tits.

I try to shake my head of any niggling thoughts. I just want to be in the moment. I want to enjoy it. I don't need to overthink it. I don't need to worry whether Jason and I will ever see each other again. Though I'm pretty certain we won't. I guess he's made himself clear. I'm the girl he has chosen to have sex with tonight. I may as well try to enjoy it. Though I have to say, I feel a little disappointed when I unbutton his shirt and place my hands onto his torso in search of the six-pack I assumed any professional athlete would have. But he just has a regular hairy belly. It's nothing special. It's not quite as fat as Eddie's but it's a far cry from the chiselled athletic body I had assumed I'd be grappling with tonight. I shake my head again… I'm such an idiot for overthinking. I genuinely feel that's why I don't enjoy my life.

I'm never *in the moment*. Even during the most special times in my life, I'm always too concerned about what others are thinking; about what this means for my future; my reputation. I'm sure the years I spent being judged as a model have affected my whole outlook on life. I always assume I'm being judged, being talked about. I'm too self-conscious. That's why I take myself too seriously; why I don't have enough fun, enough sex.

I suck in through my teeth as I feel a pinch, but the pain doesn't last too long. Literally just one second. Now that Jason is grinding slowly from behind me, it feels right. His is probably the most perfect fit out of the three I've had inside me. Men seem to be obsessed with size. From my experience now, of having three different sizes altogether, average length is what's best.

I force out a little groan, just to let him know I'm enjoying it, but I'm wary of being too loud. I don't want to alert Zach and Li from their little party. Though I'm sure they know what we're up to. They're not stupid. I'm enjoying this, enjoying the fact that I'm being a bit slutty; that I have lightened up; that I'm being taken from behind by a guy I just met a few hours ago. I don't feel any guilt, in fact quite the opposite. I think I'm actually proud of myself. I don't think I've ever been this excited. I laugh as Jason continues to thrust inside me; a laugh aimed at myself. It's the first time I've ever appreciated a bold decision that I've made. I feel myself getting wetter. Enjoying every moment.

Then the door slides open. It's Zach.

'Can I join in?' he asks. I just stare at him. I don't know why I'm not disgusted. Don't know why I haven't rolled over, pulled the duvet up to hide my naked body. I haven't said a word in response by the time he walks closer to me.

'Sabrina... do you mind if I join in?' he repeats.

I look over my shoulder, at Jason. He shrugs.

00:00

A threesome? Jesus. I'd literally be doubling the amount of penises I've had in my entire life in just one night. Isn't this supposed to be a lot of girls' fantasies? Is it supposed to be mine?

I bite at my bottom lip again, stare down at the mattress and then back up at Zach.

11

The young man dressed in all black is assisted by a young woman dressed in the same attire as he removes all remnants of lunch from the table. When they're done, the young man dressed in all black turns to the jurors and offers a slight bow again before he and his colleague shuffle out the door, shutting it tight behind them.

The jury members, left alone for the first time in ten minutes, don't immediately return to their deliberations. Number Eleven is discussing *Game of Thrones* episodes with Number Ten. Brian and Number Twelve are locked in a political debate about the state of the education system. Number Seven and Number Four are talking about their own lives. Number Five, Number Three, Number Nine and Number Eight are discussing the court system, deliberately avoiding any mention of the specific trial they are all currently serving on. Number Six has just been tuning in and out of each of the conversations happening around her as she chews the inside of her cheek. She's starting to get tired. They have been deliberating for four hours and fifteen minutes now, including their discussions through lunch, and it all seems to be getting on top of her.

Number Six's real name Cynthia Lafferty, a sixty-eight year old from Crumlin in Dublin. She was relishing being called for jury duty, even though she could have been excused on account of her age. She's almost addicted to American crime shows; felt being on a jury would be just like being an extra in an episode of *Law and Order*. Number Six has been a widow of six years; her husband Arthur finally failing to uphold his diet of fry-ups and pints of Guinness, collapsed to a massive heart attack right in front of her one Friday morning. She has two middle-aged sons who call on her more regularly than they did prior to their father's passing, but it doesn't make up for the loss. She's excited to be involved in this case — it gives her something to do — but she's been more than happy to keep herself to herself. She's been content to watch what's going on around her. As if it was on a screen. She remains in the guilty camp, though recent arguments, particularly over lunch, have led to her feeling that she's just not up to date with modern generations. She's beginning to think group sex is a phenomenon she just doesn't — and never will — understand. She thought Sabrina was the innocent party because no woman in their right mind would willingly have sex with three men in one night, but her belief has been shaken by her realisation that she can't fully comprehend Sabrina; that she can't fully comprehend the modern twenty-something. They are a far cry from the twenty-somethings Number Six knew when she was twenty-something.

The separate conversations hush when the young man dressed in all black re-enters the room.

'Now, I will lead you back to the jury room,' he says, pointing his full hand towards the door he'd just walked through. Each of the jurors pick up their notes, shuffle towards the door and then out on to the first corridor. They remain silent as they turn two corners before finding themselves inside their deliberation sanctuary again. Each of them sit back down in the exact same seat they'd occupied prior to lunch. It was akin to the habit they subconsciously adopted in the courtroom; every day the jurors sat in the same seat they had done from day one, even though that wasn't a necessity.

The young man dressed in all black lightly clears his throat to court everybody's attention and then speaks up.

'It is now two-ten p.m,' he says. 'Deliberations will continue until four p.m. today unless a unanimous verdict is reached. If not, I will be back at four p.m. to dismiss you from deliberations for the day and escort you elsewhere. If that is the case, you will all reconvene here at nine-thirty a.m. tomorrow. Does anybody have any questions?'

Number Five raises her hand and the young man dressed in all black nods at her.

'Is the judge expecting us to deliver a verdict today?'

Brian tuts, then answers her question before the young man dressed in all black has a chance to.

'Of course not,' he says. 'This young man ishn't here to answer on behalf of the judge. He's jusht talking about our itinerary; when we finish, when we restart tomorrow. He'sh not here to answer questions like that.'

Number Five swings her jaw, just about stopping herself from retaliating to Brian's condescending tone.

There are no strict time limits on jury deliberations when it comes to these kind of trials. A lot of rape verdicts are delivered within a matter of hours by jurors, but other deliberations can go on for days should the case be specifically complex. The Sabrina Doyle versus Jason Kenny, Zach Brophy and Li Xiang trial does have it's own perplexities, but it is far from as convoluted as some rape trials can get. The three defendants' lawyers will see an early verdict as a positive; as they will assume that the jury came to a quick resolution of innocence on their clients' behalf. But the time for such optimism will be just about passing them by at this stage. Both sides will be now stewing over the likely reality that the jury will not deliver a verdict today.

Gerd Bracken — and his team of defence lawyers — as well as Jonathan Ryan would have been aware that the jury requested to watch the CCTV footage of Jason and Sabrina exiting and then re-entering the Hairy Lemon either side of the 'handjob' argument as well as sought the transcripts of rickshaw rider Donagh Scott's testimony this morning. These jury actions could be seen as a positive for the defence, but Bracken is way too experienced in his field to get carried away by such thoughts. He's been through this rigmarole many times before. He'll only know the jurors' decisions as soon as they walk back into the courtroom. His tell-tale sign is that jurors who are about to reveal an innocent verdict to the court normally look to the defendants upon re-entering the jury dock, while a jury about to reveal a guilty verdict will shy away from looking at the defendants.

'So… inside the hotel suite,' Number One says after the young man dressed in all black closes the door behind him and leaves them to it. 'I mean… what can we say? We know for a fact that all three men had intercourse with Sabrina, so the big question is; did she give consent?'

'Sorry,' that'sh not the argument at all,' Brian says. 'The argument ish not whether she gave consent, but did she specifically *not* give consent.'

'Huh?' Number Five says, overemphasising her word as if she's a stroppy teenager, her face all contorted. 'Wha' you talkin' bout?'

'There'sh a considerable difference between offering consent and specifically not offering consent,' Brian says.

'He's right,' Number Twelve says, backing up the politician. 'Nobody specifically seeks consent, do they? I mean, when we're having sex, we don't stop kissing and then ask the person if it's okay if we have sex with them, do we? We just… ye know… go with the flow.'

Number Five's face is still contorted. She doesn't fully comprehend what both men are trying to explain to her.

Number Six turns to Number Five and offers a sympathetic pursing of the lips.

'What Brian and Number Twelve are trying to say is, our argument is not whether Sabrina said "yes" to sex, it's whether or not she said "no" to sex. She didn't have to vocalise her consent. She had to vocalise a lack of consent.'

Number Five turns out her bottom lip, then nods her head slowly.

'But… I mean, how do we do that?' she says.

'That'sh exactly it,' Brian says. 'That's what I've been shaying all along. We can not and will not know what happened in that hotel suite; we simply haven't been offered any evidensh whatsoever that proves beyond all reashonable doubt that Sabrina said "no".'

Number Five understood most of what Brian was saying to her, but he lost her with his use of that fucking phrase 'reasonable doubt' again.

'We can all take a guess at what happened next. But none of us can know for certain and that is why we have to find the men not guilty,' Number Twelve says, his face sporting a look that could only be described as smug.

'But you've been not guilty from the start,' Number Five says. 'You're just driving your own opinion onto others and—'

'I've been not guilty from the start, Number Five,' Number Twelve says, raising his voice over hers, 'because I knew all along that it all came down to this; the fact that none of us in this room knows what happened in that hotel suite and that the prosecution didn't do enough to convince us that their version of events happened beyond reasonable doubt. It's Sabrina's word against theirs. And listen, I feel sorry for Sabrina. I do. But we can't lock three men up for ten years each just because we feel sorry for someone.'

He was right, albeit on the high side with his projection of a possible prison sentence. Jason, Zach and Li are most likely to face somewhere between five-to-ten years behind bars if this jury deliver a guilty verdict. Seven years is the average stretch handed down to a rapist in Ireland, a number that has been ever-so-slightly increasing over the past decade. With all three men on trial now aged thirty-five, it was certainly conceivable that they wouldn't be free men for their fortieth birthdays should they be found to be guilty of this charge. If it is a case that they're found guilty, it will be Judge Delia McCormick's decision on how much time they will serve. Her reputation points to her being a judge who tends to land somewhere just over the average; if she was to go that way in this case, she would be likely to sentence all three men to eight years in prison, even though they have all had clean criminal records up until this point in their lives.

'Let's discuss what happened in the hotel room, rather than just dismiss it out of hand, Number Twelve,' Number Eleven says calmly. Number Twelve holds up his hands in agreement and then looks towards the Head Juror.

'So the defendants claim that group sex wasn't discussed at all… that Jason and Sabrina began to have sex and then Sabrina became open to the other two men joining in, that's right isn't it?' the Head Juror offers to the table.

'Well, yesh, in summary,' says Brian.

'Do we perhaps need a transcript of Jason and Zach's testimonies to make sure we get this right?' Number One offers up.

Number Ten barks the loudest "yes" in the room, bringing all eyes towards her. 'Let's get the transcript of Sabrina's testimony as well. If we're going to analyse this case as best we can, I think we'll be doing ourselves a service by having their words in front of us. Get twelve copies of each.'

Nobody around the table opposes this course of action. Number One reaches for the button in front of him on the table and as he requests the specific transcripts based around activities in the hotel room, Number Twelve brings up a piece of Jason's testimony that rang true to him during the trial to Number Ten who is sitting next to him. He waits until Number One has finished with his request to the court's assistant and then raises his point to the whole table.

'One thing that stuck out to me from Jason's time on the stand about what exactly happened in the hotel room was when he said something like "Sabrina is a lovely girl, I don't know why she is making this claim, but she only made it in the aftermath".'

'Yep,' Brian says, 'Aftermath is definitely a word he said on the shtand. I have that written in my notes here. He says Sabrina never made a claim of rape there and then. She must have only come up with the notion that she was raped after she left the room.'

'Yes,' I remember him saying that,' says Number Eleven. 'But I also remember her saying she said "no" three times.'

Rumbles of debate strike up from all sides of the table. Number One has to stand, hold his hand in the air and ask for silence. He then lets out a deep breath and sits back down just as a knock rattles on the door.

Number Nine gets up, answers the door again and takes the paperwork from the young man dressed in all black. She flicks through it as she paces the three steps back towards her seat and then stretches to hand them over to Number One.

Number One licks his thumb, then walks around the table, peeling off pages from the bundle and placing them in front of each juror. When he's done, he sits back down, clears his throat and then stares around the room.

'Whose testimony shall we start with?' he asks.

'Start with Sabrina,' Number Five says.

Number One nods his head, shuffles his paperwork until he finds Sabrina's typed script and then speed reads quietly through it.

'Okay, so if we start half-way down the page here... let me see, the fourth paragraph on the first page of Sabrina's testimony where it says "Jason took me by the hand..." — does everybody see that?'

The jurors muffle a yes and then Number One looks across the table.

'Would you like to read it, Number Eleven?' he offers. Number Eleven nods, then clears her throat.

'"Jason took me by the hand and led me to the bedroom. I had a feeling what he was after, but I didn't stop him. I didn't say 'no' – not at this point. As I already said, I fancied Jason initially. We began to kiss on the bed and he took off my suit and began to fondle my breasts before we started to make love."'

Sabrina had told the police initially that she had had consensual sex with Jason before all three men ended up having non-consensual sex with her.

"Then Zach walked into the room and started to touch me and I felt really uncomfortable. I wasn't sure what he was doing. I didn't want him to touch me. I wanted to tell him to go away, to leave me and Jason alone but... I don't know what came over me. He wanted to kiss me and I told him no. But suddenly he was up on the bed, was having sex with me while Jason just stood there and watched and I told him, I said 'no'. But nobody did anything. And then Li came in and did the same. I said 'no', I said 'no' three times. At least three times. But one of them just grabbed my hair, shoved my face into the mattress and continued to have sex with me. By the end I didn't know who was having sex with me when or even how many times any of them had sex with me, it all turned into a blur... but I know — I swear to you — I said no, I said no many times. It was hurting me. I hated it. Every minute of it. I just wanted them to stop."'

Number Eleven stops reading and looks up at the table, her eyes moist, as if what she's just read were her own words.

'Thank you for reading that, Number Eleven,' Number One says. 'So — Sabrina explicitly says she said 'no' and said that word 'at least three times'. Do we need to analyse anything she specifically says here?'

'Under cross-examination, didn't Bracken really push her on the argument that all three men were never in the room; no group sex really took part, that she had sex with the three men separately?' Number Eight asks.

'Yes, he did. And Sabrina stood firm. She never froze or hesitated on the stand, even though he did his best to push her buttons. But we can discuss the cross examinations in a second. Let's just look at her exact testimony of what she said occurred. Do we need to analyse anything specifically that she said here?'

'We only need to analyse the fact that her words aren't consistent to what Jason and Zach said on the stand — that's essentially what we're looking into,' Number Twelve says.

'True,' says Number One. 'So do you mind reading Jason's statement there...'

Number One shuffles through his paperwork again, but Brian beats him to it.

'Fifth paragraph down, where he says he shtarted to make love to Sabrina.'

'Yes… thank you, Brian,' says Number One, before raising his eyebrows towards Number Twelve.

'Okay,' Number Twelve says before taking a deep breath. '"I was making love to Sabrina when Zach walked into the bedroom. Sabrina wasn't shocked. She looked up at him and he genuinely asked if it was okay if he joined in. I mean… I wasn't happy about it. I didn't say anything, but Sabrina nodded her head. I thought it was a bit odd, this had never happened to me before. I was also a little bit disappointed. So when Zach started to make love to her, I snuck out of the room. I didn't stand there and watch as she says I did. And then me and Li just watched tele for a few minutes, before Li went to the bedroom. And… I don't know what happened. I wasn't there. But I didn't hear anyone screaming 'no' or shouting 'no'. Sabrina made love to all of us that night. I don't believe she felt at any point in the night that she was raped. I think she only came to that conclusion the next day. Sabrina is a lovely girl so I don't know why she is making this claim, but she only made it in the aftermath. I'm certain of that."'

'This is my take on it,' Number Eight says. 'Always has been. I think Sabrina only felt she was raped after the fact. She went home, thought it all through and felt a bit guilty about what happened, then rang the police.'

A slight ripple of argument threatens to erupt but Number Twelve puts an end to it within seconds.

'Let's just read Zach's version and then I think it might be an appropriate time after that for us all to get our points across,' he says.

'Yes, in fact after we read this, it may be an appropriate time for us to have a verdict vote,' Number One says.

His idea was met with a nodding of heads around the table.

'Okay… so let's read Zach's statement from the time he walked into the bedroom.'

00:05
Jason

I reach around Sabrina's back and fumble until I find the zip. Within seconds I'm snuggling in between her tits, licking at that sheen that runs right through her cleavage; something I'd been looking forward to doing all night. It was all so tempting, on show like that. I'm horny, but I'm also really disappointed — sad almost.

I'm not necessarily angry with her. I'm angry with myself.

I can't understand how I can continue to be this gullible; this stupid. I've been a celebrity for seventeen years. I should know that women aren't interested in me… not the real me.

As I'm pulling her jumpsuit off, I make a mental note to book a session with my therapist as soon as I get home. So much for having a break back in Dublin to sort my head out. Right now I feel as low as I ever have. Still, my depression doesn't seem to affect my dick.

I turn Sabrina around, into my favourite position and without any foreplay at all, I enter her. This is nothing new. When girls make it obvious to me that they're interested in one thing, what's the point in wasting time on foreplay? The only time I got engaged in that sorta thing was with Jessica. I actually used to even enjoy foreplay with her. I miss her so much. I know we argued a lot, especially towards the end, but Jesus, I'd give anything to be having an argument with her right now if it meant she'd still be in my bed when I wake up in the morning. I think it's worse to be lonely when you have lots of money. I have so much to share with someone, but nobody to share it with. When I wake up in my house in Newcastle, I can almost hear the silence. The gaff is so big that I rattle around in it. It dismays me that people equate money to happiness. It's just not the case at all. Mo' money, mo' problems is definitely accurate. Well, it is for me anyway. I hate that my friends think I should just go out and find a girlfriend, as if it's easier for me than it is for anyone else. Surely it's harder for me than the regular Joe. Tonight's a great example of that. I thought I'd met somebody interested in me, not just my celebrity. But I couldn't have been more wrong. All she's wanted was this. Me inside her. Even my therapist's advice doesn't ring true a lot of the time. I bet he'll say to me that I should have embraced the fact that Sabrina was interested in me because I am a celebrity. But that line just doesn't bridge any of my depression. It never has. My therapist isn't a celebrity, so how can he know exactly how I feel? I really can't find anybody on my level that I can talk to.

There's no way I can confide in other footballers. We just don't communicate like that. Imagine me strolling up to one of my teammates and telling him I had to fuck this hot bird because she wanted me to, but all I really wanted to do was to roll over on the bed, play with her hair and get to know her more. I'd be laughed out of the dressing-room.

I'm not so down that I've considered suicide – I'd be too afraid to hurt my mam and my little brother that way. But, sometimes I do feel as if it's the only way out of this miserableness.

I feel a tear roll down my face, so remove a hand from Sabrina's waist to wipe it away. Then I notice my crucifix bounce up and down on my chest as I continue to thrust in and out of her. I pick it up, stare at it for a second, then let it go, squeeze my eyes shut and force another tear out. I really am pathetic; fucking a hot girl from behind while crying. This would be the lowest of the low if I hadn't already been here before.... doing the exact same thing; tearing up while having sex.

I'm not even sure whether she's enjoying this – she's very

quiet for somebody being thrusted into, especially as she had told me she was looking forward to this.

I reach back down, and grab at one of her breasts to see if that makes either me or her enjoy this any more then we currently are when the door slides open. I'm not surprised to see Zach standing there, asking Sabrina if it's okay if he joins in. My dick immediately goes soft inside her. She looks back at me, as if to ask me if it's all right. I barely react. I just shrug my shoulders. I'm more intrigued to find out if she's up for this, if she's as dirty and as slutty as I assume she is from reading her text message earlier.

She doesn't say anything as Zach moves closer. I remove myself from her, and just kneel back on the bed as Zach inches even closer, almost touching Sabrina. She still hasn't said a word. Zach looks at me, then back at her. This is getting awkward. *Really* awkward. In fact, it's her making it awkward, her silence that is filling the room with suspense.

The only sound that breaks the silence is Zach unzipping his jeans. He whips his T-shirt off and flings it to the ground. I think he assumes he's being sexy. I can barely watch this. I'm so not up for a threesome. It doesn't interest me in any way. My dick is soft anyway. No way it's gonna get hard again, specially not with Zach in the room. I balk back in the bed as Zach moves in to kiss Sabrina. I don't feel jealous, just uncomfortable.

'No… no,' she says, 'no kissing.'

Zach smiles up at me. I think he's taken that as a signal that she just wants to fuck. As he inches closer, I throw my legs over the side of the bed and stand up. I can barely watch. Then Zach climbs onto the bed, knee by knee and almost crouches into the position I was seconds ago.

I tip-toe out of the open doors. I think I want to throw up.

00:10
Sabrina

I feel Jason go limp inside me. I'm not surprised. Your best friend walking in on you having sex is hardly recipe for a thrill. Though I assume this isn't their first rodeo together. I'm probably just another girl on a long list that they've doubled up on. They probably do this most weekends.

I try to think it through, but my mind is muddled. Am I supposed to say 'yes'? Am I supposed to want a threesome? Is that what most girls fantasise about? It's certainly not anything I've fantasised about. But what would I know? My sex life is about as limited as any twenty-five-year-olds could be, I'm sure. Maybe this is my ultimate test: do I want to be more light-hearted and fun, or do I want to remain the same old boring Sabrina Doyle?

I still haven't answered when Jason slips himself out of me as Zach unzips his jeans and slips them – and his T-shirt — off. I collapse my hips onto the bed and rub my hands over my face. When I lift my gaze up, Zach's face is coming towards mine. I balk.

'No... no, no kissing,' I say before I plant my face back down into the mattress. That's the second time he's tried to kiss me tonight. The second time I've swung my mouth away from his. I mean he's kind of handsome, I guess. Probably handsome to most girls. But I don't find him attractive at all. I certainly don't want to kiss him. I wish he'd go away, leave me and Jason to it. I was enjoying what we were getting up to. But within seconds of me refusing to kiss him, I feel him behind me, playing with me. I guess he took my 'no kissing' as a come on of sorts. Then again, I still haven't said 'no' to the question he asked two minutes ago. *'Can I join in?'* I still don't know why I haven't answered when I feel him insert his fingers inside me. Maybe I'm just in shock. Or maybe the little devil on my shoulder is winning out; wanting me to be more sexually active, wanting me to be the opposite of who I am.

I keep my face down, decide to be a bit more open and maybe go with it. But I can't bear to look behind me. Not necessarily at what Zach's up to, but more because I don't want to see Jason. I'm so pissed off with him. I genuinely thought I meant something to him earlier in the night. But now he's just standing there, watching as his best friend tries to please me from behind. I'm not sure if he even is pleasing me. I'm still a little wet, but I'm certain that's just the remnants of the excitement I had when Jason was making love to me. If this is supposed to be their big fantasy – a threesome – why has Jason just stopped? Why aren't we all in it together? I shake my head, decide to stop overthinking it. I can't enjoy this if I'm overthinking. I squeeze my eyes shut, shove my face firmer into the mattress and try to think of things that normally excite me.

When I masturbate, I normally imagine a rugged, handsome, tattooed man pleasing me. So that's what I imagine now. A David Beckham-type; muscular, strong arms wrapped around me, whispering sexily in my ear, telling me he wants me to cum. I can feel myself getting a little wetter. It's got nothing to do with whatever Zach is doing back there. I'm not sure what he's up to, but I try to blank him from my mind. It's not him behind me. It's my tattooed, muscular hunk. Only I don't think my hunk would be pinching me and hurting me as much. I suck the pain away through my teeth and get back to my daydream; my fantasy. I want to try and enjoy being a bit slutty for once, somebody who's not frigid. C'mon Sabrina – enjoy this. You deserve it. Two penises in one night.

I allow myself a little smile. The devil on my shoulder will be so happy I'm giving in. I might regret this in the morning, but for now I owe it to myself to have some fun.

00:15
Zach

Jason steps off the bed and stands aside, almost inviting me to go ahead and get stuck in.

I'm not sure how this is supposed to play out. If this is a threesome, shouldn't Jason still be on the bed? Shouldn't we be doing what I've seen done in loadsa porn movies? Shouldn't Jason have his dick in her pussy, maybe I should have my dick in her mouth? Maybe she shouldn't be just lying there with her ass in the air. Maybe she should be sitting up, pleasuring both of us at the same time.

I guess none of us know what we're doin'. None of us have ever been on this rodeo before. Sabrina is on the bed, me and Jason off it. So much for a roasting.

I stare at my best mate, but he's just gazing down at his feet. I don't deliberately look straight at it, but I can sense through my peripheral vision that his dick has gone soft. I'm not sure he's up for this. Maybe I should take the lead. This threesome was my idea after all.

I climb up behind Sabrina, one knee at a time while I begin to tug away at my dick. The atmosphere is a little too weird. I can't seem to get it up. It won't stand to attention. Which is really weird. One of the hottest girls I've ever seen is lying in front of me, fully naked, her ass in the air, but I just can't seem to get my mindset right.

I watch as Jason shuffles out of the room, tip-toeing quietly as if we're all asleep. I initially wanted a threesome, wanted group sex, just to try it for the sake of trying it. But now that he's leaving the scene, I feel a bit of relief wash over me. Sabrina and I can just get on with it. I'm about to have sex with a bird that looks like a fuckin' glamour model.

I cast my eyes down the back of her neck, her spine, her

ass, the backs of her thighs – just in search of a blemish, maybe even a freckle. Nothing. She genuinely looks as if she stepped out of my TV from one of those *PrettyLittleThings* commercials or somethin' .

So why the fuck isn't my dick hard?

I continue to tug away, tickling at my balls in an attempt to turn myself on, but it's just not happening. I decide to play with Sabrina, maybe turning her on will turn me on. I'm not great with foreplay, rarely use it with Tina. Our sex life consists of me saying I want it and her just giving it to me in whatever position I fancy. When we first started going out, we'd spend ages in the bedroom, finding out what each other's fantasies were. But now we just try to get it over with as soon as possible. Our sex life is basically an assisted wank for me. That's basically it. When I cum, we're done. I'm good at getting sex, but not necessarily good at sex itself. I don't need to be. What can I say? I'm a lazy, selfish fucker. But I want to try to turn Sabrina on. She deserves to enjoy this as much as I do.

I start by rubbing my fingers gently against her inner thighs for a few seconds, hoping that will get her groaning. But she's still quiet, still face down on the bed. She's a little wet, a little slippy down there, so I allow my finger to enter her. Still no groans of satisfaction. I enter another finger and begin to thrust them in and out. It feels weird. Not her insides, but the whole atmosphere. I can only hear the muffled beat of the music Li is playing in the other room. It's all very eerie.

I try to imagine what Sabrina must be thinking. She said she was up for this. Why is she just lyin' there, saying nothing? Maybe she's not as slutty as she led us to believe.

I stare down at her, willing myself to get hard as I take in her perfect skin, but… nothing. My dick falls even limper in my hand. I try to force it inside her, still limp, hoping my fingers can guide the way. Once I'm inside her, I'll harden up, we'll get this going. We could both be cumming soon, cumming together. But it's not working. I can't get myself in. This has never happened to me before. I'm so glad Jason left the room. I'd be mortified if he knew I couldn't get it up for a hottie like this. It's unnerving me that she's so quiet. Maybe she just doesn't want this. Maybe she's going to regret all of this in the morning.

'Are you okay?' I ask her. She doesn't move a muscle, not even a nod of her head. She didn't say 'yes', though she also didn't say 'no'. So I try again, try rubbing my dick on the back of her legs, hoping the smoothness of her skin turns me on, turns me on enough to get hard; hard enough for me to slip inside her.

12

Number Eight holds his hand to his mouth, clears his throat rather noisily and then begins to read Zach's testimony.

"'I walked into the room because it was clear to me that Sabrina had wanted more than just straight sex with one of us that night. She had flirted with both me and Jason through most of the night. And Li. She got on really well with Li. Probably got on better with him than anyone. We didn't discuss sex, but the fact that she came into the hotel, with just one bed, and went straight to it with Jason led me to believe that my suspicions were right all along. So after they were in there for a while, I popped into the bedroom and asked her out straight. I asked if it was okay if I joined in. I asked her, one hundred per cent. I just said 'would it be okay if I joined in?' She looked at me like in a really sexy kinda way, then she nodded her head. So, I just did... I joined in. I got on the bed, no real eh... what's-the-word... eh foreplay, yeah, foreplay, nothing like that. I just started having sex with her. She was kinda face down on the bed, but she was enjoying it. We both were. At no point did she say the word 'no'. I swear. I swear. We probably only had sex for... I don't know, it wasn't much longer than five or six minutes. It was the first time I'd ever had sex with the same girl as somebody else in the same night and it just didn't feel right so I... y'know didn't cum, like. I just stopped.'"

Number Eight looks up, awaits a response.

'What was it Zach said about Jason being in the room at the same time?' Number Three asks as he scans through the page.

'It doesn't say it here, but he was pushed on that in cross-examination. Joseph Ryan asked him if he ever felt uncomfortable having sex in a bedroom alone with a girl before and when he replied 'no', Ryan asked him why he felt uncomfortable this time,' Number One said.

'Yeah and before he was given time to answer Ryan said something like: "I put it to you that you felt uncomfortable and didn't climax because your friend was in the room looking at you performing sex with Sabrina, isn't that right?" but Zach just denied it,' Number Twelve says.

His summoning up was pretty accurate. Joseph Ryan was intent on tripping both Jason and Zach up in cross, trying to get them to admit, albeit through a slip up, that there was more than one man in the room at any point while acts of sex were being carried out; much like Sabrina testified had happened, which totally opposed the men's account. While Zach hesitated and stuttered quite a lot on the stand — and came across as lacking in any kind of sympathy, unlike Jason — Ryan still didn't catch him out quite as he would have hoped.

It was a dangerous game for Jason and Zach to play, putting themselves on the stand and open to cross-examination, but they managed to get through it. It couldn't be said that they passed the test with flying colours, but they passed nonetheless. The media reported Zach's testimony as being quite 'insensitive', noting his lack of sympathy and all but painting him as guilty – well, as much as they legally could. The reporting of his testimony spiked the #SheSaidNo social media movement. The day after his testimony — which was the day the national newspapers reported it — #SheSaidNo was posted 113,068 times in Ireland alone. A national record for any hashtag used in one day by quite some distance. There was no doubt about it; in the eyes of the general public, all three men were guilty of this crime. Yet the public only had scraps of evidence that could legally be reported to base their views on, which were — more often than not — sensationalised by the print media.

'Lishten,' Brian says, standing up. 'I know we're going to do a verdict vote now, but I jusht want to suggest that we should discard the option of 'undecided' this time. It'sh not an option the judge has necessarily given us. We can go guilty or not guilty, so maybe they're the only two options we should use. And I'd just like to add that in order to vote guilty, you have to be certain beyond reashonable doubt that the three men raped Sabrina. That's all I want to shay.' He holds both his palms towards his fellow jurors as he sits back down.

For once, Number Five doesn't react to Brian's lecture. She sits in silence and contemplates the vote ahead, just like everybody else around her. Number One removes the box from the middle of the table and proceeds to walk around the back of each juror, placing a pen and a slip of paper in front of each of them.

'Okay,' he says, returning to his chair and standing behind it. 'I agree with Brian's suggestion tha—'

'Bout time you agreed with him on something,' Number Eight says. It raises a chuckle around the room, cutting at the tension.

'Well, I don't think it'll be the last time I agree with him today, I must say,' Number One says, only to be met with 'ahhhhs' from each corner of the table. Number One was practically admitting that he was about to change his vote. At least that's what everybody was assuming.

'Calm down, calm down,' he says. 'I agree with Brian that we should all only have two options now. Guilty or not guilty. When you are done writing down one of those two verdicts, please fold your slip of paper in two, like this,' he says, showing them a run through of how to fold paper again, 'and then place it back into the box.'

He shoves the box into the middle of the table and then sits back down. The room falls deathly silent. Most jurors immediately begin to write. Number Three, Number Eight, Number Nine and Number Four stew on their thoughts, the latter twisting the top of his pen back and forth as he stares into space. Folded slips of paper are being tossed into the box and by the time Number Three, Number Eight and Number Nine have finally finished, Number Four is still contemplating his vote.

'Take your time,' Number One says, when he notices Number Four is the only juror not to have delivered a slip of paper yet.

'Don't rush him!' Number Five says.

'I'm not rushing him. I wasn't being sarcastic. I was being serious. Take your time, Number Four. This is as important a decision as you will likely ever make.'

Number Four groans, then fills each of his cheeks with air, before letting it all rasp out through his lips.

'Fuck it,' he says. 'I gotta do it. I don't want to… but I gotta write this.' He scribbles down his verdict, doesn't fold his piece of paper, he just flicks it towards the box, missing it by inches and then holds his head in his hands and folds himself forward, leaning on the table as if it's nap time.

'I didn't like doing that,' he mumbles into his own

armpits. Number Seven reaches out a hand to the back of his neck, offers him a subtle massage as Number One begins his count.

'This is so tough,' Number Seven says tutting. 'Tough on us all. I never would have thought being a juror would make me so… depressed, I guess.'

Number Four rises from his slouched position, reaches out his two hands to hug Number Seven. They hold each other until Number One declares he has a result.

'Okay guys. A significant shift,' he says. 'Nine not guilty; three guilty.'

Almost every juror strains their eyeballs around the table. They're all asking themselves the same question, but nobody dare ask it aloud. Not yet anyway. Brian was finding it hardest to hold it in; the question poised to dive off the tip off his tongue. Yet part of him was feeling more relieved than annoyed. He felt things were finally heading in the right direction; the direction he had argued for from the very beginning.

Though at this stage in a trial, after four hours and forty minutes of deliberations, he didn't need to be that smug. Leads of nine:three had been won over before, and will be won over again in this room. There was still a chance that it would be won over today.

'Who are the three that voted *guilty*?' Brian just blurts out. He couldn't hold it in any longer.

'That was a secret ballot,' Number Five snaps back at him.

'Well I know you're one for a start. I don't think this needs to be a secret anymore. We need to openly discuss this. Who are the other two?'

'Whoa, whoa, whoa,' Number One says, standing up again. 'Let's calm down. Please.' He sighs, rubbing each of his eyes with the thumb and index finger of his right hand and then says, 'I agree with Brian again here. There is no need for this to be a secret. It needs discussing. After all we have discussed over the past four hours or whatever it is, who now genuinely thinks that we should convict Jason, Zach and Li?' he asks, then sits down.

Number Five raises her hand. Number Three lets a sigh force its way out of her nostrils and then raises her hand too. It was quickly followed by Number Eleven's. Not quite the three ladies who had opted for 'not guilty' in the very first verdict vote, but almost. Number Three and Number Five haven't wavered from guilty, Number Eleven has gone from undecided into guilty — the only juror who has fallen that way. Number Six, who had been guilty in the original verdict vote, had now had a total change of heart. She figured she couldn't base her opinion on her own experiences, that she'd never understand the modern twenty-something and had come to the conclusion that it's absolutely possible in this day and age that a pretty young girl like Sabrina would offer her body up to be used by three men she met one night.

'Okay,' Number One says. 'I guess my fair question to you three is, why do you think it has been proven beyond reasonable doubt that these three men raped Sabrina Doyle?'

The three women look towards each other, none of them keen to speak first.

'Listen, it's my opinion that you all dismissed the internal cut too soon', Number Eleven finally says. 'I think the cut points to beyond reasonable doubt that Sabrina was forced into a situation she didn't want to be in.'

'No but that—' Number Twelve starts to say, but he's cut short.

'Shhh,' Number One says, 'let Number Eleven make her argument.'

'We saw the pictures of all those cuts that Doctor Johnson showed us. I know they weren't pictures of Sabrina's cuts, but similar cuts and they just have to be the result of... I don't know... forced sex. I can't get away from that. It's strong evidence for me. I'm not sure why we haven't discussed this in more detail around this table. We seemed to dismiss it a bit.'

She stops talking and purses her quivering lips.

'Okay, well if you don't mind me replying to that,' Brian says. 'It's jusht that although Doctor Johnson said that in his opinion Sabrina's cut was likely to be from forced penetration, he did alsho admit on the stand that these cuts can occur in consensual sex too. He also said they happen more regularly than anyone knows because most females don't get checked after consensual sex, do they? These checks are only really carried out for those who have been raped or are claiming rape.'

'Despite what he said,' Number Eleven says, almost getting animated now, 'he still concluded that in his expert opinion Sabrina's cut was from the result of forced penetration.' She raises her eyebrows at Brian, shrugs her shoulder.

'I understand what you are shaying and I really appreciate your point—'

'She's dead right,' Number Five chimes up with. 'I'm with her. Ye can't argue against a doctor's opinion anyway, can ye?'

Number One stands up again, holds both of his hands out and brings them down slowly; his way of reducing the tension that's threatening to erupt. It works. The room falls silent again.

'We appreciate you making your arguments, ladies. What about you, Number Three? Would you like to tell us why you feel the men should be found guilty?'

Number Three scratches her fingernails against her left temple and then stares down at the wheels of her chair.

'If I'm being honest — and I obviously need to be one hundred per cent honest — I opted for guilty because I knew almost everybody else... I could sense it... was going to vote not guilty and I eh... I just want the discussion to continue. I feel... I feel Sabrina is owed more than the time we've spent here. Maybe we should all sleep on this, come back to it tomorrow. We're only four and three quarters of an hour in, trying to break down a trial that lasted five weeks... it just doesn't seem fair to her... it's not fair on Sabrina.'

Her eyes don't leave the wheels of her chair as she speaks.

'So you voted guilty to hold off a unanimous decision?' Number Twelve asks her, his tone calm.

'If I'm being honest, yes... yes I did.'

'Okay... but if I can ask you, what do you *genuinely* think the verdict should be based on the evidence we discussed?'

She looks up from her wheels, takes in a few faces.

'Based on what we've discussed, it would be...' she hesitates, shakes her head, almost as if she's disagreeing with herself. '...eh... it would have to be *not* guilty. I don't think the case was proven, but I'd like for us to give it more time.'

An intake of breath can be heard from both sides of the table.

'Well I'm sticking with guilty,' Number Five chimes in with, shifting what had been a mature tone. 'I agree with Number Eleven that the cut is huge and points to guilt and I also know in my own heart, deep inside my soul, that these men are guilty. So I'm not changing me mind. I told yous earlier I wouldn't change.' She shrugs her shoulder towards the centre of the table.

Number One speaks up. 'Well, we all appreciate everybody's opinion here. I guess the one thing we need to discuss, given where we are now, is the doctor's evidence about the cut as that seems to be the dispute here. That is — I guess it's fair to say — what is stopping us from making a unanimous decision. Shall I eh... call it in, request the doctor's testimony?'

'Yesh ring it in', says Brian. 'But if you don't mind me saying in the meantime while we wait on Number One to make that call, I think one thing we should make fully clear here is that Gerd Bracken didn't overly push Doctor Johnson on the stand for a particular reashon. I believe that once he got the doctor to admit that these cuts can occur in both consensual and non-consensual acts of penetration it meant he felt he did enough here. It gave us reasonable doubt. And that means we can't really convict based on this piece of evidensh alone. The defence really won with Doctor Johnson.'

'He still said that in his expert opinion that this cut was likely from forced sex,' Number Eleven says.

'You're right, he did. But he could only offer opinion, he couldn't say for sure. And then Bracken of course got him to basically admit to us — to the whole court — that this cut *could* have been from consensual sex, so he did almost contradict himself on the stand.'

The jurors quieten down when a knock is heard at the door. Number Nine rises to answer it, takes the paperwork from the young man dressed in all black and then hands it over to Number One.

'Hmmm,' Number One mumbles as he flicks through the notes. 'It's only one page of testimony, he wasn't on the stand for long.'

'That's quite telling,' says Number Twelve.

'In what way is that telling?' Number Eleven asks.

'I don't believe that even Joseph Ryan felt Doctor Johnson's testimony was enough for a conviction. I think he was a witness who could help their cause, but he knew that Doctor Johnson would also testify that these cuts occur in both consensual *and* non-consensual sex. I don't believe anybody thinks this was as big a deal as we are making it now. I appreciate,' he says holding his hand up, 'that Number Eleven feels it *is* a big deal, and for that reason we are discussing it, but…'

He tails off, begins to read through the testimony like everybody else seems to be around him.

'Here,' calls out Number One. 'See here, paragraph three. He was asked about these types of cuts and he said they only occur when there is "no or little cervical fluid being produced by the female". The cut is confirmation that Sabrina wasn't producing these types of fluids and therefore wasn't turned on.'

'Yeah, so doesn't that make forced penetration more likely, if she wasn't turned on… wasn't enjoying the sex?' Number Eleven asks.

'Yeah – but look, he was asked that specifically by Bracken. He was asked if it was true that a woman wouldn't necessarily be producing cervical fluid even in consensual sex, and when the doctor replied "yes", Bracken then said, "so, just to clarify, these cuts do quite often appear in females during consensual sex?" and the doctor said "yes". This,' he says, turning his page over to face his fellow jurors, 'gives us reasonable doubt. We can *not* convict based on this testimony. The prosecution didn't win this witness. Doctor Johnson didn't prove rape. I'm sorry… I am. I wish we had more definitive evidence for everybody to stew over, but we didn't discuss Doctor Johnson's evidence in fine detail because we knew it sort of evened out the playing field. It doesn't give us grounds to find these men guilty beyond reasonable doubt. Does that help change your mind?' He directs his question towards Number Eleven.

Number Eleven can't hold in her emotions. Snot and tears began to fall down her face. She pulls both of her jumper's sleeves on to the palms of her hands and begins to wipe across her nose. As she does, she nods her head.

'Yes,' she sniffs when she removes her hands. 'You're right. It's not enough... not enough to convict.'

'So ... are you saying you are now changing your verdict?'

She continues sniffing, then nods her head again.

'Not guilty,' she whispers.

'I'm not guilty too,' Number Three says, slapping her palms against the armrests of her wheelchair.

An audible intake of breath is heard around the table, then everybody's face turns towards Number Five.

'I'm not changin' me mind,' she says.

'Number Five!' Number Eight shouts out. But he's quickly hushed.

'If you don't mind me shaying,' Brian pipes up as he flicks through his notes. 'I scribbled down the judge's final directions to us here, the speech he gave us this morning before he set us off on deliberations... I just think this will sum it up for you, Number Five. Do you mind if I read it to you?'

Number Five just nods her head, her face still showing signs of hostility. But inside she was shaking; was wondering how she was going to wriggle out of the situation she was finding herself in. She wanted to vote guilty based on the fact that she just happened to believe Sabrina over the three men in question, but she also knew that the backbone of her argument relating to 'gut feeling' and 'opinion' wouldn't get her anywhere.

Number Five's real name is Teresa Brennan, a twenty-seven-year-old shopping centre shelf-stacker from Coolock in north Dublin. She's normally cocky, even though she doesn't have the look to carry it off. She's tiny — only five foot one — has mousy brown hair and a face filled with freckles. She had to adopt an argumentative manner from a young age to stave off bullies at school. By the time she'd completed her Leaving Cert the adopted personality had become a permanent fixture. It's a shame she feels the need to constantly rebel, but that's what her personality has evolved into. She could have been a much more amenable person. Much more likeable. She's been in the guilty camp from the outset, took an instant dislike to the three men, but particularly Zach. She hated him as soon as she clapped eyes on him, feels he has the word guilty tattooed across his oversized forehead. Her temperament makes her come across as rash, hence the amount of times she's been shut down by fellow jurors during these deliberations. But she's starting to melt; the hard exterior she adopted as a kid in school is dissipating in this room.

Brian begins to read from his notes. 'The judge said to us, "your only task is to decide whether the prosecution has made you certain of the defendants' guilt. Do not allow yourshelves to be distracted from that task, do not allow yourshelves to be dishtracted by unproven opinion, do not allow yourshelves to be dishtracted by opinions you may have heard outside of this courtroom or the jury room, do not allow yourselves to be dishtracted by your own gender, by your own experiences, by anything other than the evidensh provided in this very courtroom over the past five weeks." Number Five – Judge McCormick was telling us that there wasn't enough evidensh. Just as I've been saying from the very start. He's telling us we can't decide this trial based on our own gut feelings. He was bashically telling us that we should be looking towards a not guilty verdict. The prosecution did not prove this case. I'm sorry. I am. I wish there was more to go on, but there simply isn't any evidensh.'

Number Five hangs her head.

'Number Five, at some point the judge will come back and let us know that eleven-to-one is enough for a verdict, so you hanging out is not—'

'Why don't we just hang on till tomorrow like Number

Three said... all sleep on it?' Number Five offers up. 'We need to—'

'No,' Number Three says, reaching down to her wheels, moving her chair backwards to get out from under the table and then pushing forwards towards Number Five. When she rolls up beside her, she reaches a hand out to hold one of hers.

'I'm sorry, Number Five,' she says, tears rolling down her face. 'Like you, I believe these three men raped Sabrina. I'd like to see them behind bars. But our job is to look at the evidence and there simply isn't enough evidence for us to reach a guilty verdict.'

Number Five begins to sob, then stretches across the wheelchair to grab at Number Three, holding her in a tight embrace. She nods her head on Number Three's shoulder and whispers.

'Okay. Okay.'

'So that'sh it, is it? We're all not guilty?' asks Brian.

A slow tsunami of heads nod around the table.

'Not guilty, Number Five?' Number One asks, his tone sombre.

She releases herself from Number Three's hug and lets out a deep breath, spraying some of her tears on to the table.

'Not guilty.'

Everybody soaks in the reality; the room falling silent, but for the sound of Number Three and Number Five sucking up their tears.

'Shall I ring it in?' Number One asks, breaking the silence.

'Ring it in,' says Number Twelve.

Number One holds down the button and takes a deep breath.

'The jury have reached a unanimous verdict,' he says.

00:25
Sabrina

I'm wondering why I'm breathing so calmly when inside I feel flames are starting to ignite. I can hear my breaths reverberate from my nose onto the mattress and then back into my ears. I'm getting annoyed by the fact that I can't get my train of thought on to the right track. I should either be enjoying this, or… totally incensed. But I'm neither. I'm just tired, sinking my head further into the mattress while Zach attempts to turn me on. Why am I being so indecisive? Maybe I'm not cut out for being the easy-going, fun Sabrina. Maybe I'm supposed to be dull, supposed to be frigid.

'You okay?' Zach asks. I take a moment to think about his question, but I actually don't know the answer. Both the angel and the devil on my shoulder have gone quiet. I think I'd be too embarrassed to say 'no' at this point anyway. So I just say nothing, keeping my face firm against the mattress. Jason enters my mind. I wonder how he is feeling as he stands back and watches his best mate try to have sex with me. But I can't look behind, can't even bring myself to raise my nose from this bed. I feel Zach rub himself between my legs. He's all warm, clammy. This is far from sexy. None of it feels right. I'm supposed to be turned on — I'm anything but. Then he enters me. I think it's his penis. Could be his fingers. It's not a nice sensation… quite rough actually, but I turn my face sideways just to give my nose more space to breathe through, resting my right ear on the mattress instead.

'You're so hot,' Zach says as he writhes around behind me. I don't answer him. He groans. I'm not sure whether it's with satisfaction or out of frustration. Maybe he's not enjoying this either. Threesomes are bullshit. Well this one is anyway. I certainly won't be having another one in a hurry. My whole sex life has been shit. I'm beginning to think sex is the most overrated and sensationalised act humans bang on about. Or maybe it's just me... after all, I am the common denominator in my shitty sex life. I am the only one who's been there with all three men I've let inside me. Or four. It's four now, I guess. Two tonight. Wow. I wonder when that will sink in for real. Four penises. All of different length, girth, and all these sizes have been vastly overrated. I haven't really enjoyed any penis that has entered me. Not really. Sex with Eddie was all right at the start, but it soon got boring. Maybe I'm the boring one. Maybe I should get up off my face, turn around, pull Jason and Zach on to their backs and jump on top of them, one at a time. Ride them like a cowgirl. Be a proper dirty little slut. But I actually have no interest in having sex with any of them. Not any more. My mojo is gone. All I want to do is go home, curl up into my bed and fall asleep. Maybe I'll wake up in the morning and regret this. Or maybe I'll wake up and feel disappointed that I didn't give it my best shot. It's really annoying me that I don't know how I feel, how I should feel, how I will feel.

I want to say 'no'. I want to repeat the word fifty times. Tell Zach to get away from me, tell him and Jason to get out of the room, that I need time to myself. But the word won't come out. I can hear myself say it, over and over again. But I know it's only inside my head, nobody else can hear it.

Then Zach takes me out of my thought by letting out a loud groan. I'm pretty sure it's out of frustration more than anything. He's not groaning in ecstasy. He's not even inside me anymore. No part of his body is. I think he's just kneeling back on the bed, panting— letting out sharp, heavy breaths.

'You're amazing,' he says, then he pats me on the back as if I'm a little pony he's just been on for a ride around. I let out a deep sigh — the only significant sound I've made in the past twenty minutes. I look up when the music grows louder. The door's swiped open again. I manage to move my head to look behind and make out Li's silhouette. I wrap one arm around my breasts so he can't see them; hold my other hand down by my crotch. But aside from that, I can't move. I know my ass is still hovering above the mattress, my knees, head and shoulders still sunken into it.

Then I feel him crawl up on to the bed, changing positions with Zach.

This can't be happening. Li's not going to have sex with me. Is he? We get on with each other like brother and sister. This can't be right. I hear myself scream 'no' inside my head. Then I feel him enter me. What the fuck is going on?

I raise my head fully from the mattress for the first time and stare back at Li. His glasses have steamed up, he's thrusting into me as quickly as he can. It's not hurting me, in fact I seem to have moistened somewhat. But I know I'm not turned on. I know I don't want this. I take a deep breath and brace myself to say the word that has been circulating in my head for the past five minutes. I don't know why it won't come out. I shake my head. But I don't think he can see me. My breathing gets quicker, then sharper. Speak for fuck sake, Sabrina. Speak. Say it. Say it!

'No, no, no!' I scream.

00:25
Li

There's something not quite right about tonight. Both myself and Jason are flat out on a sofa each; neither of us talking. We're just drowning in the shite music blaring from the TV.

I can't believe Jason gave up on Sabrina, allowed Zach to take control. For somebody who's been a huge success as a professional athlete, he really can be such an easy pushover at times. Especially when it comes to Zach.

I imagine what Zach's up to now. Probably getting an amazing blowjob from one of the most beautiful women I've ever seen. I was starting to get jealous when Jason took her into the bedroom about twenty minutes ago, but I'm not jealous now. I'm just frustrated; frustrated with Jason, frustrated with Zach, *definitely* frustrated with Sabrina. She seemed like such a nice girl. I can't believe she's just another slut. The world seems to be full of them these days.

I should have just gone home when we left the airport and curled up in bed beside Niamh. I was actually looking forward to going to Homebase in the morning. Maybe we still can. We got to get that paint for the bathroom.

Jesus. I really am getting old — worrying about the state of our little apartment. Can't believe I'm going to be a dad soon, going to be a married man not that long after. I'm so lucky. But I'm aware of my luck, so that's okay. I don't live with any guilt that I've managed to find everything I've ever wanted in life. I've got a decent job, an adorable family, great mates, an amazing girlfriend. There's nothing I would change about my life. And I know there are not a lot of people who could genuinely say that.

I stare over at Jason. I know he certainly couldn't say that. He's definitely depressed. His eyes are closed, but I know by the way he's slouched on that couch that he's crying inside. Maybe we all just need to get the fuck out of here. Get Jason home. I'll call into his mam's tomorrow afternoon when I'm back from Homebase. Have a proper heart-to-heart with him then.

I drop my feet to the ground and muster enough energy to get myself to a standing position, stretching and yawning when I'm finally upright. There's no noise coming from the bedroom. I step closer to it, try to gauge if Sabrina and Zach are finished. I think they are. I'll tell them we're checking out, heading home.

But when I slide the door open I see Sabrina in doggy position, her skin as perfect as any models' I've ever seen. It looks as if Zach has just finished. He's steadily getting himself to a standing position after popping his cock back inside his boxer shorts. It's not a smile he shoots in my direction, it's more of a gurn. Then he taps me on the shoulder as he passes me and makes his way towards Jason. I don't look at him because I can't keep my eyes off Sabrina's ass. I've never seen anything like it.

I start rubbing at myself, my dick standing to attention. She hasn't moved. Maybe she's waiting on me. I look behind me at the boys, then back at Sabrina. I wonder if I owe myself this — my last hurrah before I get married. But before I've stewed the thought fully around my head, I'm on the bed, my dick in my hand. I'm not even sure when I pulled down my zip. And now I'm inside her. I can't believe it. I never thought I'd have sex with somebody this hot. It feels so good. I want to take a snap shot of this moment, so I can play it over and over in my head for the rest of my life. Though I can't really see Sabrina's beautiful face.

She raises her head from the bed. She's panting. She really is enjoying this. What a dirty slut. Three dicks she's had tonight and is still gagging for more. Or is she? I watch her shake her head. Her breaths becoming sharper.

Then she snaps her face back towards me.

'No, no, no!' she shouts back.

I twist her hair around my hand and grip it tightly. Then I force her face back down on to the mattress and hold it there while I continue to thrust in and out of her.

'Shh,' I whisper. 'Keep quiet. I won't be long.'

THE END

It is believed, though it can't be proven, that in 92 per cent of rape cases reported to police, the claimant is *not* lying.

However, despite that, only *18 per cent* of rape trials ever end in a guilty verdict.

FIND OUT WHAT HAPPENED TO THESE CHARACTERS NEXT...

Watch an exclusive interview with author David B. Lyons in which he discusses this story in finer detail and explains what may have happened to the characters following the trial.

To watch, just click here:

https://www.subscribepage.com/shesaid

DAVID B. LYONS'S BOOKS INCLUDE

Midday

Whatever Happened to Betsy Blake?

The Suicide Pact

She Said, Three Said

View them all at

www.theopenauthor.com/my-books/

ACKNOWLEDGEMENTS

It took the support of a small army to make this story come to life.

Firstly, a massive thank you to my wife Kerry who looked me square in the eye in February of 2018 when I raised the initial idea for this novel and said: "You *have* to write that story."

I wasn't convinced I could do the subject justice, but Kerry can make anyone believe anything is possible.

Almost two years on, I'm convinced I did do this story justice. But that's because Kerry drove me to that belief. Thank you.

I should also thank my daughter Lola who really didn't do anything to help me write this novel. But someday – in the distant future – she will read my books and wonder why she wasn't mentioned in the acknowledgements… so here y'are Lolipops.

Barry O'Hanlon, Hannah Healy, Margaret Lyons and Yvonne Taylor read very early drafts of this book way back when and gave me superb pointers on where the arc needed improvement. *She Said, Three Said* is a much more refined novel for your input, guys.

I also need to thank Brigit Taylor, Mary Howes, Liv Sbrabaro, Deborah Hart and Roz Casagrande for their input in this novel. Each of them read my third draft and helped me round off the jaunted edges.

I need to specifically mention lawyer Johanna Ryan who shared, with me, her amazing knowledge of the legal landscape when it comes to these types of trials. This book would not have been possible without your input.

I'd also like to mention Samantha Sherlock and Glen Moore who shared their experience of sitting on major trials as a juror in Dublin's Criminal Court with me — helping me steer the juror chapters towards reality.

I must also mention my mother, Joan and my sister Debra... just cause.

The Rape Crisis Network Ireland provided me with the stunning statistics that appear throughout this book - thank you for all the marvellous work you do.

And a big thank you also goes to the editors of this novel: Maureen Vincent-Northam and the aforementioned Brigit Taylor.